*The*

# WATCHMAKER'S
# DAUGHTER

DIANNE HALEY

*The*

# WATCHMAKER'S DAUGHTER

bookouture

Published by Bookouture in 2022

An imprint of Storyfire Ltd.
Carmelite House
50 Victoria Embankment
London EC4Y 0DZ

www.bookouture.com

ISBN: 978-1-80314-243-2
eBook ISBN: 978-180314-244-9

*For Martin.*

*November 1942. Winter is coming, and German troops have occupied Vichy France, ripping families apart and sending Jews to concentration camps in Poland. But as desperate refugees try to enter neutral Switzerland, the Swiss authorities, fearful of provoking a Nazi invasion, close their borders.*

# ONE

## VALÉRIE

**Geneva, Switzerland**

Valérie tugged open the heavy wooden door and peered along the cobbled street winding through the old town towards the Cathédrale St-Pierre. The rain had cast a blanket of grey mist over the city and she could see no sign of life in the gloom.

Emile's instructions pounded through her brain.

'Don't run or draw attention to yourself. The police will question anyone acting suspiciously.'

She pulled up the collar of her old woollen coat, stepped on to the street and turned left, past the dark windows of her father's workshop at the side of their townhouse towards the steep lanes leading down the hill to the wide boulevard running along Lac Léman. Her heart was hammering, only now appreciating the risk she was taking.

*It's no more dangerous than passing messages*, he'd said.

But he was wrong. The Swiss police had clamped down on their citizens helping the French Resistance since the fall of Vichy France. They might turn a blind eye to secret messages, but if they thought she was helping refugees escape from occupied France, they'd put her on their watch list and she might never be able to help the Resistance again. And worse than that, she could lead them right to the door of the terrified people who relied on her for help. If the refugees were discovered in Geneva, less than ten kilometres from the border, the police would hand them right back to the Nazis.

The worn soles of her boots slid on the wet cobbles as she hugged the ancient stone walls of the old town, instinct guiding her steps. The darkness only underlined how strange a place her beloved Geneva had become, with war raging all around them. Fear of a German invasion was a constant presence and nobody wanted their names to be on a list of Resistance fighters, to be handed over to the victorious Nazis.

Her mouth pursed at the sides. She thought of her father always trying to please his German customers and getting her to do the same. Propping up his watchmaking business by taking Nazi gold. Her small fingers curled into fists. *If I were a man, I'd be in the mountains defending my country like Philippe, not left behind in Geneva delivering watches to the enemy.*

A door to the Hôtel Les Armures opened on her right, casting a faint arc of light into the narrow street. A blast of warm, beer-soaked air washed over her face. She ran across the road and jumped lightly down the flight of steps opposite the hotel, avoiding the treacherous piles of slippery leaves. She hid behind the small statue, taking deep breaths to still the pounding of her heart. Gruff German voices filled the alley a few metres away and she grimaced in disgust. They might not be in Nazi uniform, but she had seen both Germans and Swiss citizens sporting Nazi badges and saluting one another in the street as if Geneva was already theirs. And no German would let a shower of rain put them off their beer, not when they were enjoying a comfortable life in Switzerland while their compatriots ravaged occupied Europe.

The door slammed shut and the clatter of boots on the

cobbles grew louder, coming towards her through the darkness. She crouched down, trying to melt into the stone wall, heart thumping so loudly in her chest that she could almost hear it above the noise of the rain. If they saw her and followed her for some reason, she might as well sign the death warrant of the refugees trying to escape.

The noise of heavy boots passed above her head and grew fainter as the Germans walked away towards the Cathédrale Saint-Pierre. Valérie let her breath out in a long sigh and stepped out from her hiding place. She reached the wide boulevard skirting the Jardin Anglais without meeting anyone else and stopped where she'd been instructed to wait. This was where she would be most exposed, wondering if Emile would arrive or if something had gone wrong. She looked up and down the boulevard running between the Pont du Mont-Blanc and the south bank of Lac Léman, ready to hide in the gardens if she saw a patrol approaching.

She heard a light step behind her and before she could move, a hand pressed down on her shoulder, trapping tendrils of her hair in a claw-like grip. Stifling a cry, she twisted round, trying to break free. Then she heard a familiar voice and recognised the tall, lanky figure.

'Sssh... do you want to give us away?'

Relief flooded through her body and she grasped his arm. 'You frightened me. I thought it was the police...'

He winced and she caught him as he staggered backwards, his lame leg almost giving way. When she lifted her hand, it was streaked with blood.

'You've been hurt...'

Emile turned as she spoke and she saw four bedraggled children cowering behind his thin frame.

'The border guards were waiting. We were ambushed as we came across from Annemasse. They knew we were coming.'

The town on the border with Switzerland was one of the

main routes for refugees escaping from Vichy France and was heavily guarded by German soldiers.

'And the other children?'

'Shot by the Germans waiting in the woods. They nearly got us too, but we ran for our lives. We were lucky to escape...'

She clutched his arm, the horror of his blunt words making her catch her breath.

'They were shot?'

He wiped the rain from his face and shook his head, as if he was trying to wipe the scene from his memory.

'I couldn't help them...'

A cacophony of sirens drowned out his words and they instinctively ducked down as three Swiss police cars burst on to the boulevard and raced towards them.

'Come on, we have to get out of here. Just keep close to the wall.' She grabbed the smallest child, whose cold little fingers clutched her hand as if she would never let go, and led them up into the heart of the old town, avoiding the main streets, twisting and turning through the narrow lanes to lose the policemen. The sirens behind them grew fainter.

She stopped when they reached the heavy door to the small courtyard at the back of her father's old workshop and groped for the key in her pocket, fingers shaking as she thrust it into the lock and tried to turn the rusty bolt. To her horror, it wouldn't budge and she fought to twist it round.

'They're behind us, Valérie. We need to get inside.'

'The key won't turn. It's stuck.' She couldn't hide the panic in her voice and felt a sob rising in her throat. The shouts grew louder, cutting through the low ripple of the pouring rain.

Emile lifted her to one side and she gave him the key. He pushed it into the lock and twisted with all his strength, releasing the heavy door with a muffled crash. They pulled the children through the narrow opening and Emile closed the door behind them, just as they heard the sound of voices at the end of the street. They all stood rigidly in the pouring rain, water streaming down their faces, listening to the sound of the police banging on the doors as they worked their way along the narrow lane towards them.

Breath catching in her throat, Valérie stared up at Emile, her panic mirrored in his eyes, and then dragged her shocked gaze down to his hand as he tried to relock the door before the men could reach them. She felt a cold prickle of fear snake down her back as the key slowly turned; she had no idea if the door was properly locked.

An ear-splitting crash filled the air and the old door shook in its rusty hinges. A small hand grasped hers and she clutched it tightly, willing none of the children to make a sound. This was why Emile was risking his life leading refugees across the border and why she was prepared to help him. Children like these were being herded on to trains as if they were animals and taken to the concentration camps in Poland, shot if they tried to escape and then murdered when they reached their destination.

She looked at the still faces staring up at her and felt ashamed of her fears and her doubts. The little girl who'd clutched her hand in the boulevard leaned against her as if she was too tired to go on and Valérie bent down to hug her close, feeling her thin shoulders through the threadbare coat. Valérie shivered as she looked down at the dark head, her heart filling with pity. She was so young to have seen her friends shot in cold blood, to be running for her life and dependent on the mercy of strangers. It wouldn't be the last time Valérie would let Emile use the storeroom below the old workshop.

The door held firm and the police moved on, working their way up the street. They stood in the pouring rain, drenched and shivering, until Emile allowed them to tiptoe cross the courtyard and go inside.

Valérie helped the exhausted children into the dry storeroom and turned to leave.

'Aren't you staying?' Emile held open the door.

'I'm sorry, Emile, but I have to get home. If my father finds out what I'm doing, he'll try to stop me.' She glanced at his torn jacket. 'Will you be all right?'

He nodded. 'Marianne will patch me up.'

She hesitated at the door and watched the children lie down on the thin mattresses she had set out at the back of the store-room, too tired even to eat the stale potato bread she'd sneaked out from the kitchen. They weren't safe yet, wouldn't be safe until they were up in the mountains with a family willing to take care of them.

'How long will they be here?'

'Only tonight. Someone will come for them early in the morning. If they stay in Geneva and are found so close to the border, they'll be sent back.' He frowned in the dim light. 'Is that a problem? You said it was safe here, that your father had closed up the building and nobody would find them.'

'Nobody comes here now,' she confirmed, glancing towards the stairs to the upper floor, remembering how the building was once a noisy, industrious place, people working upstairs in the daylight streaming through the huge windows and the store-room bustling with deliveries.

She started to close the door behind her.

'Valérie?' He grasped her arm and she turned to face him.

'Thank you. I'd never have got them here without you. I don't know the back streets of the old town like you do.'


As she ran back home, the white faces of the children swam across her vision. Her step faltered when she thought about the ones who hadn't made it, killed at the border as they'd tried to escape. Little children, hunted and shot dead like animals.

She knew it was dangerous helping the French Resistance, but at least she was doing something to fight the Germans. For the first time since Philippe had gone, she could see clearly how to fill the emptiness he'd left behind.

She unlatched the front door to the tall townhouse she'd lived in all her life and slipped inside, leaning against the stone wall, waiting for her breathing to get back to normal. After a few moments, the hall flooded with light and her father came out with Dieter Runde, the official at the German Consulate who approved his export licences and was an increasingly frequent visitor.

'Valérie, is that you? We were wondering where you were.'

She glanced at Dieter, her attention caught by the edelweiss pin he always wore on his lapel, glinting in the hall light, before she returned his warm smile.

# TWO

## VALÉRIE

Valérie sat on the edge of one of the sofas in the parlour, feeling damp and cold, waiting for the inevitable questions and rapidly making up the most credible story for her absence. The heat from the fire crackling in the open hearth filled the room and she stretched her arms towards the warmth like a cat basking in the sun.

Dieter stared at her, the smile still warming his blue eyes, and she dropped her gaze. Her father believed the reason the German came round so often was that he wanted the watchmaking trade between Switzerland and Germany to continue uninterrupted during the war, but Valérie sometimes worried it wasn't the only reason for his frequent visits and flushed under his lingering stare.

She smoothed the skirt of her dark blue suit, rubbing the oil stain left by her old bicycle. She'd been careful to wear her darkest clothes, in the hope that nobody would notice her sneak through the old town. And even if someone did see her, she knew that she looked younger than her twenty years so after one glance they would never think she could be doing anything suspicious.

Her father draped her wet coat carefully along the back of the carved wooden chairs near the fire, his face turned away from her.

'This coat will be too thin when there's snow on the ground. We'll need to get you a new one.'

She looked up at him in surprise, unable to remember the last time she'd had anything new to wear. Everyone had to repair their old clothes rather than buy new ones and they'd all become experts in fashioning skirts from old coats, patching thinning elbows and mending worn hems. Her friend Geraldine had even managed to find some parachute silk and her clever fingers had created a cream silk dress they all coveted.

Her rain-soaked hair dripped down the back of her neck and she twisted the damp auburn curls between her fingers, stealing another glance at their visitor. His well-cut suit fitted his slim figure to perfection and she felt a stab of resentment when she looked down at her stained skirt. No scrimping and saving for Consulate staff, unlike most of their friends and neighbours. For once, he didn't seem interested in her. He was watching her father as Albert took out a bottle of the local Vaud white wine to share with his guest, squinting through his spectacles to check it was the bottle he wanted. Behind him, through the open door to the dining room Albert now used as his workshop, the safe was open, its contents scattered over the workbench next to the delicate tools, as if he'd been surprised by Dieter's unexpected visit.

Valérie could see the strain her father was trying to hide under the veneer of courtesy, with newly etched lines on his brow and his lips a thin line below the dark moustache flecked with grey. She opened her mouth to ask what was going on, but he spoke first.

'You were a long time. I was almost coming out to look for you.' He filled the glasses with a steady hand, waiting for her answer.

'Geraldine was busy, so I had to wait for her.'

'These young ladies, Albert... always talking and laughing.' The German waved his glass at her father. 'I never know what they can find to talk about.' His smile broadened and her father allowed himself a small chuckle.

Valérie had heard Emile talk about German civilians snooping around and reporting back to the Gestapo the names of Swiss citizens suspected of helping the Allies or the Resistance. They would be the first to be shot when the Germans added Switzerland to their list of conquered countries. Looking at Dieter sharing a joke with her father, the picture of conviviality, she wondered how Emile could think all Germans were the same. Some of them were good people, who would never agree with what their country was doing. Dieter was one of her father's best contacts and had become a close friend to him as he'd helped keep their business with Germany alive.

Her father handed her a glass.

'It's not safe out there at night. How many times have I told you that? I heard the police sirens earlier on, chasing someone. You don't want to get caught up in any trouble.'

'I'm sorry, Papa. I didn't mean you to worry.'

She tried to loosen the bow on her soft cotton blouse, the wet material uncomfortably tight around her neck, her breath coming in short gasps.

'Quite right.' Dieter leaned his dark head forward. She could smell the wine on his breath and sat further back in the sofa. 'You Swiss need to take care of your own people, protect your country until this war is over. Then everything will get back to normal.'

She smiled at him weakly, thinking of the little girl with the frightened eyes and dark mop of hair who had clung to her in the old workshop. It was easy for Dieter to say those words, but she knew that things would never get back to normal. Not when there were children lying dead in the cold and rain only a few kilometres away from their warm, comfortable room. Blinking back sudden tears, she squirmed out of her chair.

'Excuse me, but I need to go and change these wet clothes.'

Ignoring her father's angry stare, she left them together, resisting the urge to slam the door behind her. Dieter might be kind, but she could never really be his friend and pretend that everything was all right.

In her bedroom, Valérie stripped off her wet clothes and flung them on to the back of a chair, shivering in the freezing cold. She got dressed as quickly as she could and was rubbing her hair dry when she heard Dieter's voice in the hall and the sound of her father bolting the outside door, then the clinking of glasses as he cleared them away in the parlour. She sighed, knowing she couldn't put off the inevitable scene, and came out of her room, still drying her hair with the thin towel.

Her father was restoring the parlour to its usual meticulous order, putting the clean glasses away in the large, oak dresser and straightening the embroidered cushions on the sofa. The fire was low in the hearth but she knew without looking that the copper coal scuttle would be empty. She would have to try to find fuel somewhere in the city tomorrow.

'He's gone then.'

'Yes, he's gone. And it wouldn't harm you to be polite to him. He was only trying to be pleasant. You know he likes coming here and I can't afford to turn him away. If he stopped giving me export licenses, I'd lose too much business.'

'I'm sorry, Papa. I'm just tired. He just seems to be here all the time. I know he's nice, but he is a German... I can't understand why you have to invite him here and not just meet him at the Consulate.'

'He's interested in watchmaking.'

'I know.'

'And he talks to me about his wife.' He shook his head. 'It's been almost two years and he still misses her desperately. I feel sorry for him, so far away from his family and his home.'

'I know he criticises the Nazis and says he doesn't like what's happening across Europe, but Emile says we can't trust any of the Germans.'

Her father swirled round, his dapper figure no longer able to contain the stress bottled up inside him. An even-tempered man, it took a lot to rouse his ire, but when he snapped, it happened in an instant. Valérie could read the signs and sighed, waiting for the torrent.

'The only person you listen to these days is Emile. That boy does nothing but stir up trouble. Ever since his father died in that accident on the farm, he's always seeing villains around every corner. You can't believe everything he tells you. I just hope he's not dragging you into any of his mad schemes.'

Her father had always disapproved of Emile and the scrapes he'd encouraged Valérie to share since they were children. Her mother had had a soft spot for him and was more tolerant, but since she'd died, Albert's strict political neutrality always made him stiffen in the face of Emile's freely expressed opinions. She thought of Emile's bravery, risking his life to get the children to safety. He could so easily have been shot by the German border guards. Anger rising within her, she couldn't stop the protest spilling out.

'Papa, you know why he doesn't trust the Germans. What happened to his father may not have been an accident. Everyone knows that German spies were operating in Vichy France, watching anyone they suspected of helping the French Resistance. It wasn't a coincidence that the Swiss police were forever searching the farm. And you know how much it hurts him that he couldn't join the army with Philippe. You shouldn't be so hard on him.'

But she could tell he wasn't listening to her, as he turned

away and continued fiddling with the cushions and straightening out the rug.

'And that's another thing,' he said, turning back to her and sighing. 'Philippe came to see you when you were out. He looked for you at the Café de Paris but Geraldine said you hadn't been there all evening. You said that's where you were going, but did you lie to me? Where were you, Valérie?'

She stared at him, mouth open, grasping the arm of the sofa as the bitter disappointment hit her like a blow.

'Philippe was here? I didn't know he was due to be on leave. He didn't say anything in his last letter. Why didn't he let me know?'

Her father's voice lost its angry edge and he took a step towards her.

'It was very sudden. I'm sorry *ma chérie* but his grandfather had another heart attack. He got special leave for twenty-four hours to come and see him.'

'Only twenty-four hours and I missed him.'

Valérie sank on to the sofa and picked at the fraying edge of the towel. Philippe had come to see her for the first time in months and she hadn't been there. She felt her eyes prickle with tears and bit her lip to stop them spilling over. After the night she'd had, if she finally started crying, she didn't think she'd be able to stop.

'Was he very upset?'

Her father nodded and came to sit beside her on the sofa. He reached out his hand to still her fingers pulling the towel.

'Shocked and upset. They aren't sure if his grandfather will survive this.'

'I wish I'd been home in time to see him. But it's too late now.'

'It's a pity you went out at all. And did you have to be so rude to Dieter when you came back, leaving the room like that?

You know he's an important colleague. I'm only asking you to be pleasant to him.'

She blinked away the tears.

'I am pleasant to him. I just don't understand why you care so much about what he thinks. He's German, Papa. You know what his countrymen are doing all across Europe, what they'd do if they took over Switzerland. How can you just ignore that?'

'You know our situation, Valérie. We have little enough money as it is without alienating some of our best clients. I can't sell watch mechanisms to any of my German customers without Dieter's help.'

Valérie knew the setbacks her father had faced since her mother had died five years ago, had seen him losing customers to the larger watchmaking manufacturers. The little money he made hardly covered the cost of their food and the meagre amount he paid Agathe to look after the house. Even when she'd tried to persuade him to take in lodgers to supplement their income, he wouldn't agree to have strangers stay in the house, whatever she said.

'I know Dieter is harmless, but he is *German*. They could invade our country any day. Why can't you just sell to the Allies?'

'Because I need business from all sides in this war. We have more and more competitors every year and we can't afford to lose customers, whether they are Swiss, German or English. And if our country doesn't do enough business with the Germans, they might decide to walk all over us, just like they did everywhere else in Europe. Why do you think the whole Swiss army is protecting the mountains if General Guisan isn't expecting a German invasion? Is that what you want? To become like France, beaten into submission?'

'Of course not! But you've read the stories in the papers about the death camps in Poland, where they're taking all the

Jews. It's been on the radio since before the fall of Vichy France. You can't deny what they're doing...'

Images of the children she'd helped escape flashed through her mind and she could almost hear the screams of the ones who hadn't made it. Where did they come from? What had happened to their families? What were their names?

But the emotion in her father's face had hardened into resolve.

'You listen to that British radio station too much. You don't understand my position. I have no choice. I have to work with everyone to protect our business or I won't have a business left.'

'You wouldn't be doing it if Mother was still alive... She wouldn't have let the Germans anywhere near the house.'

Her father pulled away his hand and she saw the pain in his eyes before he turned his head away.

'That is enough, Valérie. I am not going to argue with you anymore. I expect you to be polite to all of my customers, whoever they are. I have a business to run and employees to support. What would happen to Agathe if I decided only to sell my products to one side in this war? She's too old to get work anywhere else and would starve. Is that what you want?'

Valérie had known her father's oldest workers all her life. They were part of her family and had looked after her since her mother died. 'Of course not. But...'

'I have to find ways to feed everyone, Valérie. We cannot survive on our principles and the sooner you learn that the better. More than anyone, your mother would have agreed with that.' He put up his hand to end the argument. 'And now you should go to bed. You have a busy day tomorrow with all the deliveries.'

Seething at his dismissal, Valérie rushed to her room and stared at her stormy features in the dressing table mirror, picking up her brush and running it through her curly hair. Her father didn't seem to care about anything but his precious customers. Sometimes it felt like they had nothing in common at all. How could he care so little about the lives of so many people? She looked at the small black and white photo of her parents before the accident, laughing at the camera. Picking it up in its ornate gilt frame, she touched it and sighed, remembering how she used to sit on her mother's bed and talk about everything – her worries, her friends, her hopes for the future.

It was only five years since her mother had died in the car accident, but so much had changed since then. It was as if a part of her father had died with her. He was always so serious and distant now, working for hours on end, unwilling to look beyond his small world and see what was happening around him.

Her mother had filled the house with books that overflowed from the old bookshop where she used to work. Valérie went across to the shelves that lined one of the walls in her room, stroking the spines of the books, her fingers moving from English to French to Russian names. Her mother had read the English books with her and encouraged her to learn the language. Valérie turned away from the shelves. So much for her dreams of travelling to England or America. She hadn't even managed to begin her English course at Geneva University because war had broken out. Her plans for the future seemed further away than ever and she began to doubt that she'd ever get out of Geneva and travel together with Philippe, as they had once talked about. What would the world be like in a few years' time, if Germany won the war?

Valérie fiddled with the black knobs on the wireless next to the window but wasn't in the mood to switch it on. She stood up restlessly and walked towards the window, trailing her fingers over the radio's smooth surface of polished wood. Suffocated by the confines of her room, she went to the window and threw open the wooden shutters, leaned on the windowsill and lifted her face eastwards towards the fresh air coming from the Vaud mountains. The rain had passed through and the night air was cold and frosty. Philippe would be on his way back to the Alps by now. She would give anything to feel his arms around her again.

Gazing down the cobbled street, she smiled, thinking about the first time he'd said he loved her, on their favourite bench looking out to the Jet d'Eau and the lake. She could still feel the intense warmth that flooded through her at that moment. Before the war had taken him away, they'd done everything together and she couldn't have imagined life without him. But when he was called up and left her behind, all she had was his letters. She bent down to pick up his last letter, lying next to the radio, and held it against her cheek.

Then a noise in the street below made her look up, but there was nobody there. She leaned right out of the window and in the pale moonlight saw a thickset figure disappear around the corner and into the night. She was sure it was Bernard, the grocer's son.

Whoever it was could have listened to her arguing with her father and heard her criticisms of the Germans. Bernard was the last person she was afraid of, but could he be one of the Swiss who saw it as his duty to gather the names of those who expressed anti-Nazi views, ready to hand the information over after a German invasion?

As she closed the shutters, she felt a pang of hunger and thought again about the children she'd left in the storeroom. She should have left them more food for their journey out of Geneva. Would they make it to safety in the mountains or would they be stopped and sent back to occupied France? She closed her eyes to banish the image of the little girl shoved on to a train and waiting in terror for what would await her in Germany or Poland. She must have been only eight or nine years old. With the taste of blood on her bitten lip, Valérie shivered and pulled her wrap tightly around her shoulders.

# THREE

## VALÉRIE

A dank, low cloud hung over the city the next morning. By the time Valérie had collected the orders, placed the larger boxes into the basket on her old bike and the smaller more precious packages in her leather satchel, her fingers were numb and stinging.

Agathe fussed over her, warming her gloves over the stove in the kitchen, misshapen fingers smoothing the thin wool. It was years since she had been able to do her skilful work assembling delicate watch mechanisms in the workshop. Valérie's father found other tasks for her to do and the old woman saw it as her duty to look after Valérie. Wearing an apron tied across her old black dress and her grey hair caught back in a tight bun, she stabbed the air with a bony finger and repeated the warning Valérie had heard a hundred times before.

'Keep your bag close to your side, don't let anyone snatch it away. They'd thieve the clothes off your back if you let them, some of the characters they're letting across the border these days...'

'Agathe, I'll be fine. I've done this for months now.'

'And call into the *charcutier* down from the station on your way back. I hear they're getting a delivery this morning. You might have to queue but you should be able to get something for supper.'

Her father's last delivery man had gone off to join the army so Valérie had taken over his job, as well as spending hours each week queueing for food. She never knew how Agathe heard which shops were getting deliveries, but she was uncannily accurate in directing her to the best source of supplies.

'I'm off now.'

She lingered in the warmth of the workshop, but her father didn't look up. He just waved a hand, hunched over his work-bench and peering through an eyepiece, assuming as always that she would do what she was asked without a murmur. The argument from the previous evening still hung in the air between them, unresolved and bitter. She delivered as many packages to the British as to the Germans but being even-handed didn't make things any better.

The previous night, she'd been completely unable to sleep and was tossing and turning in bed until the clock struck four. When she did fall asleep, the hollow, frightened face of the little girl who had leaned against her haunted her dreams. She didn't think she could ever forget her. She'd resolved to help Emile hide refugees as often as she could, even while she delivered watch mechanisms to her father's German customers. Hugging Agathe's thin shoulders, she left the workshop.

Taking a detour round by the Café de Paris, Valérie saw Geraldine, one of her oldest friends, under the green canopy at the door. She was deep in conversation with Bernard, who was putting down a box of groceries, his muscular arms bare despite the cold. She quickened her step to ask why he'd been snooping around outside her window late at night, but by the time she reached the door, he'd slunk back across the street. Geraldine was setting out the metal tables and chairs, in case the late autumn sun grew warm enough for any customers to be tempted to sit outside. She turned around in surprise when Valérie accosted her without a greeting, the welcoming smile fading from her face.

'I thought you didn't like Bernard. You used to say he was always bothering you.'

Geraldine shrugged and tossed her wavy blonde hair. '*Bonjour* to you too, Valérie. Bernard's all right. We've been having problems getting some of our food deliveries and he's helped us out. He can get hold of goods nobody else can.'

It was a struggle keeping the café supplied with enough food to carry on. It was bad enough trying to feed your own family with their meagre rations, far less cater for paying guests. Valérie sighed. It seemed like everyone was sacrificing their principles to keep their businesses afloat.

Geraldine pushed open the wooden door and gestured towards the back of the café where an open fire was crackling in the hearth, before closing the door firmly to keep in the heat.

'We got a delivery of fuel yesterday. Do you want some coal?'

Valérie nodded and smiled at her friend's generosity.

'Yes please. We've run out and it's so cold at home. But can you spare it?'

'For one of my best friends? Do you need to ask?'

'Thank you so much. I'll come round later and pick it up.'

Geraldine glanced down at the basket on Valérie's bike.

'Where are you off to?'

'Just doing the usual delivery round for my father. I'll be back in the afternoon. Do you want to meet up with Marianne? She said she'd come over when she finishes work.'

Geraldine stared at her speculatively.

'Yes, of course – but wait, Valérie. Philippe was back here looking for you last night. Did he find you at home?'

'No, I was out...'

'He looked very handsome in his smart uniform. I wouldn't take him for granted if I were you. I keep telling you that if you're not careful, some other woman will steal him from under your nose.'

'I don't take him for granted...' Valérie protested, but Geraldine wasn't listening. Her friend was looking over Valérie's shoulder at two Swiss soldiers standing in the street, her face lighting up. *'Guten Tag mein Herr...'*

*'Guten Tag,'* a deep voice responded in a strong Swiss-German accent. 'Could we come in for coffee?'

Geraldine stood back to let them in and hissed at Valérie. 'Got to go. These two are on leave from guarding the Lötschberg tunnel at Kandersteg with money to spend.'

'I'll see you later then.' Valérie spoke into thin air as Geraldine hurried inside.

Valérie's first delivery was to one of the long-established watch manufacturers in Geneva, based in a large art deco building on the Rue du Rhône, south of the city centre. For years, the company had bought watch mechanisms from her father for their luxury models and was still one of his most valuable customers. She had known Monsieur Levy, the senior commercial manager, since she was a little girl and looked up expecting to see his tall, elegant figure come out of his office and greet her with his usual warm smile. Monsieur Levy always used to fill out the forms while she was there, discussing the state of the industry and telling her the latest news of his grandchildren who lived in Lausanne. He turned a business encounter into a meeting with an old friend.

But it was his assistant who came out to take her package and hand over the paperwork, completed before her arrival. She stared at the man's crisp, expensive looking suit.

'Where is Monsieur Levy? Is he unwell?'

'Monsieur Levy has retired. I'm the new commercial manager.'

'I didn't realise he was due to retire.'

She knew he was quite old, but it seemed strange for him to leave without telling her.

'The management felt it was a good moment for him to go. We have to move with the times, respond to our customers' wishes.'

'Your customers' wishes?' She smiled brightly, while inside something tightened in her stomach.

He bent his head closer. 'People here don't wish to do business with a Jew any longer.'

'Oh... I see.'

He frowned as if sensing her dismay. Swallowing, she thought of her father and how much he relied on this man's goodwill and forced a smile back on to her face.

'If it was damaging your business, then what else could you do?'

He smiled back at her broadly.

'Indeed. We have to make sure we can trust our employees and our suppliers. It's why we are delighted to continue to do business with you and your father. We are happy that you share our concerns and would do everything possible to protect our business.'

'Yes, of course.' She glanced through the forms, her fingers trembling, and checked they were in order before shoving them into her satchel. Acid was rising up in her stomach and she willed herself not to be sick. Monsieur Levy was being retired early because he was Jewish. Things like that didn't happen in Geneva. It was as if the Germans were in control. Was this just the beginning of something far worse?

Valérie cycled back into the centre and across the end of the lake towards the Rue du Mont-Blanc, the boulevard running from the edge of Lac Léman up to Cornavin station. Her next stop was the imposing post office building, stone frontage and large arch windows dominating the street. She had to send a bundle of packages to companies all over Switzerland and pick up some supplies. A regular customer, she knew most of the people who worked here, the chatty ones, the efficient ones and those who successfully managed to combine friendliness with efficiency. She joined the longest queue to wait for Amélie, curbing her impatience as she made her way slowly to the front.

'Hello, Valérie.'

The slim, young woman smiled and reached out for her parcels, blinking behind her large, thick glasses. While Amélie was filling out forms and stamping labels, Valérie looked around the spacious hall. People were moving through the marble space, the low murmur of conversation punctuated now and then by a greeting or a sudden laugh. A large portrait of General Guisan, commander-in-chief of the Swiss armed forces and native of French-speaking Switzerland, looked down on them benevolently.

'Is Marianne working today?'

Amélie nodded.

'I saw her come in earlier.'

The telephone exchange was on the third floor of the post office building, and a team of girls put calls through and chatted to callers while they waited. Marianne passed on to Emile any information she heard on the telephone calls that could help the Resistance.

The girls usually knew who was working upstairs. Amélie in particular could be relied upon to take an interest in everyone's business.

'They should be going for lunch in a few minutes. Do you want me to tell her you're looking for her?'

'It's all right. I'll wait.'

Outside, Valérie bent down to fix the chain on her bike. She looked up when she heard someone call her name.

'Valérie. Over here.'

It was Marianne, coming out of the staff door at the side of the building with a group of girls, all shrugging into coats as they came outside. Taller than the others, her friend looked just like the farmer's daughter she was, with a riot of dark curls framing her face and a flush of colour across her cheeks. Valérie left her bike and ran across to her friend, linking arms and turning away from the group.

'Come on. Let's get away from all these people.'

She led Marianne towards a wooden bench between the PTT building and the Anglican church further down the Rue du Mont-Blanc.

'I was desperate to see you. How is Emile?' Valérie kept her voice low. 'I'm so worried about him. Did he get back home safely last night? He said it wasn't just the Swiss police waiting for them at the border, but German soldiers too. Did he tell you what happened to the children? Are they out of Geneva?'

'Yes, they're safe. And Emile's all right. My first aid skills managed to patch him up. It wasn't the first time I've put my little brother back together again and I'm sure it won't be the last.'

'You look after all of us.' Valérie squeezed her friend's arm, comforted by her calm voice.

Marianne smiled, but Valérie could see her anxiety in the deep shadows under her eyes and her hands twisting in her lap. 'He was lucky to escape this time. They've put on more border patrols.'

'He only had four children with him. They shot the rest, Marianne. They killed them.' Valérie's voice broke.

'Yes, they killed them. These Germans don't see Jewish people as human. Not even the children. The poor things had no chance once they were seen. And their guide was captured. He's a member of the Resistance so we don't know where he was taken.' She didn't need to go on; both of them knew that few Resistance fighters ever escaped from the Gestapo with their lives. 'I'll see what's said on the calls today, I might be able to find out what happened to him.'

She stared at Valérie. 'You're looking very pale.'

Valérie avoided her friend's steady gaze. Marianne had an uncanny ability to sense how others were feeling.

'I had another argument with my father last night. After hiding the children. And hearing about the others being shot...' Valérie shivered.

Marianne suddenly looked a lot older than her twenty-two years. 'Valérie, I know you want to help, but maybe you should stick to taking messages for us. If the Swiss border police suspect for a second what we're doing, then you're putting us all in danger. You know that the Germans have already got the Swiss police to search our farm twice this month. They suspect anyone with land along the border. And they're not afraid to shoot anyone who helps the Resistance. You know what happened to Papa. I can't lose Emile too.' Her voice wavered and she looked away.

Valérie clutched her friend's arm. 'No, I'm fine. I can do it. I want to help. You said yourself that doing all the deliveries for my father gives me the perfect cover for going across the city, as well as being able to use the old storeroom. No one would suspect me.'

Marianne looked away, her eyes distanced and troubled. 'We think someone tipped off the authorities last night. Someone on the inside.'

'Do you know who?'

'Not yet. Emile and I went over the whole operation, again and again, considered everyone in the chain, but couldn't work out who might have done it. Someone in the Resistance could have betrayed us, but we only know Jean. He's helped lots of groups escape, risked his life again and again, so I can't believe it's him.'

She shook her head. 'Other members provide false papers and safe houses along the route, but we don't know who any of those people are. The person who takes the refugees out of Geneva is our cousin who lives in Lausanne. She works in the Red Cross and comes to Geneva by train all the time. I trust her implicitly.'

Valérie saw one of the other girls appear at the corner of the building behind Marianne and point at her watch. 'You need to get back.'

Marianne glanced behind her and hurriedly stood up.

'I said to Geraldine that we could meet up later,' said Valérie.

Marianne frowned. 'I'm not sure we should discuss any of this in front of Geraldine.'

'Don't you trust her? Marianne, we've known her since we were children.'

'She's becoming very friendly with some of her customers. I hear them talking on their telephone calls at the exchange when I listen in. They like the pretty lady in the Café de Paris who gossips about her neighbours. You know how much she tells us about the conversations she overhears in the restaurant? I'm beginning to wonder how much she talks about us to other people...'

With that parting shot, she turned and ran up the staircase to her office. Valérie jumped on to her bike and pedalled up the Rue du Mont-Blanc past the Cornavin station towards the east of the city centre. She saw none of the people she passed, her mind racing as she thought about a traitor in the Resistance, someone who could betray those desperate children.

Valérie took the long way round to her next visit, through the park along the north bank of the lake, cycling under the russet cover of the horse chestnut trees. through the burnished leaves that had fallen from the branches. She glanced across at the opposite bank of the lake in occupied France. It might look calm now and it was hard to imagine the horrors of war on a day like this. But she knew the lives of the people living under Nazi tyranny were anything but peaceful. Whatever she could do to help them fight back was worth the risk.

She cycled past children playing at the edge of the park, their mothers chatting together on the nearby benches. One of the women waved at her and she returned the wave, recognising one of their neighbours who lived in an apartment on their street. How many of her neighbours would be rounded up and herded on to trains to Poland if they were invaded?

Turning out of the park on to the Rue de Lausanne, one of the main routes out of the city, she finally reached her destination, a handsome cream manor house backing on to the lake, surrounded by trees. This was the base for Henry Grant, one of her father's English customers. He was tall and dark-haired, his serious expression softened by eyes that held a sparkle of fun. Valérie instinctively liked him. She looked forward to her visits, the chance to practise her English and to forget for a short time the difficulties surrounding her.

She cycled through the ornate front gate, up the long drive to the front door and jumped off her bike. As she waited at the grand entrance for someone to answer the bell, she stared at the names of the businesses and press agencies operating from the building, most of which were unknown to her.

Henry greeted her at the door. Behind him, she saw a man go into what she assumed was an office and close the door. She caught the sound of a typewriter clicking before the door silenced the noise.

'I saw you ride up the drive. Come in and have some tea.'

'Thank you.'

Henry led her through the tall atrium and wide hallway to the veranda running along the back of the house. The lawn sloped down towards the lake, grass cut short for the winter to come, but would turn into a meadow of wildflowers every spring. An ancient brick wall enclosed the garden. She stood in the pale late autumn sun, gazing at the peaceful waters of the lake until Henry waved her towards a round table where tea had been laid out. They sat down and Valérie reached into her satchel.

'I've brought your orders.'

She handed over the packages and received two sealed envelopes, one with the payment due and the other with new orders, before they concentrated on their tea. She tried not to gobble like a little girl, but these days she was always hungry. Henry could still get the delicious plum tarts that used to be available everywhere in the city. They were virtually impossible to get these days.

Henry handed her some magazines and switched to English. 'I thought you might like to read these. You said that your English was getting rusty so they might help. One of my colleagues has just come back from London and brought them over.'

'Thank you. That's very thoughtful.' She put them carefully in her bag.

He looked like he was about to say something else, but changed his mind and switched back to French. 'So how is life in the old part of the city?'

'The same really... the food shortages are making things very difficult. The shops and bars are struggling.'

'Even with the imports from our German friends?'

'It's still difficult.' This kind of talk made Valérie squirm, knowing that her country was working with his enemy, but Henry never seemed to pass judgement.

'I hear there were some more refugees caught trying to cross the border last night.' He was pouring her tea and the fine china teapot stopped in mid-air as he waited for an answer. Marianne's warning came flooding back. Valérie might like Henry

Grant, but she didn't really know anything about him. He didn't usually ask so many questions, nor stare at her so intently.

'Really?' She kept her tone light and curious.

'I understand a few managed to get across to safety, but some didn't make it.'

She didn't reply.

'They said that the Germans caught one of the Resistance fighters, but didn't catch the Swiss *passeur* taking the children across the border.'

His dark eyes watched her closely and there was a heavy, oppressive silence before he carried on.

'My sources tell me the Germans have been ordered to find all those who helped the refugees to escape. And the Swiss police are assisting them.'

'Who is your source?' Valérie asked him.

'We talk to lots of different people in the course of our buying and selling. People like you. We hear things,' he said, shrugging.

'I see.'

'You can't trust anyone these days, not even your friends.'

Valérie put down the last piece of her cake, unable to swallow anything else. She placed her napkin slowly down on to her plate.

'I think I should go now.'

He smiled, but his eyes had lost their sparkle.

'Don't take any chances, Valérie. Now that Vichy France is occupied, the Germans control everything there and they aren't always respectful of borders. If you do get into trouble and you need help, you know you can always come to me.'

She stared at him in confusion. How could he help?

'Say thank you to your father for his excellent work. It is appreciated as always. I have written to him about some new orders we will need him to supply.' He broke into a gleaming smile. 'You haven't finished your cake. You must take it with you.'

He fussed over her, giving her a piece of plum tart in a small box, holding open the door and waving as she rode up the drive back towards the road. When she glanced back at the house before turning out of the gate, she saw a curtain in an upstairs room swing shut.

# FOUR

## VALÉRIE

Valérie cycled back through the centre of town, brooding over Henry's words and the intensity of his face. The corners of the magazines he'd given her dug painfully into her side when she stopped at a junction in the city centre and waited for a tram to pass.

Following Agathe's instructions, Valérie cycled to the charcuterie down from the main station but stopped when she saw the long queue of women snaking along the pavement and around the corner of the block. Her heart sinking at the prospect of standing in line for hours, she tried to remember if they had anything else in the larder for supper.

'There you are... Agathe said you'd be here'.

Her heart leapt in her chest and she turned towards the familiar deep voice. Philippe caught her to him in a fierce hug, lifting her off the ground.

'Philippe, you're still here. Oh, I've missed you so much. I thought you'd gone back to the Fort and I wouldn't see you for months.'

She flung an arm around his neck and kissed him, breathing

in his familiar smell. Her stress and worries were forgotten as she pressed herself closer to his tall frame.

'How long have you got?'

'I can only stay for an hour, I'm sorry, Valérie. But I wasn't going to come all this way without seeing you.'

Keeping one arm around her, he leaned over and placed a package into her basket.

'A pie from my mother. You can't spend time queueing up for food when I'm only here for such a short time.'

He kissed her again until a mocking laugh from the other side of the street made them look up. Valérie saw a group of soldiers joking and pointing towards them. She caught the disapproving looks of the women in the queue outside the charcuterie.

Philippe grinned down at her.

'Let's go somewhere quieter.'

She nodded and he turned her bicycle towards the Quai du Mont-Blanc, keeping her hand in his grasp as if he couldn't let her go for a moment.

Valérie cast a look up at his face, thinner now, but just as handsome. They hadn't seen each other since the summer. He seemed older and more self-assured. For a moment, he seemed a stranger to her rather than the boy she'd grown up with, the one she'd shadowed on the ski slope and the shooting range, who had kissed her for the first time and nervously shared his love for her before he joined the military. Then he smiled down at her, his hazel eyes tender and warm, and he was the same Philippe who had shared all her adventures and claimed his place in her heart.

They sat down on their favourite bench, where they'd first kissed, and looked across at the Jet d'Eau fountain shooting up into the blue sky, the cascade of water sparkling in the crisp autumn sun. Even now, in the middle of wartime, a few tourists were staring at the familiar landmark and the weary locals paused for a moment to watch the waterfall glitter in the sunlight.

'I'm sorry about your grandfather. My father said he had another heart attack. How is he?'

He shrugged.

'You know he's been living with my parents since he had the first attack, but he had another one last week. That's when they sent for me. They thought he wouldn't last the night...'

He cleared his throat and couldn't carry on.

'I'm so sorry, Philippe. I love him too.'

He gripped her hand.

'I know you do. The doctor doesn't know how long he has left. And I won't be able to get any more leave so they said I'd better come now.'

He bent his head and she knew he was close to tears. She smoothed his dark hair and kissed his cheek, breathing in the smell of his skin.

'At least you got to see him.'

She thought about the times they'd spent with Philippe's grandfather before the war, listening to his rambling stories and laughing at his jokes. Philippe had helped tend his small piece of land, feeding his chickens and cutting logs for the fire. She'd cooked supper for them all and had begun to feel a real part of their family. They were always over at his house in Vessy, south of the city. Either that or hanging around Emile and Marianne's farm near Presinge, only a short bike ride away. It all seemed such a long time ago, their old way of life snatched away so abruptly.

Philippe clenched his hands together.

'I could have done more if I'd been here. If I'd been able to help him like I always used to, he might not have had the heart attack...'

She grasped his hands and smoothed out the curled fingers.

'You can't blame yourself for having to go away. You did everything you could when you were here.'

'I suppose so.'

'And you know how proud he is of you, always boasting about how his grandson is the best marksman in the Swiss army. He wouldn't have missed that for the world.'

He chuckled and turned towards her, with a sparkle back in his eyes. 'Do you remember that time when he wouldn't accept you'd beaten me in the shooting competition until you'd shown him your cup? It was years ago, but I still remember how angry you were.'

'The look on his face when he saw the cup with my name on it and had to accept that I'd won. I'll never forget it.'

They fell silent again and she glanced at him, relieved to see that the stricken look had gone from his face, although heavy shadows gathered underneath his eyes.

'I had to go out to his house this morning. There were things he wanted me to collect. I'd have come to find you earlier, but he insisted I get them.'

'That's all right. I've been out doing deliveries all day anyway. I've only just finished.'

'I called round to see Emile while I was there.'

She hesitated for a second, wondering what Emile had said to him.

'How was he?'

'A bit shaken. He told me what happened last night.'

He stared at her and took her hands in his

'He could have been killed crossing the border, Valérie. The Germans have orders to shoot anyone trying to get into Switzerland. Do you realise what you've got yourself into?'

She sighed, wishing their precious time together didn't have to be clouded by talk of Germans and death, that familiar knot in her stomach tightening once again.

'I don't want to talk about Emile. Not now, Philippe. Let's just enjoy the time we have together.'

But Philippe wouldn't let it go.

'It's not just Emile. He told me you're helping him hide the people he brings across.'

He tightened his grip on her hands and she could see the worry in his eyes

'You know I support the Resistance and what they're fighting for, of course I do. But I worry about you getting so involved. It's dangerous going out on your own late at night. Geneva isn't the same as it used to be. You know that there's a good chance Germany might invade before long, and if they have you down as an enemy... it doesn't bear thinking about. I know you want to help Emile, but I worry that he might not realise how much danger he's putting you both in.'

'It's not about me, Philippe. I'm not the one in danger. If only you had seen those children last night, you would understand. I'm not going to stop. Please don't spoil all this.'

She gestured at the backdrop of elegant townhouses and hotels skirting the edge of the lake; the deep blue of the water reflected the brilliant sapphire of the November sky and the sound of children's laughter rippled across the surface.

'You're leaving so soon and who knows when we'll see each other again.'

She leaned over to kiss him, but he pulled away.

'Please, Val. I can't go away knowing you're putting yourself in danger. I worry about you too much.'

'I know you do, but you shouldn't. I can't sit on the sidelines and watch events as they happen. I have to try to change them, just like you. You're in the army, defending our country at Saint-Maurice while I'm stuck here making deliveries every day, some of which end up in Nazi hands. At least we get news of what's happening all around us, unlike the poor people over there. I simply can't ignore it, Philippe.

His face had clouded over when she mentioned Saint-Maurice. Was life in the military so hard? She thought he enjoyed it – the camaraderie, the chance to serve his country. But perhaps something had changed. He was based at Fort de Dailly, one of the forts that was part of the Fortress Saint-Maurice complex guarding the south-west flank of the Grand Redoubt. It was one of the major defences protecting the Alps from invasion and maybe the imminent threat of a major battle was becoming hard to bear.

But Philippe seemed far more concerned about her safety.

'You're risking your life. Is it worth that?'

'Of course it is. You've heard what they're saying on the radio, about the concentration camps in Poland and Germany. They're herding women and children into trains like animals, just over there across the border. Nobody ever sees them again. Their only escape is to come to Switzerland. We have to help them. We just have to.'

The wide-eyed children standing in the rain looking at her and Emile for guidance filled her mind. '*I* have to.'

He pulled her tight. 'I know you do. And I love you for that. I just worry about you. But I would do the same, if I were still in Geneva. At least promise me you'll take care? Don't forget how important your life is too.'

'Yes, of course I will.'

He looked at his watch and shook his head.

'I can't believe it. I need to go and get my train already.'

'I'll come with you...'

'Are you sure?'

She tried to lighten the mood.

'You don't think I'm going to miss a minute with you, do you?'

He laughed and they stood up together, turning back towards the station. They walked slowly, arm in arm, putting off his departure for as long as possible. Outside the station, he turned towards her.

'Don't come inside. I hate goodbyes on station platforms. They're always cold and miserable with too many people in tears.'

'I know.'

She took his face between her hands and kissed him softly.

'You be careful too. Remember I love you.'

'I love you too.' He dug into his pocket and handed her a letter. 'I was going to send this, but I thought I could give it to you.'

She clutched the thin envelope and put it into her satchel.

'Thank you. I'll read it later. I've just sent you a letter so it should be waiting for you when you arrive.'

He pulled her to him in a fierce hug. 'I need to go.'

'I know.'

One last kiss and he turned and walked away. Valérie brushed away tears and trudged away from the station. She didn't think she'd ever get used to him going away, the pleasure of the time they spent together overshadowed by his imminent departure. She just hoped it wouldn't go on for years. They were spending too much of their lives apart, not knowing how long the war would last or how it would end.

# FIVE

## VALÉRIE

Valérie pushed her bike up the steep cobbled street into the Place du Bourg-de-Four and saw Marianne and Geraldine ensconced at their favourite corner table inside the Café de Paris. They waved at her out of the window before she could pretend she hadn't seen them and she waved back, the chilly air catching her breath in the gathering dusk. The last thing she felt like was being sociable, but she couldn't ignore her friends. She leaned her bike next to the stack of chairs piled up against the ancient stone wall and, taking a deep breath, walked under the dark green canopy and into the wood-panelled inn, breathing in its comforting warmth.

'Sit down, you look frozen.' Geraldine pulled her towards the table and Valérie sank on to the wooden chair, hardly aware of the hum of chatter around her, seeing only Philippe's retreating figure at the station.

'You know Dieter, don't you? He was just leaving.'

She looked up to see Dieter leaning on the polished wood-panelled bar, his clear blue eyes smiling down at her. Marianne squeezed her arm and she automatically returned his smile.

'I am sorry to have missed you, mademoiselle.'

He shook her hand, holding it for a few moments in his warm grasp, before he bowed to each of them in turn and went towards the door, shoes clicking on the wooden floor. Geraldine scrambled to her feet and went after him. Through the heavy glass partition at the entrance to the café, Valérie watched her wave to Dieter, her figure distorted by the round panes.

'Are you all right?'

She realised with a start that Marianne was speaking to her.

'Yes, I'm fine.'

Before Marianne could reply, Geraldine bounced back inside, grinning widely at her unsmiling friends and placed a steaming cup of hot chocolate in front of Valérie.

'There you go. That should warm you up. You weren't exactly friendly to him were you?'

'Thanks.' Valérie cradled the hot cup between her fingers and sipped the liquid slowly, closing her eyes for a second. The Café de Paris still served the best hot chocolate in Geneva, rich and velvety and dark.

She nudged Valérie. 'He's always asking me about you.'

Valérie felt herself flush. 'I don't know why. He helps my father get export licenses, that's all.'

'All right then. I won't say anything, but he's very good-looking. And he always has lots of money, I've seen him buy everyone drinks in the bar. You want to be nice to him if he's that important to your father's business.'

Valérie glanced at Marianne, who was frowning, her dislike of gossip palpable. Geraldine, practical to the core, was only giving her what she saw as good advice and was blithely unaware of Marianne's disapproval.

Valérie took another sip of the chocolate, which was too delicious to resist, and tried to change the subject.

'I thought you had no more hot chocolate left?'

'Bernard got me some. I don't know where he gets his stuff from, but it's good.'

Marianne cleared her throat. 'And what does Bernard get in return?'

Geraldine pursed her red lips. 'I don't know what you're insinuating. He isn't looking for anything in return. He likes me and wants to help us out. We all need to stick together if we're going to survive this horrible war.'

When she got no response, she jumped to her feet and swept up the empty glasses from the table, clinking them together in her grip.

'What's the matter with you two?' Geraldine's eyes filled with tears as she looked from Marianne to Valérie. 'You're supposed to be my friends but I can't say anything these days without you being disapproving. And you're always whispering secrets together. '

Aware of the curious looks from people at the neighbouring tables, Valérie spoke hastily. 'Don't get upset, Geraldine. I'm just a bit tired, that's all. It's been a difficult day.'

She was talking into thin air. Geraldine had turned away and disappeared into the kitchen behind the bar, slamming the door after her.

After a few minutes of silence, Valérie glanced at Marianne, who was ripping a serviette into small pieces and staring across at a table of Swiss soldiers who were chatting loudly in German.

'Do you have any news?'

Marianne shrugged. 'I heard nothing about who was arrested last night. No one mentioned it on any of the telephone calls I put through. God knows what's happening to them right now, if they're even still alive.'

Valérie looked over her shoulder to watch for Geraldine coming back, her words coming out in a rush. 'One of my father's customers knew someone from the Resistance was captured last night. He asked me what I knew about it.'

Marianne stared at her. 'One of his German customers?'

'No. An Englishman. At least I think he's English. A man called Henry Grant. He works over in one of the large manor houses in the park on the north bank. He said that the border police were looking for the people on the Swiss side who were helping refugees cross the border.'

'Who is this man? How could he know all that if he's just a businessman, buying and selling goods?'

'I don't know. Maybe he's working for the Allies.'

Marianne frowned. 'He might actually be spying for the Germans, fishing for information to pass on.'

Valérie sighed. 'That's possible. I don't know him that well. I've made a few deliveries to him for my father and we have tea. He gives me English magazines. He seems nice, Marianne. But who knows, these days?'

'Can you ask your father what he knows?'

'I'll try... but you know what my father's like. He won't see things that are right in front of his nose if he doesn't want to.'

'What else is bothering you? It isn't just Henry Grant, is it? '

Valérie hunched her shoulders and didn't reply.

'What else happened today?'

'I saw Philippe. He came back to see his grandfather. It was lovely to see him, but it was such a short time. And I won't see him again for months.'

She looked up at Marianne.

'He worries about me helping the Resistance, said it was too dangerous.'

'You can't blame him for being concerned, even if you're staying on this side of the border.'

'I suppose so. It just feels like we're so far away from each other now. I barely know anything about his life at the Fort.'

'He's not allowed to talk about it, Val, not even to you.'

.   .   .

Valérie didn't stay in the café for long. She crossed the Place du Bourg-de-Four and pushed her bike through the cobbled streets of the old town towards home, pausing in front of the bookshop where her mother used to work. It looked bare and empty, the books carefully displayed on either side of the door a distant memory. She would give anything to be able to talk to her mother about Philippe, ask her advice and share her hopes for the future. She leaned on her bike and squinted through the dusty windows, remembering when the shop had been warm and cosy, the shelves full of books and magazines stretching up to the ceiling. It was a place where people had time to browse, linger over rich, dark coffee and debate the news of the day, unafraid of who might be listening.

Today, she could hardly make out much inside the shop aside from some old packing crates leaning against the cracked window. She stretched out a hand to touch the window frame and the dark green paint flaked off in her hand. She wondered why no one had taken over the shop when Monsieur Steinberg had left, though when she checked behind her, she realised that not many people passed through this lane. Perhaps it wasn't so attractive a location as it had seemed all those years ago.

She pushed her bike away from the window then stopped when she thought she glimpsed a flickering light at the back of the bookshop. She glanced at the door and saw with a jolt of surprise that the lock on the door wasn't old and rusty like the rest of the building, but new and shiny. Someone had made sure that the building was secure. She stared again through the dusty shop window, half expecting her mother to appear behind the glass and beckon her to come in, but the light had gone and she gave herself a shake. Maybe it had passed into new hands.

When she got back home, Valérie hung up her coat on the rail next to some dark overcoats made of fine cashmere. She ran her fingers across the soft wool and wondered who was visiting her father. Walking softly through the house, she heard low voices coming through the closed door to his workshop. None of the doors in the old townhouse fit their frames snugly and she paused outside the door, listening intently.

'It's too much Albert. I can't source the number of jewel bearings you're asking for... I wouldn't have enough for my other customers.'

She recognised the voice of one of her father's major suppliers, Pascal Dumont, a man she'd known all her life. He was part of the close network of artisans supplying the delicate individual watch parts for *établisseurs* like her father, who assembled them into watch movements which he sold on to the larger watch manufacturers. Her hand hesitated on the door when she heard the other voice, one she didn't recognise.

'Well, I can't give you more at the price you're paying. We need to focus on our larger customers, the major factories in Chaux-de-Fonds. The industry is changing Albert, you can't escape the facts. It's moving away from small specialist workshops like yours to large conglomerates, companies that produce to scale, manufacture all their own components rather than buy everything from smaller specialists.'

She heard her father sigh.

'You know my view, Monsieur Weber. There will always be demand for the high-quality watch mechanisms we produce, even if we don't manufacture the plates or bridges ourselves. I know that the number of my customers has reduced, but those who remain continue to demand high-quality products. The big factories can't replicate the level of workmanship I can produce.'

It was an argument that Valérie had heard for years, but she wondered how long her father's business could survive while he ignored what was happening all around him. At the start of the war, he'd closed down the large workshop and turned her mother's elegant dining room into a makeshift base, employing a couple of his old workers to make components in their own homes in the traditional way. While the industry was going for scale and automation, he seemed to be stepping back in time.

'I'm sorry, Albert. You'll need to find another supplier for your jewel bearings...' The harsh voice grew louder and she heard the noise of heavy footsteps coming towards the door. She ran lightly up to the first landing and heard the door crash open, then bent forward to glimpse a large man she'd never seen before stride towards the front door and pull a coat from the rail, his bulky frame filling the hall. She watched as her father followed him down the hall and caught his arm. They walked out together and she could hear the murmur of voices outside, though she couldn't make out what they were saying.

She walked slowly down the stairs, wondering why her father was ordering so many expensive watch parts when she knew that his order book was thinner than ever, and almost collided with Pascal as he came out of the parlour. He smiled broadly when he saw it was her, kissing her on both cheeks.

'Valérie, I didn't know you were there... How are you, my dear?'

'I'm well, Monsieur Dumont.' She looked at his hunched figure and lined features, trying to hide her shock at how old he seemed.

'How is your father's business holding up, Valérie?'

'We're managing. We still have most of our old customers and a few new ones.'

'He is an artist, your father. He will never accept that price is more important than quality to most buyers these days.'

He looked as if he was about to say more, when Albert came back into the house, shutting the door firmly behind him. Pascal clasped his old friend's hand. 'You didn't agree to pay that crook what he was asking, did you?'

Her father sighed. 'No, but I probably paid more than the bearings were worth.'

'How can you afford it, Albert? The volumes you're asking for...' Pascal shook his head.

'Don't worry, my friend. I can pay. I still have plenty of customers. My business isn't finished yet.'

When Pascal had gone, Valérie sat on the side of her father's desk and told him about each of her visits. Yesterday's argument faded as she talked, passing on news about each of their customers, whether they were happy or worried, what they'd said and what she'd seen. Her father had taught her that it was important to share all the information gleaned from her visits to customers, however small or insignificant the information might seem. She put the packages she'd collected on his desk and he opened each of the boxes, checking that the parts were what he had ordered.

'Did you know that Monsieur Levy has left Universal Watches?'

Her father looked up and sighed. 'The last time I saw him he said that he probably wouldn't be there for much longer.' He paused. 'He was a good man.'

Valérie bit her lip. Monsieur Levy had known her father for decades and she was dismayed to see how little emotion he displayed at this news.

'I saw his assistant today. He seemed very pleased to get the job, said that some of their customers didn't want to deal with Monsieur Levy any longer because he is Jewish.'

Her father didn't reply so she changed the subject, swallowing her frustration.

'And I sent everything off at the post office. Then I delivered the packages to Henry Grant. He said to thank you for your valuable work. He wanted me to tell you that specifically.'

'Very good. He's another important customer.'

Valérie hesitated, then asked. 'How much do you know about him?'

He took off his glasses and polished the lenses, thinking about her question.

'Henry Grant? He works for an import-export business and is the main buyer for several English watch companies. He's been here since before the war. Why do you want to know?'

She shrugged. 'I just wondered. He was asking lots of questions when I was there today.'

'What kind of questions? Were they about us?'

'Not specifically. More about how things are in Geneva generally.'

'Valérie, that's his job. His customers rely on him for the supplies to keep up their production so he needs to be aware of what's happening here. If something happened to us or to the other companies he deals with, he would have to find alternative suppliers. That isn't easy in wartime.'

'I suppose so.' She clapped a hand to her forehead, 'I completely forgot. I saw Philippe this afternoon and he gave me something for supper... from his mother. It's in my basket.'

She could feel her father's eyes follow her as she went out to fetch the pie and place it in the larder.

'I'll heat this for supper later on...'

'Are you all right, *mignonne*? You must be pleased you saw Philippe after missing him last night?'

'Of course, it was wonderful to see him. But we didn't have long together and I'm just a bit tired, that's all.'

She bent down and pulled the English magazines from her bag with the letter Philippe gave her.

'Henry gave me some new magazines so I'm going to go up to my room and read them.'

She kissed her father and left him smoothing out the stack of invoices she'd brought back.

In her room, she tossed the magazines on to the bedside

table and threw herself on to her bed, lying in the darkness and clutching Philippe's letter, replaying in her mind the sound of his voice and the feel of his lips. She opened his letter and lit the small brass lamp next to her bed, which cast a pool of light on to his familiar writing.

*Ma chère Valérie,*

*I hope you're well. It's been months since I've seen you – I miss you so much. Thank you for your letter, I love hearing all your news. I'm sorry that you're worried about your father's business. I hope he's managing to sort out his export licences.*

*You'll never guess what happened to me last week. We were out near your uncle and aunt's farm on an exercise and our truck broke down. Then it started to snow and we had to find shelter for the night. So, six of us slept in their barn! When your aunt realised it was me, she asked us in for supper. She reminded me so much of you – I almost felt like you were with me. They killed some chickens and we all had a feast. It was the best meal I've had in ages. You must say thank you to her from me when you next write.*

*That was the first proper snow before the winter. They're expecting some fairly heavy falls before Christmas so we'll be on skis a lot more. Don't be too jealous – it's all work! And it isn't the same without you anyway. No one to have a proper race with.*

*Some of our unit can't ski very well so we're all encouraged to practise regularly. It's the best way to get around the mountains for reconnaissance. We even have a film unit coming to make a newsreel for the cinema showing how important it is that we all ski well to be able to defend the mountains.*

*I'm writing this on the train on my way to Geneva! I'm sorry to have to tell you but they think my grandfather has had another heart attack. The minute Monsieur Favre heard about it, he talked to my senior officer to ask him to give me leave to come home and see him. He's been very kind. I'm going straight to visit grandfather in hospital but will come over to you as soon as I can and I'll give this letter to your father if I can't see you. I'm so worried about my grandfather, but really excited to see you.*

*Avec tout mon amour,*

*Philippe*

The sharp sound of pebbles scattering across the shutters on her bedroom window made her sit up. A louder crack came from a large stone hitting the bottom of the shutter and she leaped out of bed and pushed open the window. At first, she couldn't see anyone, but then a figure peeled out from the shadows and she recognised Emile's uneven gait.

'What are you doing here?' she hissed, glancing at the light from her father's workshop downstairs.

'I need to speak to you. It's urgent. Can you come out?'

'Now? I'm not sure if I can.' She could hear someone laughing in the next street and hissed. 'It's not safe here. There are too many people around. I suppose I could come and meet you in the storeroom.'

Anything was better than lying on her bed missing Philippe. And she wanted to have a word with Emile about giving away her involvement in the Resistance. Philippe had enough to think about, without being worried about her.

'Throw me the key.'

Valérie took the large key out of her satchel and dropped it out of the window into Emile's hands. Without another word, he disappeared into the shadows. She checked up and down the street to make sure that nobody was following him, then closed the shutters. She crept downstairs and took her coat from the hook in the hall, glancing at her father through the door to the dining room. His head was bowed, his elbows resting on the table and despite her annoyance with him, she felt a stab of concern. Perhaps he felt more than he was prepared to admit.

Swallowing her guilt at adding to his worries, she tiptoed across the floor. She'd just have to take the chance he wouldn't come to look for her before she got back.

Hunching down against the cold wind, Valérie walked the few hundred metres to the old workshop without meeting anyone. She looked up and down the street to check she wasn't being followed before she opened the door to the courtyard and ran to the building. When she pushed the door open, a hand shot out to pull her inside and slam it shut behind her. She grasped his arm to steady herself and looked up into Emile's strained face.

'Why are you here so late? What's happened?'

He half-turned to look behind him and Valérie saw a woman appear out of the shadows, hardly older than she was, staring suspiciously at them and saying nothing. She was tall, with straight, dark, shoulder-length hair, dressed in men's clothes, the trousers held up by a thick leather belt around her waist. The hilt of a knife stuck into her belt caught the glow from the old lamp which lit up the back of the storeroom.

Emile cleared his throat. 'This is Simone. She's just escaped across the border. The Germans have been trying to catch her for months and came very close tonight. Jean decided it was too dangerous for her to stay in France any longer. He asked me to help her escape.'

Simone sat down on the bottom step of the wooden stairs leading to the upper floor. She stared at them, then took out a cigarette and lit it up, breathing in the smoke and blowing it out in a cloud that almost hid her face from view.

Emile lowered his voice. 'She says she's smuggled out a list of traitors in the Swiss army who are passing secrets to the Nazis. The Germans are desperate to find it and destroy the evidence before she can give it to the authorities here. She needs to hand it over fast before these traitors give away information that could damage our country.'

'*Non.*'

They both turned towards the Frenchwoman, who was staring at them through the smoky air and shaking her head.

'Not to the Swiss authorities. They are not to be trusted to act on it. My mission is to hand the list over to the Allies.'

She gesticulated towards Emile with the cigarette, the burning end jerking in the shadows. 'That's why I came to you. I was told you delivered funding from the English or the Americans to the Resistance. The list must be given to your contact.'

He nodded and looked uncertainly at Valérie.

'I needed to get her as far away from the border as I could and this was the safest place I could think of. Can you hide her for a few days until I hand the list over? Then I'll arrange to get her out of Geneva.'

Caught up by the urgency in his voice, she nodded.

'Valérie, this could be more dangerous than anything I've ever asked you to do. The Swiss police have been told she's a criminal and a danger to anyone who approaches her. She doesn't trust them enough to tell any of them about the list, and they're determined to find her and send her back. It's crucial to maintain their relationship with the Germans and anyone hiding her will be prosecuted. This could mean jail. And it would certainly mean you're on record as anti-German. Philippe will never forgive me if I drag you into trouble with the police and put you at risk. When he came to see me, he asked me not to get you involved in hiding Jewish refugees, far less something like this. But I don't know what else to do.'

Without needing to look, she was aware of the woman's fierce gaze, waiting for her answer; Valérie didn't hesitate.

'Of course, I'll help.'

A sudden clatter on the floor made them turn towards Simone and they saw that she'd crumpled back on the stairs in exhaustion, a hunting knife dropped at her feet. In that moment, Valérie understood with sickening certainty just how far the Frenchwoman was prepared to go to fulfil her mission.

# SIX

## PHILIPPE

### **Saint-Maurice, Valais, Switzerland**

'Drinks all around. You boys deserve a break, working all these hours up in the mountains to defend our country.'

Philippe glanced at the white-aproned bar owner behind the large wooden counter grinning down at the group of soldiers crowded around the table in the corner. So much for keeping a low profile. The whole place was looking at their unit, including the German soldiers at the other side of the bar, who had sneaked into the warmth instead of standing on the freezing platform guarding the goods train passing through Saint-Maurice station. He hadn't seen them come in, nor had he noticed the two businessmen in dark suits sitting at the table in the other corner, staring across the room at the group of Swiss soldiers.

'These German soldiers shouldn't be in here. They're supposed to stay on their trains when they cross Switzerland,' one of his unit muttered to Philippe. He nodded. They all knew the conditions the Swiss imposed on German trains entering their territory, the price of being able to operate in a neutral country.

Shielded by the arms raised around him ordering drinks – the loudest shouts coming from Olivier, their unit leader – Philippe got up and headed for the door. He didn't like Olivier and knew that the feeling was mutual, so the last thing he wanted to do was to share a drink with him. He bent his head down to pass under the low doorway when he felt a steely grip on his arm.

'Hey soldier, don't you want a free drink?'

'No thanks.' He saw Olivier wander across to speak to the businessmen in the corner. 'I don't like the company.'

The bar owner took an instinctive step backwards at his expression, smile fading, and Philippe escaped into the cold night, breathing a sigh of relief as he closed the door to the Café de la Gare. He knew he had to control himself and not attract too much attention, but with so many worries and secrets buzzing around his head he felt on edge, ready to blow up at the slightest provocation. His low mood since parting again from Valérie didn't help, their time together so brief and hurried. He gazed up at the sheer cliffs framing the town, feeling calmer now he was outside and alone.

He walked to the corner of the street and leaned on the building directly opposite the main station, pulling out a cigarette and lighting it up. He stared at the elegant building in front of him, the carved balustrades and simple lines of the stonework designed to welcome tourists seeking the ski slopes and the thermal baths across the Rhône in Lavey-les-Bains. There weren't many tourists these days and only a smattering of hardy pilgrims visited the ancient abbey in the town. Even the citizens of the local area and the surrounding mountain villages were outnumbered by soldiers.

In some ways, the town of Saint-Maurice hadn't changed

much since Philippe had come here as a boy, helping Valérie's aunt and uncle on their farm up the mountain in Gryon. The annual pattern for the farming community was the same as it had been for centuries, herding the cattle high into the mountains in the summer and letting them graze the sweet Alpine grass, then bringing them back down to the valley in the winter. There was still the constant struggle to bring in enough harvest in the summer to feed the cattle in the cold months, made worse by the men being called away for military service.

In other ways, everything had changed. The town had always been an important strategic location for trade and defence as the gorge narrowed in this part of the Rhône valley. Now the steep cliffs concealed powerful guns and hundreds of men living in tunnels dug into the mountain on both sides, ready to repel an invading army. Saint-Maurice was where they spent their time off, trying to forget the weeks living in underground tunnels, punctuated by military exercises in the mountains and shooting practice at a nearby shooting range.

Philippe sighed when he thought about Valérie and how frustrated she felt not to be able to join the army. He would have been just the same in her position and felt a thrill of pride in her bravery despite his concern for her safety. It was dangerous to help the Resistance, not just because of the Germans guarding the border with France and the possibility of being blacklisted as an enemy just before an invasion, but also because of the *passeurs* who took refugees across for thousands of francs. They could be ruthless and had a reputation for leaving refugees stranded if they thought they were going to be caught, making sure they kept the money they'd been paid. Emile was setting himself up to stamp all over their patch and deprive them of that money and now Valérie was mixed up in it too.

Philippe knew that his father, like a lot of the canton police, had little patience with the French Resistance, far less with

Swiss civilians helping refugees cross the border. He could still hear the lecture, repeated to anyone who would listen: *We are struggling to feed our own people, far less those escaping from France...* Three years into the war the Swiss were tired, scared and hungry, and more and more often these days were ready to turn their backs on people they could ill afford to help.

He heard a noise behind him and spun around, then relaxed when he saw Christophe.

'Where did you appear from?'

Christophe glanced behind him towards the streets that formed the main part of the town and Philippe saw a small blonde woman slip into the shadows at the end of the block.

'You've been meeting someone?'

'She's called Nathalie.'

Christophe grinned at him, white teeth gleaming in the street light.

'Who knows when we might get down here again?'

He frowned at Philippe, who was hunching his shoulders against the cold wind blowing down off the mountains and funnelling through the narrow gorge between the high peaks.

'Are you all right? Why are you standing here in the freezing cold?'

'You know I don't trust that barman. Trying to get us drunk and then encouraging us to talk about what we're doing up at the Fort. All those people in there listening and watching, ready to report back on what they hear.'

He thought about the businessmen at the corner table talking to Olivier and the German soldiers, sitting comfortably as if they had a right to be there.

Christophe punched his arm. 'You don't trust anyone these days. You'll be accusing me of selling secrets to the Germans next.'

Philippe grinned and shook his head.

'You know what the chief said. You've been working non-stop for months and need a night off. We all do. Sleeping and eating in that rabbit warren of tunnels in the mountain for months on end. It's enough to make you go mad.'

'It's not that bad. And you know how important the work is,' said Philippe grimly. 'We have to be prepared for a German invasion. You heard the briefing. They could strike at any time, particularly now France has fallen. Switzerland is surrounded. What we're doing up here is more important than ever.'

Christophe answered, but his words were drowned out by the sound of the train on the platform in front of them powering up its engines. It loomed like an awakening monster in the darkness. The two German soldiers burst out of the bar and ran past them towards the train, jumping into the nearest carriage. Inside the train, they glimpsed a group of German officers wearing the black coats of the Gestapo moving to the front.

Christophe stubbed out his cigarette with the toe of his boot. 'I wonder what they've got on that train they're so keen to hide. More German weapons going to France. Or maybe treasures from Italy they're planning to sell.' He dropped his voice to a fierce hiss. 'Kept safe for them by their nice Swiss banker friends until the end of this godforsaken war. I sometimes despair of our countrymen. They'll take money from anyone.'

Philippe looked at Christophe, marvelling at how his mercurial temperament plunged from happiness to despondence in an instant, the change in his mood reflected in his expression. He knew that Christophe's father had died just before the war and his mother didn't have much money. The proceeds from the sale of his art dealership had been used up over the subsequent years and she was struggling to feed his younger brothers and sisters, relying on the few francs Christophe could send home out of his army pay.

Before he could reply, an army truck careered round the corner of the building and screeched to a halt at the front of the bar. The driver jumped out of the cab, leaving the engine running and ran towards them.

'You've been ordered back. There was an explosion at the Fort. They think it was deliberate. Everyone needs to come back now.'

Christophe grasped Philippe's arm.

'I need to find Stefano. He came out with me when I met Nathalie. We can't leave him behind.'

'You go and get him. Hurry up or we'll have to leave without you.'

Christophe had gone before he'd finished speaking and Philippe strode back to the Café de la Gare, walking into some of his unit who had heard the truck and were crowding out of the bar, pulling on their coats to protect them from the cold.

'What's going on?' Olivier barged through the group.

'We've been called back to the Fort.'

Philippe turned to the café and saw the naked interest of the other patrons and the bar owner craning his neck to see what was happening outside.

'Why? What are you talking about? Out of my way...' Olivier pushed past him to speak to the truck driver and Philippe turned to the other men.

'Is everyone here?'

They looked at one another and then one of them spoke.

'Stefano isn't. He went off with Christophe.'

'Anyone else missing?'

They shook their heads.

'All right. Everyone into the truck.' They all obediently trooped out towards the truck and started climbing into the back.

Philippe glanced up the street to see if Christophe and Stefano were coming. Stefano was one of the youngest in the unit, from Ticino, the Italian-speaking region of Switzerland. A quiet boy, he seemed to look to the others for guidance. He was the last one Philippe wanted to leave alone in the town late at night, with German soldiers walking around.

'Come on... get in!' Olivier yelled at Philippe. 'What are you waiting for?'

'We haven't got everyone here yet.'

'Too bad. They'll be left behind. Our orders are to get back immediately.'

Philippe didn't move.

'We're still missing two men. We can't go until everyone's here.'

Olivier sneered and came up close to him.

'Who exactly do you think is in charge here? I'm ordering you to get into the truck because we're going now.'

Philippe still didn't move and clenched his fists behind him. The men were looking curiously out of the truck, a few of them smiling in anticipation at the likelihood of a fight. It was certainly turning out to be a more interesting night than they'd imagined. But Philippe wasn't going to give them the satisfaction and he uncurled his fingers and walked slowly towards the truck, stopping in front of Olivier.

'We're missing Christophe and Stefano.'

'Then they'll have to find their own way back, won't they?'

A shout echoed across the street and they both turned around. Christophe and Stefano raced towards them and they all finally clambered into the truck. It started up and lurched its way around the station square. Out of the back, Philippe saw the train edge its way out of the station towards Geneva on its way to France. He, too, wondered what was inside it. Was it on its way to pick up innocent people and take them away to the camps in Poland?

'Thanks for waiting.' Christophe and Stefano were panting.

'You're welcome.'

'You almost caused a fight.' Walter, a weather-beaten farmer from the German-speaking area near Brig, grinned at them. 'Pity you turned up when you did.'

'Who was going to fight?'

Walter glanced to check he couldn't be overheard by Olivier, who had chosen to travel in the comparative warmth of the cab, then pointed at Philippe.

'Your friend here. Didn't agree with Olivier that we should leave without you.'

'Quite right too.' Antoine, a thin-faced lawyer from Lausanne and one of the older men in the unit, nodded in approval. 'The first rule of leadership, don't leave anyone behind.'

Christophe shook his head when Philippe didn't make any comment. 'I keep telling you that Olivier has enough reason to resent you without making it worse. You shoot better than him, ski better than him... now you're showing up his total absence of leadership ability.'

'Did you want to be left behind?'

His friend rolled his eyes.

'Then stop complaining.' Philippe grinned at Christophe.

The men fell quiet as the truck wound its way through the deserted streets and towards the bridge over the Rhône. It was a clear night and the frost on the banks of the river glistened in the moonlight as they crossed the bridge. Philippe stared out at Lavey-les-Bains and the grand spa resort at the bottom of the mountain road, the warm ochre colour of the hotel building glowing in the dim lights. Its popularity hadn't been diminished by the war, with English tourists being replaced by visiting dignitaries and senior military personnel. Philippe could see people laughing and eating inside the restaurant, a world away from the war raging all around them.

They reached the bottom of the narrow road that snaked up the side of the mountain to the Fort perched high above the valley and the truck started to climb the hill through the icy branches of the fir trees.

He felt a sharp nudge in his ribs.

'Here, have a bit of chocolate…' Christophe broke off a piece from the bar he was hiding in his jacket and handed it to Philippe.

'Thanks…'

'You look like you need cheering up. Don't tell me you're still pining for the beautiful Valérie?'

'How did you guess?'

'Not difficult. You're always like this when you've been back home.'

'I don't really want to talk about it.'

Christophe shrugged and leaned back against the side of the truck.

Philippe frowned in the darkness. He wasn't about to tell Christophe that he was more worried about Valérie than he'd ever been. He was afraid of the danger she could get herself into and was frustrated that he was so far away and wasn't there to protect her. What if she started going across the border herself to help the refugees across?

The noise in the truck intruded into his thoughts, the soldiers' voices making a racket all around him.

'So what happened up there?'

'There was an explosion at one of the entrances to the funicular railway. Caused a fire. Deliberate, they said…'

'Anything to stop us defending ourselves…'

'How did the Germans get near the place? Whoever was on duty won't live this one down.'

'Just as well it wasn't us.'

'Did they catch anyone?'

'No one knows. That's why we've all been called back. The last chance we'll have to get a drink for months.'

'And a kiss…'

The men all howled with laughter at the forlorn voice.

'Has old man Favre taken you to Lavey yet?' said Christophe.

'Not yet. How do you know that's where he goes?'

'Everyone knows. Regular as clockwork every Thursday. Has his session in the medical centre and then a smart dinner to follow.'

'He deserves it, Christophe. He works harder than anyone else in the Fort.'

In late spring, when their commanding officer had asked to speak to Philippe, he'd thought it was about his shooting. He knew he was one of the best marksmen in the camp and already spent a lot of his time training his fellow soldiers and showing his skills off to visiting military dignitaries. Maybe he would be sent to another unit to train their marksmen. But instead, he'd asked Philippe to help cartographer Roger Favre document the weapons and explosives they were planting in the mountains so that they had a record of the Alpine defences they could deploy in the event of an attack.

It was a big honour to be chosen for the work. Favre was a friend of one of his old geography professors and when he'd complained about the standard of every assistant they'd given him so far, his professor had suggested Philippe. And although they didn't say it, Philippe guessed it was also because they knew his father was in the Geneva police and they could trust him to keep the work secret.

The work was more interesting than Philippe had expected but he was relieved that he could still go out on exercises in the mountains with his unit. He couldn't have faced being cooped up in their airless office all the time, the only sounds breaking the silence the occasional scratching of their pens. Favre was a national hero and a hard taskmaster. He drilled into Philippe so many times the importance of accuracy, because the lives of their countrymen could depend on their work. He himself barely took a break for hours on end, his sense of duty and service underpinning everything he did. Philippe knew how much pressure Favre was under and had decided early on that he would have no reason to complain about his work. Since they'd been working so closely together Philippe had seen the man's softer side. When he'd heard about his grandfather's heart attack, Favre had given him immediate permission to go and visit him.

The truck was still grinding up the road, twisting and turning its way up the thousand metres to the Fort perched at the top of the northern side of the valley. There were over twenty hairpin bends on the road to the top and the men all swayed in one single movement when the truck sped up and swung around each corner. Philippe caught sight of an old barn in a clearing next to one of the bends. It would be full of winter feed for the cattle in the area, like the others dotted along the single-track road. Many of these barns could only be reached by horseback, particularly when the snow fell at lower levels. Most of the farmers still relied on horses and carts to feed the cattle, just as the army relied on horses to move equipment around the mountains.

As they approached the Fort and the driver waited for the guards to open the gate, Philippe wondered why the Germans had tried to blow up one of the entrances to the complex. It could have simply been an attempt to destroy part of the network of tunnels and fortifications. But how did they get close enough to do it without being seen? Could they have someone on the inside helping them? He glanced round the young faces in the truck and wondered who among them could think of betraying their friends and their country.

Favre had said it was vital that Philippe didn't talk to anyone about his work on the maps, not to his family or his friends. Not even to the fellow soldiers in his unit, although they must have all guessed where he was going every other day.

He knew they were right to be cautious because if the Germans found out what he did, they might find a way to threaten him to acquire his secrets.

He wished he could have told Valérie all about it. They'd always discussed what they were doing, shared their worries and concerns, but now they seemed to be leading separate lives, each fraught with their own secrets and dangers.

# SEVEN

## PHILIPPE

The truck roared through the main gate and slid to a halt. There was a covering of snow on the ground at this higher altitude, hardening in the freezing temperature. The doors swung open and the men all jumped out of the back. Philippe was the last to climb down and he found himself in a crowd of soldiers milling around the open space, huddled together to protect themselves from the bitter wind scything across the mountainside. The Fort must have been evacuated and the men were only now being taken back inside, unit by unit. He glanced up at the mountain but there was nothing but blackness above the main entrance, no indication of where the saboteurs had tried to strike.

The camouflaged entrance to the Fort was relatively small and gave no indication that it opened up into a huge complex of thousands of kilometres of tunnels going deep into the mountain leading to dormitories, restaurants, equipment rooms, kitchens and even a hospital.

One of the soldiers had said that the bomber had targeted one of the ventilation shafts at one end of the funicular railway that was used to transport men and artillery around the inside of the hillside. If they'd wanted to delay the work being done to build defences, then that was the place to strike, thought Philippe. Perhaps it was as simple as that, an attempt to slow them down.

'Come on, we need to get inside before it starts snowing...' Christophe tugged his arm and he saw Olivier shouting at them to go to their dormitory. His voice was whipped away in the wind, but everyone obediently turned towards the entrance. Olivier glared at Philippe as he followed his friend through the door, the other units queuing up behind them to go back inside. Glancing around him at the moving figures filling the rock tunnels lit by strings of lights, Philippe knew that once they had reached their quarters, he would have no opportunity to go back out that night. He followed Christophe for a hundred metres or so through the damp access tunnels, then pulled his sleeve. 'Cover for me, will you? I'll be back soon.'

'What? Where are you going?'

But Philippe slipped away without answering. It was easy to peel off into the crowd and tag on to a group going in the opposite direction. If he was asked, Christophe could say that he got split off from his unit and would probably catch up in a few minutes. It would be enough time to let Philippe check the map room, just to make sure that it hadn't been disturbed. He had a chilling thought that the Germans could have been after his maps. It could change the whole future of Switzerland if they fell into enemy hands.

He followed another unit and then turned away from the main tunnels into a narrower cul-de-sac, where they worked on the maps, next to a smaller storage room and rifle room. He felt in his inside pocket for the key, which he always kept with him and slipped it into the lock, turning it slowly and checking behind him to make sure he wasn't being followed. Inside the room, the heater was on and the bright lamp shone down on a bald head.

'Monsieur Favre... I didn't expect to see you here.'

The older man looked up and gestured to the papers in front of him.

'The work never goes away.'

He studied Philippe and his eyes softened.

'How was your grandfather? I hope you managed to see him.'

Philippe sank on to a chair near the door and ran his hand through his hair.

'Yes, I saw him, but he was very weak.' He cleared his throat.

'They're not sure he'll last much longer.'

'I'm sorry to hear that.'

Philippe looked around the room, bare of all but the required furniture: two long wooden tables, a few chairs and the large wooden cabinet with wide, shallow drawers where they stored the maps. Everything seemed in order, nothing was left out on the tables an intruder could steal or photograph. He glanced again at Favre and saw that he was studying one of the maps Philippe had completed the previous day, showing the detailed bomb positions marked along the main ridge down one side of the Rhône valley.

'I wanted to check that everything was all right here. When I heard that someone had damaged part of the Fort, I was concerned that they were looking for the maps, that they may have found this room.'

'You were completely right to be concerned, but all is well. I have been here all evening checking your work and have not been disturbed. But I'm glad you came back. I have a package to be collected in Geneva on Thursday. I wondered if you'd like to fetch it for me.'

Favre smiled.

'I know you just came back up, but I thought you might like to go and see your grandfather again.'

'Thank you, sir. I would like that very much.' He felt a spurt of gratitude towards the old man. If he planned it properly this time, he could also see Valérie for longer.

'And Philippe, I plan to go down to the baths at Lavey the same evening. You can join me when you get back. You have done some excellent work here and I think you deserve a reward.'

He felt a thrill of anticipation at the prospect. By all accounts, he could look forward to a real treat, as the cartographer usually had supper in the expensive restaurant where they served as good a meal as you could hope to get in wartime Switzerland.

'I'll speak to your unit leader about it tonight. Now go to bed.'

Outside the fortified door, Philippe reached into his pocket for his key. They always locked the door behind them when they left the map room. But his key wasn't in his pocket, or on the floor. And he hadn't left it in the lock. He heard Favre move inside the room.

'Don't bother locking the door, Philippe. I'm just coming out.'

At the end of the cul-de-sac, he turned the corner into one of the larger tunnels and thought he saw Christophe in a group of soldiers walking away from him.

'Hey, Christophe.'

His shout disappeared into the noise of marching boots as another unit came up behind him and he quickened his pace to keep ahead of them.

It took Philippe an age to reach the door of his sleeping quarters, pushing past several units still making their way through the tunnels. It was much busier than usual, which must mean that some of the complex had been damaged and was out of use. At least it gave him an excuse to be late. He pushed open the door to his dormitory, hoping his absence hadn't been noticed, but Olivier's harsh voice greeted him as he came in.

'You're here at last, are you? Where did you disappear to? What makes you think you're different from everybody else and don't have to follow my orders?'

'Sorry Olivier. I got stuck behind a large group and was told to wait until they had gone past.'

He threw his backpack on to his bunk and picked up the letter on his pillow, planning to save it for later, before glancing at the men reading their own letters at the other side of the room.

'Who collected the mail?'

Antoine, the lawyer from Lausanne, raised his hand without lifting his head.

'Thanks.'

Olivier frowned at him and was about to speak when Philippe stalled his question. 'Someone said the tunnels round the funicular railway are damaged so everyone needs to pass through this way. It's mayhem out there.'

Before Olivier could reply, they heard another unit leader just outside their door shout at his men to move on, followed by the noise of shuffling feet, which faded away after a few minutes. Olivier glared at Philippe and stomped towards the door. 'You'll be woken up at six o'clock in the morning for shooting practice at the Saint-Maurice range. You'd better all get some sleep.'

When he'd gone, the men relaxed and started speculating about what had happened. Philippe turned to Christophe, who was quietly reading a book in the bunk below his. He must have been mistaken when he thought he'd seen Christophe in the tunnels outside.

'Thanks for covering for me. How quickly did he notice I wasn't with you?'

'Not long after you'd gone. I've told you, he's always trying to land you in trouble. And that was before you showed him up tonight. If you hadn't appeared when you did, it would have been another formal complaint. And you know he's trying to stop you from working with old man Favre. Seeing you go off to sit in a warm office when we're all freezing outside on guard duty has made him ten times worse.'

Philippe threw his belt down on to his bed. 'I know it has, but he can't do anything about it... and anyway, I'd much rather be out with all of you.'

'I'm just saying, you need to watch out for him. He'll get you into trouble if he has the chance.'

Christophe turned around and then cursed as Philippe saw a roll of banknotes slither off the bottom bunk on to the floor. Christophe swooped down and gathered up the notes before anyone else could see, then stared at Philippe as if daring him to ask where he'd got the money, his face flushed from bending down.

'I didn't think you had any money left...'

Christophe turned away and carefully put away the notes and folded his jacket. 'I won it playing cards down in the valley. You were all drinking in the bar, so I decided to make better use of my time.'

They didn't speak again and Philippe lay in bed trying to imagine how Christophe could have made so much money playing cards within such a short time. Had Christophe lied to him? That possibility bothered him, like a nagging pain. Maybe he had seen Christophe out in the tunnel. What could he have been doing there?

He pushed Christophe out of his mind and turned over on the thin mattress, thinking instead about what his friend had said about Olivier's jealousy. He'd have to be very careful in future.

Unable to sleep with so many thoughts chasing through his head, he reached down and picked his knapsack up from the floor. When he plunged his hand to the bottom, he felt an unmistakeable hard shape and pulled out the key to the map room. He couldn't remember putting it there at all, but he must have been more distracted than he'd thought. At least he wouldn't have to admit to Monsieur Favre that he'd lost it.

His hand felt the thin paper of the letter from Valérie and he propped himself up on his bunk to open it.

*Mon cher Philippe*

*It's getting colder now, even in the city, so it must be worse with you. Let me know if you need me to send you anything. Agathe is busy knitting socks – on top of the multiple pairs you must already have. I hope you're keeping warm. I wish I could be with you and see for myself that you're all right.*

*You asked me in your last letter whether I'd gone shooting again. Well, Marianne, Geraldine and I all went last week. I agree that we all have to be able to defend ourselves. We went to Veyrier and it was very strange being there without you. Monsieur Ernand sent his good wishes. He asked when you'd be back. I hope it's soon!*

*I don't know if you heard but an Allied plane crashed just north of Geneva a few weeks ago. We heard it fly overhead – it was very low. It sounded like they had engine trouble. Thankfully they didn't hit any houses and crashed in a field. The pilot and crew were taken to hospital but no one knows if they were all right. The Germans have asked us to keep to the blackout rules because they don't want the Allied airmen to have any lights to guide them if they fly over Switzerland. We're lucky they didn't land in Geneva! I hope they weren't too badly injured.*

*It's almost December and it will soon be Christmas. Will you have any time off? Let me know. Aunt Paulette has asked us to spend Christmas with them in Gryon. That will be good if you're staying in Saint-Maurice because it's really close, but if you're coming back to Geneva, I want to stay here. I don't want to miss the chance of seeing you.*

*Write to me when you can. It's not as good as being with you but I love hearing your voice in your letters.*

*Avec tout mon amour*

*Valérie*

# EIGHT

## PHILIPPE

By the next morning, the rumours sweeping round the Fort about the explosion and the likely perpetrators had reached fever pitch. All through breakfast and as they collected their rifles from the rifle room, the soldiers speculated about the cause of the explosion, passing titbits of news between them and repeating all kinds of theories.

'I heard they were targeting the new machine guns which had just been delivered. They were stored near the funicular railway,' said Antoine to Philippe as they waited for their turn in the shooting range. 'Someone must have leaked the information to the Germans because how else would they have known about the guns? Or where they were being stored?'

Philippe didn't reply and tried to clear his mind of everything but his shooting, seeking the familiar stillness that enabled him to focus and get his best results. The shooting range was the one place where he could block out everything else and he realised how much he depended on the few hours spent in the familiar hangar. It felt almost like his second home because he'd been coming to this range in the valley near Saint-Maurice with Valérie since they were children. Despite the place being filled with soldiers, he still expected to see Valérie come and stand next to him, smiling up at him, her eyes lit up with anticipation. He pushed away the thought of her, seeking the inner quietness that produced his best shooting.

'And if they catch the traitor who gave them the information, he'll be taken out and shot,' carried on Walter. They all knew the price paid by Swiss soldiers if found guilty of treason. They faced a firing squad made up of members of their own unit.

Antoine was still waiting for an answer. 'Hello, are you still with me? You haven't heard a word I've said, have you?'

Philippe snapped back into the present. 'Yes, I have. Whoever was responsible for leaking the information, they'll have to find him first. Not that easy when there must have been lots of people who knew about the gun delivery.'

'I heard it was someone from Ticino. Leaking information to his Italian friends.'

He stared at Walter's weather-beaten face. They all knew that since Italy had joined forces with Hitler, the spies in Switzerland weren't confined to German sympathisers who believed Switzerland rightly belonged to their larger neighbour as part of the Third Reich, but included Swiss who were admirers of Mussolini. Before he could reply, he heard a shout from the other side of the hangar.

'Philippe, come over here.'

Max, the owner of the shooting range and the man who'd taught Philippe how to shoot, raised his bushy eyebrows in despair and moved out of the way to give him some room, his long, wavy grey hair rippling as he shook his head, his nose wrinkling in disgust.

'Whatever I say to this lot, it isn't helping them to shoot any better than when they came in an hour ago. You need to show them how to do it properly. I've got another three groups waiting outside so I can't spend any more time on your unit today.'

Philippe moved to the front and the men crowded behind him to watch.

'Aim for the furthest target,' Max instructed. 'Three shots.'

Everyone fell silent and collectively held their breath as he steadied the rifle. After a few moments, he fired the gun three times in quick succession. Max raised his arm and checked the target.

'All dead centre.'

A cheer went up from the group around him and Philippe grinned.

'That's what we need from every soldier...' Max growled. 'All right, move along now.'

When his unit had filed out of the hangar, Philippe caught up with Max at the door.

'Not like you to be so critical. They aren't the worst I've seen.'

His smile didn't prompt the usual response; Max looked unusually grim. He shrugged and stubbed out his cigarette, twisting his boot in the dirty snow.

'What's the point?' He waved his arm around to indicate the groups of men shivering outside, waiting for their transport. 'If the Germans decide to walk all over us, what are we able to do about it? This lot can hardly point a rifle in a straight line, far less kill a man at distance with one shot. This strategy of pulling back and defending the mountains. We haven't got a chance, my friend, not a chance.'

Philippe stared at him, wondering why he was sounding so hopeless.

'And if we do manage to stop their invasion, what will be left of Switzerland? A few mountains and a depleted army, most of us dead. Hardly worth fighting for.'

Philippe tried to think of something to cheer Max up and

take his mind away from the interminable lines of soldiers filing through the shooting range in front of them, heavy boots churning up the mud.

'You know that anyone can learn to shoot with the right training. It just takes time and application. Valérie and I used to come here when we were kids, so we've been learning for years...'

'Aah, Valérie.' Max's breath came out in a long sigh. 'She is a lovely shot that one.' He nudged Philippe, a smile chasing away the gloomy expression.

'Both of you, fighting to be the best. And each so different, she quick as a flash to aim and shoot and you taking your time, slow and considered. Her skill comes from reactions as fast as lightning.' He clicked his fingers. 'Like this. While yours comes from a place of calm and concentration.'

He slapped Philippe's shoulder. 'And more often than not, she would win. You are a good shot *mon ami,* but she... she is the best.'

Max's smile faded again. 'And this lot... They will never be as good. However many times you show them, they will never rival the lovely Valérie.'

'But Max, they're trying their best. And they only need to be good enough. If we have sufficient numbers, then we'll have a chance of beating back the enemy and protecting the Alps. We can't afford to lose. Just look at what's happening all over Europe...'

He got no reply and realised that Max wasn't listening to him but was staring up at the mountains towards the Fort.

'I hear things when people come here to shoot. There was a man in here the other day who was telling his friend that someone in your Fort was spying for the Germans, passing secrets to them and nobody suspected him.'

He looked again at Philippe. 'Could that be true? I hear that the Germans are prepared to pay a lot of money for information. They can buy anything they want because we Swiss are now so poor, after so many years of scraping a living.'

Philippe felt suddenly cold when he heard Max's words, thinking not about the explosion in the camp but about seeing Christophe outside the map room.

'Did they say anything else? Who was leaking secrets and what information they were handing over?'

Max shook his head.

Philippe remembered the roll of banknotes that had fallen out of his friend's pocket. He didn't believe Christophe could have won all that money in a card game, but nor could he bring himself to believe he would sell information to the Germans. They were friends, they watched each other's backs. But if he was the culprit, then Philippe would have to turn him in. He felt sick when he thought he might be ordered to be part of the firing squad that executed his friend. He shook his head to dislodge the thought. It couldn't be true. Christophe would never betray his country.

'I don't think you should be talking like this. These lies could be spread to weaken us, to make us mistrust one another because we think our neighbours and our friends are betraying Switzerland.'

Max stared at him, his expression impossible to read, before he spoke. 'All I know is that you can't trust anyone, not even the people you think are your friends.'


Philippe's unit returned to the Fort at lunchtime. He saw Favre in the dining room eating with another senior officer, a sandy-haired, hard-featured man who reported directly to the Fort Commander. He peeled away from the queue for the canteen, ignoring the smell of food and his hunger pangs, and headed straight to the map room. He had lots of work to finish if he was going to be allowed to go back to Geneva so soon.

Once he let himself into the map room, he looked in the wooden cabinet and pulled open each drawer in turn, to find the map he was working on. The maps were numbered in order so, while he was going through them, he checked that they were all there. He found the right one and laid it on his table.

He glanced over at Favre's desk, where the professor kept the second copy of the smaller maps. There was nothing left out on the desk. He knew the professor kept all his equipment locked up and his desk meticulously tidy. Philippe gathered up his pens and rulers and settled down at his table.

A moment after he sat down, he heard the key in the lock and Favre came in. He seemed surprised to see Philippe.

'Are you not having your meal? I saw your unit come in just now and didn't expect you for some time.'

'We were longer at the shooting range than planned. I didn't want to waste any more time because I need to finish off this map. It's the one of all the bridges in this section of the Redoubt. I've almost finished marking the bomb locations.'

The two men worked silently for the rest of the afternoon. Philippe struggled to stay awake, the restless night and early start making his head droop. That seemed to sum up military life, he thought, endless stretches of tedium interrupted by bursts of urgent activity. He was relieved when Favre started to gather his things and signalled an end to the long afternoon. He carefully stowed away the map he was completing and let himself out of the map room, heading towards the canteen.

He could hear the noise of laughter and chatter growing louder as he got closer and the warmth of the room hit him when he walked inside. There was almost a febrile atmosphere in the large room, speculation and conjecture swirling from group to group. There had been rumours for weeks about a German invasion and the attack on the Fort had brought those rumours to life.

He grabbed a tray and some cassoulet before squeezing into the space between Stefano and Christophe.

'We're on guard duty tonight,' said Stefano, his sallow features crinkling in disgust.

Christophe looked up from his plate, carefully wiping the last drop of cassoulet with a chunk of potato bread. 'On the upper part of the road to Morcles, to make sure the Germans can't sabotage another part of the Fort.'

Philippe stared at them. 'Why us? It can't be our turn yet.'

One of the routine tasks for each unit was to guard the key access points to the Fort. Everyone disliked it, especially at night in the autumn and winter, but they all had to take their turn.

'Orders from the top. Some of the other units are checking the bridges round the Fort to make sure an intruder hasn't tampered with the explosives.'

Walter, the farmer from further up the valley in Brig, shook his head. 'At least we aren't doing that, wandering around the mountain all night, just like my herd of cattle.'

Philippe was about to reply when one of the senior officers came up to their table. He looked harassed and consulted his clip board.

'You're Olivier's unit? He's sick tonight and can't supervise the guard duty. One of you will have to do it... we don't have anyone else spare.'

He looked around them, waiting for someone to volunteer. They avoided his eye, all reluctant to step forward and take on the extra responsibility which meant they would miss another precious hour of sleep. Philippe glanced around and then raised his hand, sighing. He was finding it hard to sleep at the moment anyway, between worrying about his grandfather having another heart attack and Valérie being confronted by Nazi soldiers at the border.

'I'll do it.'

The officer scribbled on his clipboard, then stared at Philippe. 'You're the marksman we saw this morning, aren't you? All right, you're acting leader for tonight. I'll note it on your record. You need to be ready to leave in precisely one hour. You'll get your final instructions at the main exit.'

'Yes sir.'

As soon as the officer was out of earshot, Christophe couldn't stop himself.

'I'll bet Olivier isn't sick at all. More likely sick of standing in the cold all night and staying behind to make his report while the rest of us go to bed.'

The others were nodding and grumbling to one another.

Philippe looked around the table, suddenly irritated. Did they not understand how high the stakes were? If they didn't successfully protect the Alps they might all be under Hitler's tyrannical rule. Which of them would survive an attack if it came? Who among them had loved ones who would be sent to the camps in Poland or executed on the spot? An image of Valérie facing a firing squad forced its way into his head. He took a couple of deep breaths before speaking in a low voice.

'Whether Olivier is sick or not makes no difference. We have a job to do, so we just need to get on with it.'

Christophe shrugged, before replying, 'I suppose so.'

The others shifted in their seats.

Philippe picked up his tray. 'We haven't much time, so let's get going.'

They trooped out of the warm canteen after him.

Just under an hour later they queued up behind the other units. Philippe had completely underestimated how long it took to get half a dozen men equipped and ready to leave but they'd made it. He received his final orders from an officer who pointed to one of the trucks in a convoy of vehicles.

'You're taking over from the unit guarding the upper part of the road between here and Morcles since this morning. You'll be relieved at eight o'clock tomorrow morning.'

Philippe heard one of the men groan behind him and his lips twitched.

'You can get a lift down in that truck. He's going down to the station to collect some supplies and will drop you on the way.'

'Thanks.'

They jumped into the back of the truck and it started up noisily. A few minutes later, it dropped them just before an old stone bridge on a sharp bend in the road above a steep drop, shielded by fir trees. The puddles at the side of the road were hardened into ice and the night sky was cloudy, obscuring the moon and stars. There was snow in the air. Philippe paused to speak to the driver.

'When will you be coming back up the road?'

The driver was older than most of the other soldiers and seemed in no rush to get on his way to the station, happy to sit back in his cab and speculate about the happenings at the Fort.

'In a couple of hours, if we get the parts to repair the railway. Once that job's done, they can move the artillery. Then everything will get back to normal.'

'Have you heard anything about how the Germans knew where to strike?'

The driver shook his head. 'They don't know who gave them the information, but somebody did. Filthy traitor, giving us all this extra work...'

His words seemed to remind him that he had an important job to do and he reluctantly wound up the window. 'Better get on.'

Philippe stood back from the truck as it moved off and crawled round the sharp corner at the bridge before speeding up and disappearing down the hill, the roar of the engine fading into the distance. He turned to see where his unit had gone. There was no one on the road and he looked all around him.

'Psst, we're over here.'

On the steep side of the slope a few metres from the corner, the group of men were huddled behind a crumbling stone wall leading into the trees. They could have been the only ones left on the mountainside, with no lights shining through the trees from the nearby village to pierce the thick blanket of darkness. Although the wall protected them from the worst of the freezing wind, they looked miserable, the hoods of their white ski suits over their faces and shoulders hunched. Philippe took pity on them.

'We can take it in turns, a couple on the road at one time. That means we'll all get some rest. Whoever is on guard will need to alert the rest if anyone approaches.'

He was rewarded by a couple of lame cheers. Christophe stood up.

'I'll do the first watch with you.'

They hardly spoke after that, changing round as agreed, the men huddled behind the wall sleeping fitfully. The freezing wind had dropped but the forecast snow never arrived. It was deathly quiet, the silence only broken by the lorry going back up to the Fort, presumably carrying the necessary parts. This time the driver only waved as he passed. Everyone in the village of Morcles and the surrounding farms and chalets was safely in bed and asleep.

At five o'clock in the morning, Philippe and Christophe were back on duty. Philippe leaned on the barrier at the side of the road, staring down at the dried-up riverbed that ran down the steep slope under the bridge. Christophe sucked in his breath.

'I don't see why the Germans would try to attack the Fort again. They're just playing a cat and mouse game, trying to keep us guessing. This rumour about the big invasion is nothing more than that, just rumour.'

Philippe shook his head. 'I don't think it's just a rumour.'

The sharp crack of a branch breaking on the road down from the bridge silenced him and they stared at the spot. Rustling sounds came from the dead leaves at the side of the road and Philippe took a few steps towards the noise, his heart pounding. He felt Christophe's presence behind him as they crept towards the noise, boots making no sound on the icy road surface.

A sound like a pistol shot echoed through the darkness. Philippe ducked instinctively and reached round for his rifle.

'What is that?' Christophe breathed in his ear. He pointed to the road ahead and Philippe saw a dark shape further down the road moving towards them. Christophe clutched Philippe's arm to stop him going any closer and stepped in front of him.

'What are you doing?' hissed Philippe.

'I need to see who it is.'

'Not on your own, you don't.'

'Stay back, Philippe.'

Ignoring Christophe's warning, Philippe stayed at his shoulder and they approached the dark shape, hardly breathing.

'Stop. Don't go any closer,' Philippe hissed suddenly before taking a torch from his pocket and flicking it on to illuminate the road ahead. Two eyes shone into the light and the beam picked up two horns and quivering ears above the flash of white. The mountain goat stared unblinkingly at them for a few seconds, head tilted to one side, like an inquisitive magical creature. Then it shook its whole body before turning and jumping down the slope below the road and disappearing out of sight.

Christophe let out his breath in a long sigh.

'It was only an animal.' His voice quivered slightly.

Philippe clicked off his torch.

'Who did you think it was? I know these mountains. You

see more goats than people at this time of year. I think it was a chamois.'

Christophe gave a nervous laugh and looked away.

As they retraced their steps back over the bridge, Philippe noticed a tremor in his friend's hands. The mountains were a strange place at night and everyone was on edge at the thought of German spies lurking in the shadows. But why had Christophe been so anxious to be the first to investigate the noise in the darkness?

# NINE

## PHILIPPE

Later that morning, Philippe looked around outside the Fort for someone who could be Favre's driver. The cool air chased away the last vestiges of sleep and he pulled the collar of his uniform more tightly round his neck. Favre had promised he'd give him a lift down to the station, but Philippe fully expected he'd be too busy to remember the promise and looked around at the trucks, wondering whether any of them were heading down the valley. As he stood there uncertainly, a large black car drew up in front of him and a thin old man leaned out of the passenger window.

'Private Cherix?'

He didn't recognise the driver, who seemed almost as old as Favre himself.

'Yes. I'm Cherix.'

'Monsieur Favre asked me to take you down to the station. Jump in the back.'

The drive down the mountain was very civilised. Philippe relaxed into the comfortable seat and compared it to his usual trip in the back of a draughty truck being thrown down the hairpin bends on the mountain road. They were lucky to follow in the tracks of a larger vehicle as it had started to snow heavily and the visibility was poor. By the time they got to the valley floor, the snow was lighter but one look at the grey sky told Philippe that it would fall at lower levels before long.

At Saint-Maurice station, a train was drawing into the platform and the driver sprang out with surprising agility to open the door for Philippe, giving a jaunty salute.

'There's your train now, sir.'

Philippe nodded his thanks and strode the few metres across the platform to the train, hardly aware of the bustle around him as the other passengers disembarked and boarded. The cloud was now lying low in the valley, obscuring the mountain peaks, and wisps of mist swirled around the station buildings and the steaming train. He found a seat on the side with the view of the lake and high peaks, hoping the mist would clear once they set off. He'd probably sleep all the way but, if he did wake up, he didn't want to miss the view of the wide expanse of water stretching between Switzerland and France. As the train pulled out of the station and entered the tunnel, he smiled in anticipation. He would have enough time to collect the papers for Monsieur Favre, visit his grandfather and then go and find Valérie. He felt a warm glow of anticipation as he pictured her face, full of joy and surprise.

He slept for most of the journey, the comings and goings of his fellow passengers hardly disturbing him, and only awoke as they drew into Cornavin station. He jumped out of the train and walked through the station building that stretched along one side of the Place de Cornavin, ignoring the trams waiting in front of the station and heading down the Rue du Mont-Blanc. It wasn't the most direct route to the university in Plainpalais, but he wanted to cross the boulevard at the end of the lake rather than one of the closer crossings. Valérie said that she often sat on their favourite bench on the Quai du Mont-Blanc when she was taking a break in between making her deliveries and he didn't want to miss her if she was there.

He stopped and leaned on the bridge, looking towards their bench, thinking about the times he'd sat there with Valérie. He scanned along the Quai du Mont-Blanc but couldn't see her familiar figure anywhere. The lake opened out in front of him and the Jet d'Eau sprayed into the grey sky on his right. After a few moments, he pulled away from the bridge and carried on his way, through the shopping district and then following the ancient ramparts enclosing the old town. He crossed the Place de Neuve into the university district, past the statues of reformation figures towards the grand Bastion building. He ran up the flight of steps at the front of the imposing structure and asked at the main desk for the package for Monsieur Favre. Fidgeting impatiently, he waited as the man reached below the desk and held out his hand for the large envelope.

That hadn't taken long. Philippe glanced at the large clock on the wall before leaving the building and heading for the cantonal hospital, only a ten-minute walk away. Pausing at the entrance to his grandfather's ward, he was suddenly hesitant of what he might find. The memory of his last visit when his grandfather was hardly conscious was still vivid in his mind; his grandfather was no longer the strong, healthy man Philippe knew so well. He pushed the door open. His grandfather was sitting up in bed, washed and shaved. He turned his compact figure to the door and grinned at Philippe, his face no longer pale and grey, but a much healthier colour.

'Philippe, my boy. I'm so glad to see you're back. I can speak to you this time.'

Philippe returned the smile and went to give him a hug, which was returned as strongly as always, then sat down next to his bed.

'It's so good to see you, you're looking much better. What have the doctors said?'

His grandfather grimaced. 'I'm to keep calm, they've told

me. Or I'll have another heart attack and this time it'll finish me off.'

Philippe smiled at the irascible tone.

'For once, you'd better do what you're told.'

'I suppose so, but I don't want to talk about me. How are you getting on with Favre? He's working you hard, I hope.'

'Yes, but no harder than himself. At least I get out on the mountain with the unit. He spends all his time inside.'

'Excellent. Well I'm very glad to see you, my boy. Wouldn't have liked you to remember me from the last time you were here.'

They talked about the snow coming and how a harsh winter would impact the crops, then moved on to the recent rumours of a German invasion. His grandfather always liked to hear about the general mood among the military, especially their desire to repel any German advance. He deeply disapproved of the Swiss authorities' willingness to continue to trade with Germany and turn a blind eye to the atrocities they were committing across Europe. When his ire moved on to Swiss police co-operation with German guards on the French border, widely rumoured but never confirmed, Philippe thought it best to steer him away from the subject that had caused so many family arguments.

Finally, he asked Philippe about Valérie, a twinkle in his eyes. 'That one is a keeper,' he said as he so often did. 'Go and find her instead of spending time with an old man.'

'I'm going to see her now.'

His grandfather nodded towards a bunch of deep red flowers on the table next to his bed.

'She came to visit me and brought these. She's a sweet girl, Philippe. Don't let her slip through your fingers.'

'They're beautiful. And of course I don't intend to.'

'Get away and find her then. You can see I'm better.'

Philippe smiled. If his grandfather was starting to order everyone around, then he really was better.

Buoyed by his visit, Philippe strode back to the old town through the streets of smart townhouses, then climbed up the hill and walked towards the square in front of the Cathédrale St-Pierre. He'd check at Valérie's home first. She'd either be there or he'd find someone who could tell him where she was. He walked up to the familiar three-storey narrow townhouse, glancing at the metal rails covering the ground floor windows to see if there was anyone inside and rang the bell. Agathe came to the door.

'Philippe. What are you doing here? Did Valérie know you were coming?'

'No. It was a last-minute thing. Is she at home?'

Agathe shook her head.

'She went to the Café de Paris to meet someone.'

Impatient to spend as much time as he could with Valérie, he walked quickly along the familiar streets towards the Place du Bourg-de-Four. But when he reached the edge of the square, he stopped suddenly, his eyes fixed on the windows of the Café de Paris below the green canopy. Behind the few hardy people sitting at the outside tables, in the front window, unmistakeable through the pristine glass, he saw Valérie. She was sitting next to Dieter Runde, the official at the German Consulate. And as he watched, he saw the man lean across and grasp her hand. She smiled up at him, her head tilted to one side in that inquisitive way he loved, and Philippe felt his heart plummet.

Philippe stood for what seemed like an hour, frozen in shock. He was buffeted by the people walking around him, only dimly aware of shopkeepers greeting their customers and going about the business of the day. His fists clenched as he watched Valérie clearly enjoying the German's company, laughing and looking into his eyes. Anger burned through Philippe until he felt hot and feverish and he resisted a strong urge to barge into the café and punch Dieter's face again and again. The girl he loved was enjoying herself with another man while he was in the mountains preparing to fight for his country. He thought that beautiful smile was only for him, but he saw now that he'd been deluding himself. He watched as the German reached out and touched one of her chestnut curls and hate flooded through him. He wasn't going to stand there and watch any more. He'd seen enough.

Turning on his heel, he almost walked into a group of women coming into the square and pushed past them without saying a word. He kept his head down and strode to the station, barely seeing anything around him, his stomach churning. Was it possible he had misinterpreted what he'd seen? This was Valérie, his Valérie. Surely, she would never do this to him. And with a German! But the picture of Valérie smiling up at the man was undeniable. What a fool she'd made of him.

The train journey to Saint-Maurice was just as uneventful as before, but it was like being in a different world. All the excitement and happiness he'd felt that morning seemed so far away now. Realising he hadn't eaten since breakfast, he'd bought bread and cheese at a kiosk outside the station but left it untouched on the train. He was relieved to jump out when the train drew into the station, the cold sting of the air taking his breath away. He needed a distraction, anything to keep his mind away from Valérie. He crunched briskly across the snow and hitched a lift with a truck going back to the Fort, getting off at the Grand Hôtel des Bains at Lavey.

Philippe had never felt so betrayed or broken before, but even with his spirits so low he couldn't help admiring the incredible view that was stretched out before him. The snow in the valley made the hotel and spa complex look like a fairy wonderland. The carpet of white snow sparkled in the low lights prescribed by the authorities, which were shining against the elegant ochre-coloured building. Ornate Edwardian railings in a deep green and shuttered balconies were dusted with snow and everything was perfectly still and quiet, the only sound the crunching of his own boots on the ground.

Philippe gratefully received some coffee from a young waitress, and sank into one of the deep armchairs in a corner of the expensively decorated lounge of the Grand Hôtel des Bains with a deep sigh, closing his eyes. Tiredness enveloped him suddenly and he wondered if he could just sleep there for a while. The softness of the crushed deep red velvet under his fingers seemed a world away from the spartan surroundings he was used to at the Fort. Favre had gone to the spa medical centre for the regular treatments he received from their white-coated professionals and wouldn't be back for at least an hour. Dinner was booked for seven o'clock. The lounge was quiet in the late afternoon and there were only a few groups of guests drinking coffee and talking quietly.

Foggy with exhaustion, Philippe was dimly aware of a couple of businessmen who came into the lounge, glanced around at the occupants and walked across to sit at a table in the opposite corner of the large room. The older man who led the way was large and thickset, the younger one shorter and slimmer. They brushed snow off their heavy coats and placed their hats on to the table. He heard one of the men order drinks in German but nothing of their conversation, their hushed voices absorbed by the rich furnishings and deep carpet. Despite the excellent coffee, his eyelids began to droop and Philippe dozed until the clatter of a cup falling on the tabletop woke him up with a start.

'I'm sorry,' whispered the waitress, leaning down to pick up his cup, flushing with embarrassment. 'I didn't mean to disturb you. I'm new here.'

'That's all right.' He smiled at her, then looked around the room. It was much busier with people coming in for dinner who were being served colourful cocktails and champagne, a pianist playing softly in the background. He looked across at the table with the businessmen and saw that they were leaving. He watched them throw down some notes on to the table and turn towards the door, brushing past the young waitress without acknowledging her murmured thanks.

Philippe shook his head to try to banish the fog of sleep but he was now uncomfortably warm in his thick grey uniform and it was an effort to stir himself. He'd have to get some fresh air before Favre came back or he'd disgrace himself and fall asleep into his supper. That would be a good way to repay Favre's kindness. He glanced at the clock, which showed it was ten minutes before seven. He knew there was a door at the far end of the lounge which led outside into the grounds so he left some money on the table and walked quickly across the lounge into the garden, shutting the door hastily behind him as the cold air caught his breath.

Philippe moved away from the door into the darkness through some tall shrubs, part of a secluded garden at the side of the hotel and the thermal pools. He stood at the edge of the snow-covered lawn stretching into the darkness and looked up at the balconies above him as he lit a cigarette, remnants of sleep fading away. Most of the rooms seemed to be unoccupied but here and there, dotted along the façade of the building, he could see a lamp shining through the shutters which cast a sliver of light on to the grass. Despite himself, Philippe's thoughts drifted back to Valérie. For how long had she been seeing the German? When she was writing letters to Philippe, was she secretly laughing at him and his naïve trust in her? How could she work for the Resistance while holding hands with the enemy?

Revived by the cold air, he snuffed out his cigarette on the icy ground and turned to thread his way through the trees and bushes back into the lounge, deciding to banish his tormented thoughts with a stiff drink before dinner. His senses now fully alive, he heard the sound of boots softly crunching across snow in the darkness behind him, and then the distinctive noise of whispers in German. Without thinking, he slid behind one of the taller trees at the side of the building, expecting to see a couple of hotel guests appear out of the darkness.

The footsteps stopped at the edge of the garden and Philippe held his breath. A light flicked on in an upstairs room and the beam shone on to the grass. It was switched off a second later but Philippe had seen two figures standing in the gloom. He was sure it was the two businessmen from the lounge, the larger man unmistakeable. In the sharp beam of light, the Nazi silver eagle motif gleamed on his coat. They were waiting for someone.

He shrank back further into the bushes, then saw Favre walk around the corner of the building and come straight towards him. What was he doing here? Philippe took a step forward ready to warn him about the Nazis, but before Favre reached his hiding place, he turned away from the building and walked directly towards them. Philippe pulled back and saw one of the Germans lift his arm towards Favre. They were passing something between them. Something small and easy to conceal. He heard them whisper, Favre nodded his head and then they split up.

Philippe was terrified to move and for the second time that day, felt as if his feet were frozen to the ground. He swallowed hard to stifle a cough as Favre came back towards the building. The Nazis had gone too, vanishing as quickly as they had appeared. Finally Philippe exhaled, mist rising in the cool air, and had to take a couple of deep breaths before he could move. Suddenly panicked, he realised he had to get back inside before Favre could walk around the building or he might suspect Philippe had seen him. Philippe ran back to the door and walked as casually as he could through the lounge to an alcove near the main entrance, his mind whirling.

Consciously slowing down his breathing, he closed his eyes and sank back into a chair, feigning sleep while his heart raced.

He couldn't believe what he'd just seen. Favre, the war hero, was the one passing information to the Germans. The man he had looked up to, the man he'd respected above all others in the military. And he'd thought the old man had even grown fond of him.

'There you are.'

Philippe opened his eyes and stretched. 'I'm sorry. I must have been asleep.'

Favre gave a small, satisfied smile. 'Are you ready for dinner? You must be hungry by now.'

Philippe followed him into the dining room. He should have been starving by now and he had been looking forward to this meal for days, but he just felt sick. Was there anybody he could trust? First Valérie, now Favre. Both had betrayed him. Looking at the professor carefully putting on his glasses and studying the menu, Philippe felt desperately alone. It was horrifying to think that the dedicated and hard-working figure sitting in front of him could be collaborating with the enemy under the noses of the Swiss army.

He jumped when Favre addressed him directly.

'So how was your grandfather? I hope he was better today.'

'Yes, thank you. I think he'll recover.'

The cartographer smiled at him, inviting conversation and Philippe pushed away his disgust and tried to give his best impression of someone enjoying a rare treat.

Throughout that nightmare dinner, while he was holding a light-hearted conversation about life in the Fort, Philippe was desperately trying to work out what he should do. He had to find out what had been handed over and get absolute proof. Once he spoke out, it would be his word against the man everyone believed was a Swiss hero.

As Favre talked and laughed in front of him, Philippe's smile hid a wave of burning anger. Until he had more evidence than his own word, he couldn't let Favre think the game was up.

Favre would just find a way to cover his tracks and escape, or ruin Philippe's credibility, or worse. Red-hot anger turned into cold determination as Philippe planned how he could expose the traitor he had once admired so much. He would never trust anyone so easily again. Not a war hero, and not even the girl he loved.

# TEN

## VALÉRIE

*Chère Valérie*

*I've thought a lot before writing you this letter. I'm not sure that it's a good idea to try to keep our relationship going, with so much coming between us. We hardly see one another and when we do, it isn't for long. There never seems to be any time to be alone together.*

*I'm going to concentrate on my work here and I think you should just forget about me. I hope that this will make things easier for you.*

*Philippe*

Valérie read the letter several times, before throwing it on her bed. Her heart felt heavy in her chest as the meaning of his stark words sank in. The letter sounded like it came from a stranger rather than from the man she loved. She jumped up and paced the room, her eyes brimming over, wishing she could just see him, speak to him, try to understand what had prompted him to write such cold words. Perhaps something had happened up at the Fort to upset him. She couldn't believe it was the end, not for her and Philippe. She remembered their last lingering kiss, the feel of his arms and the warmth in his eyes and shook her head in denial, certain to the core that he must love her still. Something must have come between them to prompt his letter, but what could it be?

After a sleepless night, Valérie slipped through the door of the storeroom and closed it behind her to block out the lingering afternoon sunshine. Her eyes were red and puffy from crying and she blinked a couple of times to adjust to the darkness. She could hear nothing in the room and breathed a sigh of relief. Emile must have come back for Simone to take her out of Geneva. The escaped Resistance fighter had been in the store-room below the old workshop for three days and Valérie's nerves were stretched to breaking point, trying to hide her frequent visits from her father and make sure she wasn't drawing attention from any prying eyes. But her relief was tinged with disappointment; she had grown fond of the sharp, courageous woman with her shy smile and looked forward to their whispered conversations. As if by mutual consent, they didn't talk about the war or the resistance, but about times of peace and hope, before Europe had descended into chaos. But then she heard a small noise in the darkness at the far side of the room.

'Simone, are you there?'

'Yes, I'm over here,' whispered a voice. 'I was just sleeping.'

Eyes now accustomed to the gloom, Valérie approached the bed and placed her basket on the thin cover. 'Emile hasn't come for you yet?'

'No. I thought he would come this morning but I haven't seen him.'

Valérie took out the loaf of potato bread from the basket and passed it to Simone.

'Why are you sitting in the dark? You could go upstairs where it's light. Or sit closer to the door. If you open it a few inches you could let some fresh air in, without any risk of being seen.' Then it wouldn't seem so much like a prison in here, she almost added. She shivered in the cold air and pulled up the collar of her new coat, glad of its warmth.

Simone took the bread from her outstretched hand, broke off a piece and chewed it before she replied. 'I heard people outside. They were rattling the gate to the courtyard to see if it was locked so I came as far away from the door as I could.' She pointed at the ugly knife on the bed. 'I decided that if they managed to get in here, I'd kill as many of them as I could before they shot me.'

Valérie glanced behind her as if someone was standing over them, then gave herself a shake.

'I didn't see anybody out there now. They must have moved on.'

They looked at one another for a long moment and then spoke at the same time.

'It's too dangerous for you to stay here...'

'It's too dangerous for you if I stay here...'

They exchanged a smile, but Valérie knew they were running out of time to get Simone away from Geneva. When she'd met Marianne that afternoon her friend had told her that the search for the Resistance fighter was spreading all over the city, involving not just the Canton police but the German border guards.

'They're all talking about it on the telephone,' Marianne warned. 'They suspect someone is hiding her in the old city and they're under strict orders to search every building, whether it's occupied or deserted. They're not going to give up. I've told

Emile he's going to have to move her on or they'll find her. And if they do find her, it will lead them straight to you.'

Marianne had handed over a bag with the clothes Valérie had asked for. Valérie was too small for any of her clothes to fit Simone, but Marianne was taller and roughly her size.

'Thanks, that will at least help her to blend in. She can't go out wearing the clothes she has on now, or she'll be stopped before she reaches the end of the street.'

Marianne had given her a quick hug. 'I'm working late at the telephone exchange tonight so I'll listen in to the calls, see what I can pick up.' Then she was gone.

Valérie didn't repeat any of this to Simone. Although the Frenchwoman had at least been able to sleep and eat during the three days she'd been cooped up in the storeroom, Valérie knew she was haunted by the knowledge that she hadn't been able to hand over the list of traitors. Her pursuers were now snapping at her heels, searching day and night to prevent her from completing her mission and escaping further into Switzerland.

They heard a scuffling noise in the courtyard and in an instant Simone jumped off the bed and stood in front of Valérie, knife raised to attack the intruder. Heart beating wildly, Valérie stood her ground and stared at the storeroom door as it slowly inched open.

'Valérie? Are you in there?'

Emile slipped through the door, dark head bowed, and closed it softly behind him, pulling his thick coat out of the way. He turned awkwardly on his weak leg and almost walked into the sharp blade.

'Hey, put that thing down. It's only me. What's happened?'

Simone let out her breath in a sigh, walked jerkily to the back of the storeroom and dropped on to the bed, her shoulders rigid. She picked up the bread and tore off another piece, leaving Valérie to do the talking.

'The police were searching the area. Simone heard some

people trying to get into the courtyard. It isn't safe here any longer.'

Emile sank on to a wooden chair and sighed. 'I know. They're looking for her all over the city. Jean said the Germans have been interrogating the villagers across the border where she was hiding and he can't be sure that no one will talk.'

Valérie glanced at Simone, who was quietly watching them and was puzzled by her willingness to let them discuss her fate without making her own voice heard. She was perfectly polite and grateful for the food and shelter Valérie provided, murmured her thanks for everything she was given, but resisted all conversations about her current situation. She'd keep to safe subjects of the past and retreat to the back of the storeroom if Valérie tried to discuss the war or the future.

'All right, but the longer she's here, the more chance someone will wonder why I keep going to my father's old work-shop. Everyone round here knows it's closed up. She needs to get further into Switzerland, hide in the mountains away from the authorities.'

Emile ran his fingers through his hair and then held her gaze, unable to hide his frustration.

'I know... but I'm doing my best. My usual contacts who take the children into the mountains aren't too keen on getting involved. The police are questioning everyone they suspect of helping refugees. It's just not safe at the moment. And she insists on staying in Geneva until the list has been dealt with.'

'I am not important. It is the information I must pass on to the Allies that is important.'

Simone spat the words out angrily, her shrill voice cutting across their argument, and they turned to look at her. She was leaning forward and Valérie could see her face was flushed, despite the freezing temperature in the storeroom.

'Who is your contact in the British SOE? Or is it the Americans? Who is funding the Resistance cell in Annemasse? He is the person I have to see.'

She picked up the bag. 'I will put on these clothes and go myself to find him. Where should I go?'

Emile shook his head. 'I can't tell you that. I've left a message in the usual place. It's been picked up but there is no reply yet. I always have to wait for a reply and it can take a few days to appear. We'll just have to wait.'

'Who is your contact? What is his codename?'

She was standing up and facing Emile, as tense as a coiled spring. Valérie moved to stand in front of the bed, hiding the knife Simone had thrown down.

Emile stood firm. 'I can't tell you what I don't know. I've never met the contact who provides the money that I pass on to Jean, or picks up the information I leave. I assume it's someone in the SOE but I don't know for sure. I don't even have a code-name. We've never needed to use one before.'

His voice deepened with conviction. 'What I do know is that they'll give me instructions on how to pass it on. I have no doubt about that.'

He appealed to Simone, arms outstretched. 'You know how it works. Each person only has the piece of information they need to do their job. It protects everyone. If either of us is caught at the border, then they can't betray the other.'

She nodded and turned away, speaking so softly that they could hardly catch her words. 'It's why my copy of the list isn't the only one.'

Emile's eyes widened, and he took a couple of steps towards her, his voice raising in excitement.

'If there's another copy, then we don't have to wait. Simone, we could get you out of the city now. You can trust me to pass it on.'

'*Non.*' She spun back around, grabbing the end of the metal bedstead to steady herself. 'The other courier was also being hunted. I have to be sure my copy is passed on. I will not leave until I'm certain. People have died for this. And all the time we delay, vital information about your defences could be leaked to the Germans.'

Valérie held her breath, looking from one to the other before Simone turned away. She could see the frustration and emotion etched across Simone's face, the room full of pulsing anxiety.

'Fine. So we have no choice. We wait for your contact to respond,' Simone said over her shoulder before she went back to sit on the bed, her sudden fire extinguished.

Emile and Valérie let themselves out of the courtyard and walked back the short distance to her house through the old town, the streets empty and quiet. They didn't speak for a few minutes, each deep in their own thoughts, before Valérie broke the silence.

'That's the first time she's lost her temper. She doesn't usually say much. Every time I bring her food, all she does is thank me and she refuses to say anything else about what's going on. The only kind of conversations she'll have are about the past.'

He hesitated before answering. 'She won't want to talk to you because she knows she's putting you in danger and the more you know the riskier it gets. Jean didn't tell me every-thing, but he did say that Simone was betrayed by someone in her Resistance cell and had to go on the run. The Germans captured the rest of her cell and killed them all, after torturing them to find out where she was because they know she has the list. Everywhere she goes, they kill the people who've helped her. She's desperate to move on because they're only one step behind her and she thinks it will just happen again.'

Valérie shivered, feeling completely out of her depth and struggling to imagine how she would behave in the same situa-tion. Could she repulse everyone who tried to get close to her because it was the only way to protect them? She couldn't imagine such a lonely way to exist.

'This list she has. Are you sure you'll be able to get it to the Allies?'

He shrugged. 'They've always responded before, but it will take more time. I've told her we should pass it on to the local police, but she's insisting it needs to go to the Allies and she wants to do it herself. She doesn't trust the Swiss police, thinks they're in league with the Germans and won't act on the information.'

Valérie shook her head, thinking of Philippe's father and the last time she'd heard him lecture them about why they shouldn't try to help people escape from occupied France. She hated his conviction that it was right not to accept Jewish refugees, they had argued fiercely over that many times. But he clearly believed he was protecting Switzerland and its people.

'I'm sure the police would take the list very seriously and pass it on to the right person in the military authorities. I can't believe they wouldn't act on information like that,' said Valérie.

'I think so too, but she's convinced they don't want to annoy the Germans and will just bury the evidence.' Emile put up his hands to stop her protests. 'It's no use arguing with me Valérie, she won't listen. And you saw how she acted just now. She's a fraction away from turning on us too. We need to get her out of Geneva soon or she'll do something crazy and we'll all end up being arrested.'

He kicked a loose stone in the cobbles and it slammed against the opposite wall. 'All I wanted to do was to fight the enemy like Philippe is doing, despite my stupid leg. And I can't even help one solitary Resistance fighter get out of Geneva. Much good I'm doing for the war effort.'

Emile usually never talked about his limp and Valérie grasped his arm, trying to think of something to lift his mood. 'You're helping by working with your mother on the farm, too.

Providing food is just as important as fighting the enemy. We can't fight if we're starving to death.'

'I know, I know, but it just doesn't seem like enough.' He stopped in the street and stared at Valérie, taking her cold hands in his warm grasp. 'We can't afford to wait any longer. If no one comes to the handover point tonight, then I'll just have to persuade her to give me the list somehow and I'll get her out of Geneva myself. I know some of the safe houses in Lausanne and Montreux, so I'll take her to one of those and hope they'll take her in. Just make sure she's changed into Marianne's clothes by ten o'clock tonight and I'll come back to get her out.'

'But Emile, what if nobody comes? How will you persuade her to leave? I can't believe she'll just give you the list. You heard her. Giving it to the Allies herself is all she thinks about.'

'I'll just have to. It's too dangerous for her to stay here. And it's too dangerous for you too. Philippe would go crazy if he knew what I was getting you into. He asked me to protect you when he came to see me, not get you involved in hiding Resistance fighters. But we're taking refugees across the border and I can't be here to check on Simone every night as well. It's important we get as many people across as we can, before the weather gets worse and makes it more dangerous.'

Despite herself, Valérie felt tears prick her eyes at the mention of Philippe, the memory of his cold letter still hurting like a physical ache.

'I'm not sure Philippe cares anymore what happens to me.' Her voice choked and she looked away from Emile.

'I don't know where you got that idea from.' He shook his head. 'He said he relied on me to look after you. I know he had a lot of other stuff to worry about. I don't know how much he's enjoying life at Saint-Maurice, seems to be involved in some top-secret work. That's as much as he told me when I spoke to him.'

She tossed her head. 'It's obviously too secret to tell me anything about it.'

'You're not listening to me. He wants you to be safe. That's what's behind everything he does. I've never known anyone to love someone as much as Philippe loves you. Trust me, Valérie.'

Without giving her any time to answer, he kissed her cheeks and left her at the door to her house. Valérie stared after him as he limped up the cobbled street, brooding over what he'd said about Philippe, wondering again why he'd sent her that letter if he really did love her still. Then she closed the door behind her with a sharp snap and ran upstairs, turning the dial on the wireless in her bedroom. However bad the news, at least it would take her mind off the questions spinning around her head. She could feel a ball of anxiety growing in the pit of her stomach: for Philippe, for Emile and for Simone. She felt as if they all stood on the edge of a precipice.

The crackling sound filled the room and she turned the volume down, leaning towards the radio so she wouldn't miss anything.

*This is the BBC. Here is the news.*

*Church bells were rung all across the United Kingdom for the first time since May 1940 in celebration of the allied victory at the Second Battle of El Alamein.*

*In the Stalingrad area the Red Army has repelled enemy attacks and is improving its position against the enemy.*

*RAF bombers have taken part in the heaviest raid yet on Italy. The targets were again Turin and Genoa in the north of the country.*

*Reports are still being received of Germany's barbarous treatment of Jews. German troops have occupied Vichy France and are marching into Lyons, Limoges, Pau, Vichy and other towns.*

Valérie switched off the radio, her nerves suddenly hardening into steel. They had to get Simone out of Geneva that night.

# ELEVEN

## VALÉRIE

Valérie returned to the old workshop as Emile had instructed. Her father watched her put on her coat, his furrowed brow highlighted in the pool of bright light shining down on his workbench. He laid down the small screwdriver he was using.

'Please don't go out tonight.'

'I agreed to meet Marianne. She's finishing late.'

'Something's going on out there this evening. Philippe's father called by this afternoon and said the police are searching for an escaped prisoner. They've closed off the Pont du Mont-Blanc and are checking everyone leaving the old town. I don't want you getting mixed up in any trouble.'

He looked worried and much older as he watched Valérie. Feeling a pang of guilt, she kissed his forehead.

'Don't worry, Papa. I'll be fine. I'll only be an hour and I'll stick to the side roads. If I see any trouble, I'll come back home.' With that assurance, he would have to be content. But she knew he'd watch until she turned the corner towards Geraldine's café, where she usually met Marianne at the end of her shift.

Once out of sight, Valérie turned in the opposite direction from the Café de Paris towards the old workshop. She kept close to the city walls, walking briskly in the freezing cold, looking all around her in case she ran into the police. But there were very few people around and those out on such a cold night were minding their own business, as reluctant as she was to be recognised. She stopped and raised her head at the sound of a police siren screaming from the main boulevard at the edge of the lake, but nobody ventured into the alley. All of the cafés around this part of the old town were closed and most people were safely at home. Only Geraldine's Café de Paris stayed open this late at night, busy entertaining off-duty soldiers, so she kept well clear of it.

As she turned the last corner, a step sounded behind her and she slipped into a narrow alley, pressing herself against the cold stone wall, hardly breathing as she waited for the person to pass. A familiar figure walked right past her hiding place. It was Bernard. What was he doing here? She peered around the edge of the building to see where he was going. Two men emerged from the shadows up ahead and they shook hands, then started an intense exchange in low voices. She crept out further but couldn't make out what they were saying. One of the men handed over a package to Bernard, in return for notes that the man checked carefully before they split up.

Valérie scrambled back into the alley so Bernard wouldn't see her, the worn soles of her boots sliding on the cobbles and her breath coming in short gasps. He passed so close to her hiding place that she could smell tobacco smoke. He must be getting the extra supplies for his father's shop from the smugglers who were bringing goods illegally across the border from France. That was why he was being so secretive. The heavy police presence on the streets hadn't put any of them off. Not Bernard nor the smugglers. Everybody knew that the smugglers' chief objective was to make money out of this horrible war, whether it was by selling goods or people.

It wasn't until the noise of his footsteps had faded away that she came out, moving through the shadows more carefully in case anyone else crossed her path. She breathed a sigh of relief when she reached the courtyard and silently opened the door to the storeroom.

Simone jumped up from the bed in surprise, hand reaching for her knife.

'Why are you here so late?'

'Emile said he would get you out of Geneva tonight.'

Simone grasped her arm, a real smile lighting up her face, more animated than Valérie had ever seen her. 'He has received instructions for handing over the list?'

'I hope so.'

The woman's grip made Valérie wince.

'You mean you don't know?'

'Simone, you're hurting me. You'll have to trust Emile. If he thinks you need to get out of Geneva you'll have to leave. That's all I know.'

She passed across the bag she'd brought with her.

'These are some clothes. It'll make it easier to blend in.'

Simone picked up the bag and Valérie breathed a sigh of relief.

While she was changing, Valérie rolled up the mattress and stored it with the others in the cupboard under the stairs. She stacked the wooden chairs against the wall, leaving two for them to sit on, then glanced around the room to check there was nothing else to show that someone had been sleeping there.

'I'm ready.'

She turned to look at Simone, now dressed in one of Marianne's old skirts and jumpers. She seemed younger and more vulnerable than before; the figure hidden under men's clothes looked thinner in woman's clothes. Valérie felt a rush of pity for her, seeing for the first time the ordinary woman that she must have been before the war.

Simone was holding out her knife.

'If I'm leaving tonight, you should have this. You'll be able to defend yourself if you're attacked.'

'Simone, I can't take your knife. You might need it.'

'I have another one.'

'No.'

Simone took a step closer, her eyes blazing in the light.

'You've helped me… hidden me here. If the Germans find me, they'll come after you. I can't leave you unarmed.'

Valérie opened her mouth to argue but the intense look in the other woman's eyes silenced her.

'I already have too many deaths on my conscience. I don't want yours to be another one. You are a good person, The Resistance needs people like you.'

'But Simone—'

'You must take it… It's the only way I can pay you back.'

'All right, okay. I'll take it.'

'Here's the belt. You can wear it around your waist and it will never be seen. Then you'll have a weapon at all times.'

Valérie took the belt.

'Thank you.'

'Put it on.'

She sighed but did as she was told, adjusting the strap and sliding the knife into the leather sheath. Simone nodded in satisfaction.

'Promise me you will always wear it.'

'I promise.'

They sat down to wait. When she changed position, Valérie felt the weight of the knife at her waist and itched to take it off. She'd spent her life around guns, but this weapon was different, not intended for sport but for death. They sat for a while, listening to the wind swirling outside and a brief smatter of rain. For once, she couldn't think of anything to say to Simone, even though she knew she might never see her again.

Finally, Simone broke the silence. 'Something's wrong. He isn't coming.'

Even as she spoke, they heard a noise outside and Valérie jumped up from the chair. Thank God he was here. She ran to the door and opened it an inch or two, scanning the courtyard outside, but there was no sign of Emile. The heavy door at the other side of the courtyard leading into the alley was still closed but it shook on its hinges as if someone had pushed against it. She stepped hastily back inside and closed the door.

'Who is it?' Simone was standing right behind her and Valérie could feel the tension in her body.

'I don't know. Someone was trying to get in. Or maybe it was just the wind.'

'But the courtyard door is locked, isn't it? I thought that only you and Emile have the keys.'

'Yes.' Valérie's voice sounded hollow and unconvincing. The possibility that someone else could have taken the key from Emile hovered around them, unspoken but insistent. Valérie looked around her but knew that there was only one way out. She felt for the knife at her waist and her clammy fingers closed around the hilt. Behind her, Simone pointed her pistol at the door.

An insistent whisper came from the other side of the door.

'Valérie, are you in there? Let me in.'

She yanked open the door and Marianne almost fell inside, clutching hold of them to steady herself, her face deathly white.

Simone ran to fetch a chair and Marianne sank down on to it as if her legs could no longer carry her. She bent her head and took a deep breath that seemed to steady her, then looked up. 'It's Emile. He's been hurt.'

'What's happened? Where is he?'

'He was attacked at the drop-off point.' Marianne's voice shook as she recounted the story. 'I heard one of the police calls, saying he'd been attacked by a gang of thugs and left for dead. I went to find him and he was already making his way to me. He was covered in blood.'

She couldn't carry on and Valérie handed her the water bottle, but Marianne pushed it away.

'There's no time. He wanted me to warn you. He said the Germans were behind it, they know where you're hiding Simone and have got the police to shut off the old city. You have to leave now if you're going to get her out of Geneva.'

'Who attacked him?' Valérie tried to take in what her friend was saying, the options for where they could go running through her mind. It was up to her now to get Simone to safety.

'He wasn't sure, their faces were covered. They followed him, then they threatened him, saying they knew he was working for the Resistance.' Her breath came out in a sob. 'When he wouldn't tell them anything, they started hitting him.'

Valérie felt sick. 'How did he get away?'

'He said that one minute they were hitting him and the next they dropped him and ran away. He thought someone might have frightened them off, but he didn't see anyone. Before they left, he heard them say they were coming to the old town near the cathedral, so they know roughly where Simone is.'

Marianne swallowed some water before she could carry on. 'He looked awful, there was blood everywhere, but he wouldn't let me wait with him for more than a few minutes. Said I had to come and tell you to leave now because they'll find you otherwise.'

As if to underline her warning, police sirens screamed in the distance and they heard the sound of shouting voices only a few streets away.

'They're coming. It's too late. We'll never get out of here.' Valérie looked around the room wildly. She clutched Marianne's arm. 'He talked about safe houses in Lausanne and Montreux but I don't know the addresses. And how are we going to get out of Geneva?'

Marianne shook her head. 'He didn't say anything else. But you need to get out of the old town first... then make for the countryside north of the lake. Someone will take you in. '

She stopped and listened. 'If you don't leave now, you'll be trapped.'

They ran outside and Marianne hauled open the door to the alley. She looked outside in both directions and then pushed Valérie and Simone out into the narrow lane.

'Don't go near the Pont du Mont-Blanc. It's crawling with police. Try the Pont des Bergues, you might get across that way.'

Valérie and Simone ran along the cobbled streets that skirted along the old city wall and towards the edge of the old town. Valérie tried to look back to see what had happened to Marianne but almost tripped up on the uneven cobbles and clutched Simone's arm to stop herself from crashing to the ground.

Her panic had subsided now that they were outside and she led Simone in and out of the winding lanes, taking a circuitous route down to the water that didn't take them along any of the major thoroughfares, where she knew the police would set up checkpoints.

They avoided the elegant shopping area around the Rue du Rhône and slowed their pace to a brisk walk as they approached the Pont des Bergues, pretending to be two friends who had missed their last tram. Her heart was pounding but Valérie grew more confident as none of the police cars stopped to ask why they were out so late at night. She glanced up at the lights still on at the top of the grand post office building a few blocks away, where Marianne had heard about Emile; her step faltered as she imagined his pain and terror. She needed to be strong, like he was. What would she do once she'd got Simone to safety? She would have to take the list back to Geneva to hand it over, but she had no idea who Emile's contact was, or even where his drop-off place could be. Her mind racing, she glanced at

Simone, whose face was hard and determined, and wondered if beneath her steely exterior she was just as frightened as Valérie.

At the bridge crossing to the north side of the Lake, Simone nudged her suddenly and whispered. 'That police car has driven past us before. I think he's going to stop.'

The car slowed down next to them and a young policeman wound down his window. Valérie put her hand on Simone's arm and bent down towards the open window, forcing a smile.

'Papers please.'

Valérie handed over their documents, standing in front of Simone to shield her from the police, holding her breath as he examined Simone's false papers. If there was anything wrong with them, if someone had made a mistake, it would be all over. Already there were groups of police gathering at the end of the bridge. She tried not to let her fear show in her voice.

'What's going on? There are a lot of police out tonight.'

'We're after an escaped prisoner,' the older policeman in the passenger seat leaned forward, his voice a low drawl. 'We're from out of town but we've all been ordered out of our warm beds to look for him. He's probably miles away by now. We're just on our way to a briefing.' He snorted in disgust. 'This bloody war. We're supposed to be neutral, but it seems to me that our bosses are just following Nazi orders most of the time.'

His younger colleague interrupted the indiscreet outburst and handed back their papers. 'You'd better not hang around here, mademoiselle. With a desperate criminal on the run, it's not safe.'

Valérie nodded and forced herself to smile once more as he wound up his window. She grasped Simone's arm and dragged her away from the car.

'Come on. Let's get out of here.'

They walked across the bridge to the north of the city, the two policemen standing guard on the other side waving them through.

Unable to believe that the policemen didn't know who they were looking for, Valérie felt a surge of hope that they might get out of the city. From the old town, they cut through the Pâquis district towards the entry to the park. Valérie wouldn't normally have ventured into the red-light district at night, where the bars and clubs were still open, but she didn't look to the right or left as she walked and no one took any notice of them.

'Where are we going?' muttered Simone through clenched teeth. 'This place is too busy.'

'Don't worry. We're almost there. The path around the lakeside should be safe and we can get out of the city that way.'

'If you're sure.'

'Trust me. I'm sure.'

Their lucky escape gave Valérie a new burst of energy that lightened her steps. If the police had known they were searching for a young woman they would have seized them in an instant.

The Parc Mon Repos stretched along the edge of the lake and bordered the grounds of Henry Grant's house. Valérie suddenly remembered his words. *If you get into trouble and need help, you know you can always come to me.* She glanced through the trees towards his house, its lights twinkling through the branches swaying in the breeze. It was their best hope of escape if they could only find a way over the high wall that divided the park from his garden.

But before she could tell Simone her plan, the Frenchwoman stopped and pulled her off the path towards the large trees.

'We have to hide.'

'There's no one here.'

'I think we're being followed. And there are men up ahead on the path. Listen...'

Valérie strained to hear anything above the quiet lapping of the water against the banks of the lake. Then they both heard it.

The unmistakeable crackle of a radio coming from ahead of them around a bend in the path.

'Local police report two young women crossed the Pont des Bergues... going north... they're following in pursuit.'

They heard a sharp order to switch the radio off and then silence. Simone pointed back the way they'd come and Valérie caught her breath when she saw a group of men marching towards them. She recognised the figure at the front. It was Dieter. She shrank back behind the tree, hardly daring to breathe, her legs almost buckling beneath her. What if he'd seen her? Or if he started to search among the trees?

So Emile had been right when he said Dieter was working for the Gestapo. She had been taken in by the German's friendly interest in her father's business and his convincing criticisms of the Nazis. And she'd warmed to him when they'd met in the Café de Paris and he'd listened to her plans for travelling to England with Philippe after the war. She'd felt sorry for him as he talked to her about his late wife, overwhelmed by emotion. She'd even let him hold her hand for a few minutes until she'd come to her senses and pulled it away. But while he was smiling at her over steaming hot chocolate in the café and drinking wine in their home, the picture of civilised behaviour, he was spying on them all. And here he was, hunting Simone like an animal.

The noise of their footsteps faded and Valérie saw them disappear around the bend ahead. They must have joined the men with the radio because a larger group of ten or twelve men reappeared a few moments later. She watched in horror as they put on black masks. Valérie ducked back into her hiding place. The men were talking, obviously debating where to search next, Dieter gesticulating to the others.

She looked around her, trying to see a way out, but they were trapped between the police and the group of vigilantes. If they came out from behind the trees, they would be seen. The panic she'd felt in the storeroom surged back. She felt sick with fear.

Simone took hold of her hand and her urgent whisper cut through Valérie's turbulent thoughts.

'I'm going to give myself up. It's me they want, not you. I'll distract them. You must get away from those men. Go straight back the way we came. You're Swiss. The police won't bother you.'

'No Simone, you can't. There must be another way.'

'There is no other way. You know that as well as I do.' She clutched Valérie's arm in a claw-like grip. 'Listen to me. I hid the list upstairs in the old watch workshop. I was scared we would be caught. It's hidden behind your father's desk. You must find it and give it to the British.'

'You left the list behind?'

'I thought it would be safer hidden there. I knew I could rely on you.'

Valérie stared at Simone in the darkness and could feel the energy and steely determination that so characterised the woman. She shook her head, unwilling to accept that it could end like this.

'If we run now, we might get away. I know somewhere we could go.'

'They'll hear us. They're too close. If I distract them, you might be able to escape. But you must promise me you will hand over the list.'

'I promise, but don't do this... please, Simone. There must be another way.'

Her words fell into thin air. She desperately clutched for Simone's hand, but she grasped at nothing. Simone had marched out on to the path and left Valérie crouching and frozen behind the tree. She couldn't risk looking out from her hiding place. But she heard everything above the sound of her rapid, shallow breathing. Simone's footsteps as she walked towards the group of masked men. One of them shouting when they caught sight of the figure coming towards them in the gloom. Then a maelstrom of footsteps and scuffling as they ran to grab their quarry.

Valérie turned to flee, looking back only once. She saw Simone, a small figure in the middle of the group of masked men. In the darkness, there was the glint of a knife as it caught a shaft of moonlight. Then shots filled the air.

Valérie raced through the trees along the edge of the path, panicked and wide-eyed, too shocked even to cry. Her feet slithered on the rough ground.

Running steps behind her made her shrink further back into the trees. There were shouts all around her and she didn't know which way to turn, confused by the noise and the darkness. She had no choice but to scrabble her way further back into the trees to put as much distance as possible between her and Simone's murderers. How could her life have ended so quickly? She had been there, so fierce and alive, just minutes ago. But the harsh, cold sound of those shots at such close range left no room for doubt. Simone was gone.

Pushing away the overpowering dread that there was no escape, that she'd be caught and shot before they realised she was Swiss, she wound her way through the thicker bushes until her back was against the high wall that formed the barrier between the park and the houses skirting the lake. She looked frantically to her left and right, but there was only the wall stretching to either side topped by tangled barbed wire to keep intruders out. When she reached up to grasp the old bricks, they crumbled in her fingers and she couldn't get any grip. She sobbed in desperation as she fell back, nails torn and fingers stinging with pain.

The shouts were much closer now. Valérie whipped her head round, expecting to see masked faces appear through the trees. She could hardly breathe, fear dulling her reactions.

Images flashed through her mind, her father at his workbench smiling up at her, Philippe's warm gaze and the feel of his arms around her. She turned her face towards the men clambering through the trees. It was over.

Suddenly a hand clasped over her mouth. A voice breathed close to her ear. 'Don't scream... they'll hear you.'

Strong hands lifted her bodily off the ground and pulled her backwards into darkness. The world was turning upside down; she clutched the hand that was clamped over her mouth, forcing herself not to make a noise. Shadowy figures loomed above her and she blinked a couple of times, realising she must have come through a door to the other side of the wall in Henry Grant's garden. She jumped when a voice shouted in disgust, '*Niemand hier...* There is no one. We're wasting our time.'

Then the noises faded away.

Valérie was shaking so much that she could hardly stand up. One of her rescuers stretched out a hand to lift her up and she stumbled on the uneven ground until she could regain her balance. She stared at the three figures around her but could only see the glint of eyes above the scarves hiding their faces.

'Thank you,' she whispered, terrified that there was still someone on the other side of the wall who would hear them. 'How did you know I was there?'

'We got a tip-off,' one of the men whispered. 'Not everyone in Switzerland agrees with the Germans taking the law into their own hands.'

'Who are you?'

'Better you don't know that.'

She nodded, struggling to believe that she'd escaped, that she was still alive after what had happened to Simone. She put a hand up to rub her eyes, but it was shaking so much that she let it fall. Her breath was coming in short gasps. She could so easily have been killed if it weren't for Simone's bravery.

'Why didn't they come after me?'

'The door only opens this way. You can't see it from the other side.'

She felt suddenly very tired.

'I need to get home. My father will be worried sick.'

Two of the men led her to a van parked a few metres away concealed behind some large shrubs at the side of the large garden. She couldn't decipher the writing on the side, but it looked like some kind of delivery van.

'We'll take you across to the old town. They're still guarding all the bridges so you won't get across otherwise.' One of the men handed her into the back of the van and spoke in a low voice, as if he still expected an attack before they'd got her safely away.

'Hide in that compartment. When the van stops and you hear the door open, get out and go straight home. Don't wait and don't look back.'

The door slammed shut and Valérie held on tightly as the van accelerated sharply and bounced over the rough ground before turning on to a smoother surface. She breathed in the strong smell of cheese that lingered in the van and closed her eyes, Simone's brave face before she walked towards her death imprinted on her mind.

She didn't know who had helped her, but the door in the wall led through to the garden behind Henry Grant's manor house. As she was shaken around in the back of the van, Valérie thought about the Englishman. He had said to come to him if she needed help. Once she'd found it, maybe she should give him the list. 'Don't worry, Simone,' she whispered in the dark. 'I'll carry out your mission, I promise.'

# TWELVE

## VALÉRIE

They dropped her at the edge of the old town and she ran all the way home without looking back. She closed the front door and leaned against the wall, gasping for breath and waiting for her heart to stop racing.

Her relief was short-lived. The terror that had dogged her steps all the way home gave way to the shattering knowledge that she had failed Emile and not been able to save Simone. She knew she should go back out and make sure that Simone's list, the information she'd died for, was still where she'd left it, but Valérie didn't think she was strong enough to go out again. Not yet. Her legs felt weak and her whole body was trembling.

'Valérie, is that you?' Her father's worried voice broke into her thoughts and she looked up to see him appear at the end of the hall.

'Papa...' She ran to him and threw herself into his arms, hugging him tightly and burying her nose into his worn sweater, comforted by the familiar smell. After a few seconds, she felt him draw back.

'Monsieur Cherix is here.'

She whipped round to see the familiar uniformed figure

standing at the side of the room watching them closely. He was shorter and plumper than Philippe, the once dark hair now a shock of white, but his features were so like those of his son that she blinked a couple of times. She couldn't speak, her mind whirling from all that had happened that night, the knowledge that the Swiss police must have helped the Germans to find Simone burning in her mind.

'He came to check we were all right. It isn't safe these days to be out so late.'

'I'm not here in my official capacity Albert, but as a friend.' He turned to Valérie. 'Some officers reported that they spoke to two young women crossing the Pont des Bergues tonight. They warned them to go home, that it was dangerous to be out.' He cleared his throat. 'They didn't know who the women were, but the description they gave of one of them sounded very like you.'

'I've been with Geraldine at the Café de Paris.' Her voice cracked and she sat down abruptly on the nearest chair, her legs threatening to give way.

He held up his hand. 'I don't want to know where you were or what you were mixed up in, but I'm just glad that you are safely home.' He hesitated and then continued. 'Your friend Emile wasn't so lucky. He was attacked tonight, set upon by a gang of hooligans. He could have been killed.'

Neither Valérie nor her father spoke. She didn't trust herself to say anything, she was shaking so much. Her fingers had begun to throb as the feeling came back to them and she hid her bleeding nails in the folds of her skirt.

'I just hope that you and your friends learn a lesson from tonight. You need to understand that getting too close to the French Resistance puts you in a very dangerous position. They will work with anyone, including smugglers and criminals. Our job is to protect Swiss lives but we won't be able to protect you or Emile all the time. Incidents like those which occurred tonight make that more difficult.'

He looked like he was about to say more, but one glance at her white features and muddy clothes seemed to change his mind and his stern features softened.

'I'm relieved you're home safe.' He nodded at them both and left. They waited until the door was closed behind him before her father came and sat next to her, putting an arm around her shoulders.

'Thank God you're home.' His voice shook and he smoothed down her hair. 'Where have you been? I was so worried about you. There are police everywhere, they said they were searching for an escaped prisoner. Please tell me you weren't caught up in it? '

'It wasn't an escaped prisoner,' she mumbled into his shoulder before lifting her head. 'But that's not why I'm late. When Emile was attacked, I had to stay with Marianne.'

Albert pulled away from her a little and studied her face. 'Who attacked him? I told you not to get involved with that boy. He'll not rest until he's got himself killed.'

Valérie kept her hands in her lap so her father wouldn't see her bloody fingers. She was feeling calmer now and knew there were some things it was best not to tell him, terrified she might put him in danger too. What if he challenged Dieter? Valérie couldn't bring herself to believe her father knew about his friend's Gestapo connections and his life as a vigilante.

'Who do they think attacked the poor boy?'

'He doesn't know. They were tormenting him about his limp and he retaliated, so they turned on him.' She stared at her father before carrying on, carefully. 'Dieter was out there tonight. I saw him.'

He didn't react to her words but looked thoughtfully at her for a few moments, his eyes empty of expression.

'I can't believe he would be part of anything like that. He's an official in the Consulate, Valérie, he has a reputation to consider.'

Valérie bit her lip and tasted the sharp tang of blood.

'I don't trust him. I think you should be very careful what you tell him.'

'I am careful of him. He would be very quick to withdraw his business if he thinks we're selling more of our products to the Allies than to him.'

Her father paused and studied her tangled hair and pale features. Then he surprised her with his next words.

'I wonder whether you shouldn't go away from Geneva for a few weeks, my love. Go up to the mountains to stay with your aunt in Gryon. You've been working very hard over the last few months. This incident with Emile, the rumours flying around about his activities, it's affecting you.'

'No, Papa. I can't go away. I want to stay here with you. You can't manage the business on your own, Agathe is too old to be of much help.'

She couldn't run away now. In any case she had to find Simone's list and hand it over to the Allies. With Emile in hospital and no idea of who his contact was or how to get a message to them, she would have to trust that Henry was working for the Allies and hand the list over to him. She'd have to go back there, to the place where Simone was killed. The vivid memory of Simone extracting the promise before she walked to her death filled Valérie's mind. She looked down at the glowing embers in the hearth, fearful that her father would see something of the horror of that night in her face.

He seemed content just to plant the idea. 'You don't need to decide immediately, but your aunt would be happy to have you with her for a few weeks. You could help your cousins on the farm, get some fresh air in your lungs. It's only a few weeks until Christmas so I could come up then and join you. Your aunt has invited us already, so you'd just be going a little early.'

She shook her head and stood up to leave.

'I'll think about it, Papa, I promise, but I don't want to leave you alone here.'

When she finally escaped to her room, her fingers had stiffened up and she winced as she soaked them in a bowl of warm water. She let the waves of pain wash over her, but they didn't blot out the image of Simone's face, her dark eyes wide and determined, her thin body hitting the ground.

The next morning, as soon as Valérie had gathered the deliveries for the day, she headed straight towards the old workshop.

Wobbling on her bike, she pulled her coat up around her shoulders and stifled a yawn, tiredness making her cold and shivery. She hadn't been able to sleep much, replaying in her mind the awful memory of Simone walking out from their hiding place and the loud sudden staccato of pistol fire. When she did fall asleep her dreams were even worse, Simone's face turning into her father's, then Philippe's, then her mother's, their screams drowned out by the sound of gunshots.

She turned the corner into the alley and jumped off her bike. Before she could look for the key in her bag, she saw that the door to the small courtyard outside the workshop had been forced open, the wood splintered and cracked, and it was swinging open in the wind. Glancing along the alley, she saw that no other doors had been forced open. She felt a cold shiver snake down her spine. They had just got away in time.

Dreading to think that she was too late and Simone's list had already been found, Valérie pushed open the door and wheeled her bike into the courtyard, then ran across the rough ground to the building. The storeroom door was hanging at an angle, lock shot through, and Valérie went inside. In the empty space downstairs nothing looked any different to the previous night. Desperate to find the list and get out of the place as soon as she could, Valérie ran up the wooden staircase to the workshop on the upper floor and threw open the door.

The scene was one of chaos, work benches toppled over and boxes upended, tools strewn over the ground. It wasn't the Swiss police who had been searching here, she knew instantly. They wouldn't have destroyed her father's equipment, the oldest and most prized pieces dating back centuries. This must have been done by German spies who were searching for the list. They wouldn't hesitate to destroy Switzerland and all that it valued. And she had led them here, the destruction all around her was her fault. How on earth was she going to tell her father what had happened?

A bird flew against the window next to her head and the scrabbling noise made her jump, the shock forcing her to keep moving. She stepped over a heavy stamping machine used to make plates and bridges, now lying on its side on the floor, and headed towards her father's workbench at the far end of the room directly in front of the largest windows. They must have been interrupted and hadn't got that far. The benches and equipment at this end of the room were untouched. She sank on to the stool at the desk and looked around for somewhere Simone could have hidden the list, opening the drawers at the front of the desk with shaking fingers and lifting the boxes of small screwdrivers and metal files, but she couldn't find it anywhere. She twisted round on the stool and scanned the room for any clue Simone could have left behind her, before turning back. She had said to look in her father's desk, it must be there somewhere.

She felt under the bench, fingers straining to find any piece of paper, but there was nothing there, so she examined the front of the wood, checking the corners of the drawers, trying to find any kind of hidden compartment, growing increasingly desperate. Could she be too late? Had the Germans already found the list of Swiss traitors? Why hadn't she come here straight away last night? If the list was lost then she'd failed Simone all over again. Valérie covered her face with her hands and sat like that for what seemed like an eternity, playing over in her mind Simone's exact words... *'I hid the list upstairs in the old watch workshop... behind your father's desk...'*

*Behind* the desk, not *in* the desk, Simone had said. Valérie lifted her head and examined the wall in front of her where the bench slotted underneath the narrow window ledge. She leaned across and felt around the edge of the bench, looking for a crack between the wood and the wall. At one end she felt a narrow gap. Her heart racing, Valérie slipped her fingers inside the gap and pulled out a folded piece of paper. She started to open it and saw that it was a list of names, handwritten on lined paper, torn from a notebook. She clutched the paper in triumph, but before she could read it she heard a noise downstairs in the courtyard. Somebody was there. She stuffed the paper into her pocket and ran as quietly as she could across the workroom and down the stairs. Now she'd found Simone's list, she would guard it with her life.

She peered round the door and breathed a sigh of relief when she saw that it was only Bernard and Geraldine standing in the small courtyard. Bernard was looking sullen and Geraldine flushed and angry.

'What are you doing here?' Valérie looked from one to the other, trying to work out what was going on. 'Were you looking for me?'

'No,' burst out Geraldine, flushing a deep red colour that matched the roses on her dress.

'Yes,' contradicted Bernard, casting a look of disgust at his blonde companion. 'We came to your house and followed you up here.'

Valérie was surprised at the look he gave Geraldine, as Bernard usually hung on her every word, always eager to please and do any favours whenever he had the chance. He wasn't pandering to her now. He took Geraldine's arm in his strong grasp and pulled her roughly towards Valérie, ignoring her exclamation of protest.

'Tell her what you told me,' he ordered in a curt voice Valérie had never heard before. She dragged her eyes away from the angry figure standing in overalls, this new Bernard unrecognisable. Was this the same man she'd seen trading with smugglers late at night and sneaking round the streets spying on them all?

'It was yesterday evening,' stuttered Geraldine under Valérie's hard stare. 'In the café, some Germans came in and I heard them talking about a Resistance fighter. They said she'd escaped here from across the border and had been hiding in Geneva... They were laughing, shouting for drinks...' She gulped and then carried on. 'They said the woman had been shot. '

'And what did they say about the people who helped the woman escape?' prompted Bernard.

Valérie looked at him, wondering how much he knew.

'Tell her, Geraldine,' Bernard said.

'They said that they knew some Swiss people were hiding her.'

Valérie swallowed. 'Did they know who?'

'No. They said the German guards had picked up someone on the French side of the border who they thought had been involved and they were going to hand him over to the Gestapo. They'd interrogate him, see what he could tell them.'

If someone in the Resistance had been tortured, then they could all be exposed. Valérie's voice sounded harsh in the quiet courtyard.

'What was his name?'

'They didn't say, but it sounded like he was young, they talked about him being a boy.'

She drew a sharp intake of breath and closed her eyes.

Another child, tortured and brutalised at the hands of the Nazis. How could they be so cruel?

'And they didn't talk about anyone else?' she said slowly, after a few minutes.

Geraldine shook her head and pulled her arm out of Bernard's grasp. 'I hate you,' she spat at him and turned to look defiantly at Valérie. 'I told him that no one said Emile's name. They didn't talk about him being attacked. I didn't know he was going to get hurt, I couldn't have done anything to stop it.' She looked again at Bernard angrily. 'Whatever you may think.'

He ignored her and spoke to Valérie. 'I wanted you to know what they were saying, just in case you were worried they'd come back...' His voice trailed away and he looked embarrassed for the first time. 'I like Emile. He's always been nice to me. He didn't deserve to get hurt, whatever he was doing. Whoever attacked him didn't even know if he was involved in hiding the fugitive, but they beat him up anyway.'

'Thank you.'

Valérie felt herself redden with embarrassment. She didn't trust Bernard, had been convinced he spied on them. She'd seen him with her own eyes trading goods with smugglers and assumed that all he cared about was making money. But she wondered now whether she had judged him too harshly; maybe he had a boundary he wasn't prepared to cross and some people he wouldn't betray.

'I hate all these secrets.' Geraldine was almost in tears. 'I don't know what's going on with you. But look, that's all they said. I don't know why you had to drag me all the way here to tell Valérie that, Bernard.'

Neither of them replied that she wouldn't have believed Bernard if he'd come on his own, but they both knew it was the truth and Valérie felt herself flush again.

Geraldine pulled out a handkerchief and blew her nose loudly. 'And I don't want to know what you're all getting involved in either. I hate this horrible war and the sooner it's over the better. Making us all so uncomfortable, fighting with one another.'

At her childish complaint, Bernard's heavy features broke into a smile and he said. 'Come on, I'll walk home with you.'

Mollified, Geraldine looked at Valérie. 'Your friend Dieter came in to have a drink. He was asking about you.'

An image of Dieter leading the group of masked men in their hunt for Simone filled Valérie's mind.

'He's not my friend.'

'Don't bite my head off. I'm only telling you. He wanted to know when I'd last seen you and he was asking after you. That was all.'

They left Valérie standing in the courtyard, her mind turning over all that they'd said. Although she felt reassured that they didn't know for definite she'd been involved in hiding Simone, it felt like half the world was coming for her. Swiss police, German border guards and gangs of vigilantes had all worked together to hunt down one single woman. Simone never stood a chance.

Valérie shivered as the words of the police officer from the previous night about pandering to the Germans came back to her. She wondered again how far the Swiss authorities were prepared to go to appease their strong neighbour and keep their country from being invaded. She knew they wouldn't hesitate to hand over any French refugees they found and might turn a blind eye to undercover German activities within their borders. But surely they wouldn't endanger Swiss lives? Would they protect her, if they discovered she was the person who had hidden Simone?

Before leaving the courtyard, Valérie felt for the piece of paper in her pocket. Unable to resist a quick look at the list, she unfolded it and glanced down at the first few names. She knew that anyone proved to be a traitor would face a firing squad.

These men were betraying their country and could cause Switzerland's downfall if they were invaded. Soldiers like Philippe might not survive the war. And what for? Money? When people like Simone and Emile were prepared to give their lives to stop the Nazis? Let them be shot, she thought bitterly as her eyes drifted down the list.

The names were mainly German-Swiss, the area of the country where most of the people sympathising with Germany came from. But at the bottom of the list, there was a French name. She blinked and shook her head to check that she wasn't seeing things. But the clear black writing remained the same.

*Philippe Cherix – Fort de Dailly.*

Shock hit her like a physical blow and she put the paper back into her pocket with shaking fingers. She glanced around her to check she wasn't being watched and that a shadowy figure wasn't going to emerge out of one of the buildings and snatch the piece of paper from her hands. But the only shadows were in her mind, paralysing her physically and emotionally.

Valérie pushed her bike through the broken gate and turned towards home, walking as if she was in a dream. The deliveries were forgotten as she struggled to accept what was written on the paper. Philippe was identified as a traitor. But she couldn't believe it was true. How could it be true, that her brave Philippe who was so proud to fight for his country, could ever betray them all? It must be a mistake. What should she do now? Simone had made her promise to hand the information over to the Allies. But if she fulfilled her promise, she might as well write the death warrant of the man she loved.

Valérie walked through the familiar streets without seeing those who passed her or called out a greeting, wondering what on earth she should do. How could Philippe's name have got on to that list? There must have been a terrible mistake. He was the last person who would betray his country.

At least she had the list in her possession and hadn't handed it over to anyone without checking what it contained. Her heart lifted a fraction when she thought she could just rewrite it and delete Philippe's name. But what about the other copy that Simone had mentioned? And, as much as she hated herself for thinking this way, could there possibly be a chance that Philippe might have got caught up in something?

His last letter was so strange, so unlike him. If she could only see him, ask him, she'd know the truth from his face. But to delay handing the list over meant that the real traitors on the list had more time to pass on vital secrets to the Nazis. The image of Simone walking to her death filled her mind. How could she let her down?

When she got home, Valérie had no chance to retreat to her room because Marianne was in her father's workshop, waiting for her. When she opened the door, her friend ran to meet her, pale and solemn, eyes flashing a warning as her father came to the door at a more leisurely pace.

'You need to come with me to see Emile. They've taken him to the cantonal hospital. He's been asking for you.'

# THIRTEEN

## VALÉRIE

They cycled south towards the cantonal hospital across the Boulevard des Philosophes. Valérie was relieved that the noise of cars and trams made conversation impossible, effectively postponing Marianne's probing questions. There had been only time for a brief exchange when Valérie's father had left them to go back to his workshop.

'I thought you were captured or worse,' hissed Marianne. 'How did you get away?'

Valérie bent down to adjust her bike. 'Simone saved my life. I would have been killed if she hadn't given me the chance to escape.'

The guilt that she'd been unable to save Simone rushed back stronger than ever, weighing her down and making her dread Emile's inevitable questions. And worse than that, the knowledge that she couldn't do what Simone had asked grew into a hard lump in her stomach. She thought of Philippe, his hands tied behind his back, facing a firing squad, and shook her head to try to clear her mind. She simply could not betray him, even though she was endangering her country and their whole way of life.

She had prepared her story by the time they arrived at the hospital and her nerves were on fire as she followed Marianne through the long, rambling corridors to the ward. She was becoming adept at lying to everyone around her when they asked awkward questions. But could she lie to Emile, one of her closest friends, after she had almost lost him forever?

When she came into the ward, she saw Emile in the bed at the far end and stopped suddenly when Jean, his Resistance contact, stood up at the side of his bed and looked across at them, his expression unreadable.

Jean bent down to whisper something to Emile, shook his hand and came towards them, pulling his beret over his closely cropped brown hair as he walked. He nodded at them, his dark eyes lingering on Valérie. She stared back at him, wondering what he'd been whispering to Emile. He passed without speaking, brushing past her roughly. Marianne ran to Emile's bedside and Valérie gave herself a shake before following.

She was shocked when she came closer and saw Emile's bruised and bloodied face below the thick white bandage wound around his head. He struggled to sit up in bed and wouldn't accept their help, despite his obvious pain. She tried not to let her sympathy show as she knew more than anyone how much Emile hated the thought of being pitied, but sat down on the chair next to his bed and waited until he was able to speak.

'How are you feeling...' she started to say, but he had no time for pleasantries. His voice was harsh and he had to swallow some water before he spoke.

'Marianne said she got you out of the storeroom in time, but what happened then? Jean said an informer told the police someone was hiding Simone in the old city. Where did they find you?'

'We managed to cross the Pont des Bergues, but only

because the policemen who stopped and questioned us didn't know who they were looking for...'

Valérie hesitated as she considered the turn of events that had led them towards the park at the north bank of the lake and what had greeted them there. She gave a hollow laugh.

'We thought we were so lucky that they didn't know who they were looking for, but then we walked right into a group of vigilantes waiting for us. They were tipped off we were coming. We were trapped between them and the police.'

'And then?'

'Simone said she was going to turn herself in and told me to run away when I had the chance. I tried to argue with her, but she said that we couldn't both get away and it was her they wanted not me. She told me to save myself.'

Emile cleared his throat and swallowed another gulp of water. 'Didn't you try and stop her?'

'What do you think?' Valérie replied hotly and he had the grace to flush as she glared at him.

Marianne's voice of reason broke into the uncomfortable silence. 'We're all on the same side, remember. If we start fighting among ourselves then we're lost.' She turned to Emile. 'We all know Simone was unpredictable. How do you imagine Valérie could have stopped her once she'd made her decision?'

Emile closed his eyes and shook his head, but stayed silent as Valérie continued her story. She was grateful to Marianne for calming him down. 'She wouldn't listen to me. The next thing I knew she had walked out from where we were hiding, right towards the group of men. The minute she stepped on to the path, they surrounded her.'

Valérie gulped a couple of times, reliving the fear and emotion of that awful moment. Tears sprung into her eyes and she looked down, unable to continue.

'I heard she injured one of them,' said Marianne, squeezing Valérie's hand. 'A border policeman said it this morning when I was working at the telephone exchange. Someone was injured but he didn't say who it was.'

'Did they say who they were, the men in masks?' asked Valérie.

'No.'

'I know some of them were German. They may have been getting information from the Swiss police, but the men who killed Simone were German.' She paused and then added, 'Dieter Runde was there. He was the only one I recognised.'

'I told you all along he was working for the Gestapo.' Emile sounded grim. 'He has the perfect cover working at the Consulate, cosying up to anyone prepared to ignore the truth about what he's doing in Geneva.'

Valérie wasn't going to rise to the implicit criticism of her father but turned away from him towards Marianne. 'Did they give any names over the telephone?'

'No, but they sounded very relieved that the whole affair was over. As soon as they knew they weren't chasing an escaped criminal but someone from the Resistance, some of the local policemen refused to take part, despite their orders.'

They were all silent for a few moments with their thoughts and then Emile came out with the question Valérie had been waiting for.

'What happened to the list of Swiss traitors that we need to hand over to the Allies? Did Simone take it with her? If the Germans found it on her, then this was all for nothing.'

Valérie looked directly at Emile. 'I don't know whether she had it with her. I didn't see it... Did you ever see it?'

He shook his head. 'She wouldn't let me. Said the fewer people who knew what it contained the better.'

Valérie let out a sigh of relief and closed her eyes briefly.

'You don't think she left it in the old storeroom, do you?' Marianne was studying Valérie's face, her expression quizzical.

'I wondered that too, so I looked there this morning, but I

didn't find it,' replied Valérie calmly. 'The place was a mess. Someone went through the building searching for Simone and they destroyed all my father's equipment. I don't believe it was the Swiss police. Our place was targeted. It was the only gate left wide open and the locks on the doors destroyed. If the list was anywhere in the storeroom, they would have found it.'

'So Simone's dead and we've lost the intelligence she brought with her.' Emile leaned back against the pillows. 'Well, at least we know there was another copy of it. Although the other courier was being hunted too.'

Valérie looked away from Emile, her stomach lurching. Even if she destroyed the list, someone else could just walk into the authorities and hand over another copy.

Emile sighed heavily and Valérie felt a surge of pity. He looked exhausted, his body bruised and broken.

'Tell me what happened to you. Who attacked you?'

Marianne put her hand on Emile's thin forearm to try to stop him from sitting up again, but he ignored her.

'It was just along from the handover spot. I'd waited there for hours and had just decided I'd have to come back and admit to Simone that my contact hadn't appeared and convince her to leave anyway when a gang of four or five came around the corner and surrounded me. Called me a Jewish sympathiser. Kept asking who my Resistance contacts were, told me to stop helping people escape from France or they'd make me pay for it. Their faces were covered, so I don't know who they were. When I tried to run away, they pushed me over and kicked me while I was lying there.'

His voice trembled slightly but he cleared his throat and shrugged. 'All I remember was the kicking and punching and then it stopped. Just when I thought they'd decided to kill me.'

'Why did they stop?'

'I don't know. I thought that someone must have disturbed them and they didn't want to be caught. One minute they were hitting me and the next they'd run off. I lay there for ages, wondering if I was dead or alive and then I remembered you and Simone and realised I'd better warn you. I wasn't far from the Rue du Mont-Blanc and I knew that Marianne was at work that night so I managed to drag myself there.'

'And you didn't see anyone else?' asked Valérie.

He shook his head. 'There was an odd atmosphere in the town last night with all those police crawling around. People had been warned to stay indoors and were afraid. They didn't want to get involved, especially when they saw what I looked like.' He gestured towards his bruised face and winced at the movement.

'Was it the same group that came after us? Was Dieter with them?'

'No, this lot were Swiss. Jean said he thinks he knows them, he's warned me about them before.'

Emile clamped his lips together and glanced at Marianne.

Valérie leaned forward. 'Emile, I forgot. You need to warn Jean.'

'What about?'

'I heard that the Germans caught a member of the Resistance who knew about Simone. He might have told them where to find her and who was hiding her.'

'He's dead. Jean told me when he was here. That's why he came to see me. He doesn't think the Resistance cell has been betrayed.'

'Dead...' Valérie whispered. 'He was just a young boy. And it doesn't sound like Jean is very sure. What if they know about you now?'

'Can we ever be sure of anything, Valérie?' Marianne answered for him. 'Or of anyone? For every brave soul like Jean and Emile risking their lives helping people escape from France, there are twenty others prepared to turn them over to the authorities without hesitating.'

Valérie knew Marianne was right, that the Resistance was outnumbered by those in authority and in the wider French community who were prepared to work with the German occupier. Sometimes it was through fear of reprisals, which were often brutal, or because of the need for money to buy food. As she stood up to take her leave and glanced at Emile's tired and bruised face, she also had to accept that some Swiss even agreed with Nazi ideology and would help drive out anyone who didn't conform to their religious beliefs or ethnic identities.

They left Emile and headed back to the old city. Cycling along in silence, Valérie couldn't stop thinking about the list, and Philippe's name glaring up at her. There was only one way forward. She had to get to Philippe and warn him. And she had to admit that a shadowy part of her needed to see his face to be sure that it wasn't true. Quite how she was going to get into the Fort to speak to him, she hadn't yet worked out. She would just have to get the train to Saint-Maurice and then she'd figure out the rest.

When they finally reached her father's workshop, Marianne took her arm, her face filled with concern.

'Don't take Emile's comment to heart,' she said. 'He didn't mean to blame you, he feels so guilty that he wasn't able to come for Simone himself. And that he wasn't able to fight off his attackers.'

Valérie didn't trust herself to speak; she only gave her a quick hug and ran inside to find her father, remembering the damage to his workshop with a guilty pang. She heard glasses clink in the parlour and hurried into the room.

'Papa, I've decided you're right. I'd like to go and stay with Aunt Paulette for a little while, but there's something I need to tell you first.'

Her voice tailed away as Dieter stood up slowly and turned towards her, his arm in a sling. She grasped the door to steady herself, staring at him in horror.

# FOURTEEN

## PHILIPPE

Philippe stood at the top of the Grand Chamossaire, the highest peak above the village of Villars-sur-Ollon, and glanced down at the sheer rocky drop a few metres to his left, moving his skis to point down the slope. The sky was a brilliant blue against the snow-covered mountain. A thick layer of cloud had settled over the valley below him and even the village of Leysin, usually visible from the Grand Chamossaire, was submerged in the clouds.

He waited for the rest of his unit to clamber out of the funiluge and collect their skis. Installed just before the start of the war, the barge-shaped sledge could carry a dozen people from the Col de Bretaye up to the top of the Chamossaire, its occupants having nothing more to do than drink in the view while the cable system did all the hard work. It had been designed to attract tourists, but the only people on the slopes this early in the morning were soldiers. Every man had to be able to ski competently and know the terrain sufficiently to play his part in the event of an invasion.

He looked across at the jagged peaks of the Dents du Midi

and, beyond the ridge, at the blunt white top of Mont Blanc shining in the early-morning sun. He breathed in the icy mountain air and filled his lungs with its sweet freshness. It was good to get out of the warren of tunnels in the Fort for a few hours. Even though they were used to living so close to one another, eating and sleeping together in stuffy and poorly lit conditions, whenever he came outside he realised how strange an existence they were forced to lead. For a moment, he dreamed of never having to go back in there again, never having to spend another hour across the table from Favre, watching every word in case he revealed his suspicions, waiting for Favre to drop his guard and make a mistake. He just needed more evidence to ensure the other senior officers would believe him when he finally spoke. Every time he saw them joking and laughing with Favre, his chest tightened at the thought of how hard it would be to convince them.

The tense atmosphere in the Fort was making everyone uneasy and suspicious. Whoever had leaked information about the location of the new artillery had still not been identified and mistrust pervaded every corner of the place. It flared up in petty arguments. Philippe pulled on his gloves more tightly and flexed his fingers. But even though he strongly suspected it was Favre who was responsible, he simply did not have any real evidence.

'What are you waiting for?' Christophe shouted at him. 'Lead the way.'

Philippe slung the rifle over his shoulder, grabbed his poles and launched himself over the lip at the top of the slope, his skis floating through the fresh powder snow. He pointed his skis straight down the mountain, gathering speed as he carved his way through the snow, imagining he was all alone, then stopped at the base of the wide Bretaye bowl before the run narrowed alongside the café. Once buzzing with tourists, there were only a few locals left to keep it going. He waited for the others, watching as Christophe led the pack and skied down to join him.

All at once, his enjoyment of being outside in the mountains on such a gloriously sunny day was blighted by the worries about his friend which bubbled up to the surface. After both Favre and Valérie's betrayal, he simply could not bear the thought that Christophe might be just like them. But he'd have to confront Christophe sooner or later about the money he'd seen him try to hide. And had he taken Philippe's keys and gone to the map room? He couldn't believe Christophe was working with Favre to sell military secrets, but it seemed like he was wrong about everyone he trusted.

'I forgot to tell you,' Christophe said when he slid to a stop beside Philippe and managed to catch his breath. 'They caught the collaborator this morning.'

Philippe stared at him. 'Who told you that?'

'One of the men in his unit. They're all stunned, didn't suspect him at all. He was in the unit responsible for guarding the Fort that night. They think he told the Germans where to strike to cause the most damage to the artillery.'

'Why did he do it?'

His friend shrugged. 'Nobody knows. He kept protesting that he was innocent, that he'd been set up, but no one believed him. They all thought he'd been bribed by the Germans and done it for the money.'

'What will happen to him?'

'He'll be put on trial. And then shot, probably.'

'Christophe, I've been meaning to ask you...'

But his question was left in the air because the others had gathered around them. Olivier pushed through the front, almost knocking a couple of the men over in his haste to take charge.

'You didn't wait for my order. You can both bring up the rear from now on.'

They waited until the others had skied off.

'You'll have to slow down now,' said Christophe. 'His skiing is on a par with his shooting. We can take the scenic route.' With a cheeky grin, he fell in behind the line of soldiers skiing sedately behind their unit leader.

Philippe couldn't resist returning the infectious smile, but as Christophe skied ahead, his smile faded. Could Christophe be involved in Favre's schemes? Would it soon be him heading for a court martial?

He skied past the café, barely glancing at the few early customers drinking coffee, then dropped down on to the piste winding through the trees along the track leading down from the summit. On the mountain railway line leading up to Bretaye from Villars the trains were still running, though the timetable was reduced since there were fewer visitors to carry around the mountain.

When the unit had skied halfway down to the village, they took a sharp right-hand turn under the railway line at the Col de Soud, in front of another deserted café perched above the station. They waited in a group on one side of the railway line and then skied in single file under the line before emerging into the forest above the village.

After Col de Soud they split naturally into small groups. Christophe and Philippe were last in line and soon lost sight of the others among the trees. They stopped to take a rest above the narrow road winding around the chalets and farm buildings dotted up the slope. Through the trees, they saw a few trucks further down towards the village but it was deserted this high up where the road came to an end beside a traditional chalet. The chalet looked empty and run-down, the stone walls on the ground floor crumbling at the corners and the wood cladding on the upper floors faded and grey with age. The fragments of cloud dispersing above the village floated around the chalet, adding to its air of decay.

When they'd got their breath back, Philippe turned to Christophe.

'There's something I wanted to ask you.'

'What?'

A large, black Mercedes trundled slowly up the road towards the chalet below them.

'Hang on. It can wait.'

Philippe pulled his friend further back so they were shielded by the trees and whispered, 'Don't move.'

'Why not?'

'I think I know that car.'

The car turned off the road and stopped next to the dilapidated chalet. Philippe checked each of the windows to glimpse any sign of life in the building, but the shutters were all closed. He saw Favre's driver jump out of the car and take out a roll of brown paper from the front seat, concealing it under his coat as he walked around the chalet out of sight. Philippe drew in a deep breath. It had to be a map; he recognised the paper. And maps were never to be removed from the Fort. A few moments later he came back out with another man and they stood talking together. The man was tall and heavy-set and looked all around them as they talked. It was the man Philippe had seen outside the Grand Hotel meeting Favre.

'Who is it?' breathed Christophe.

'It's Favre's driver. Handing over one of our maps to a German spy.'

'I knew it. I suspected him all along.'

'You suspected him?'

Serious for once, his friend nodded. 'Yes, I did. All those trips down to the spa would have been a good cover for something. But it was just a guess and I didn't want to say anything to you. You seemed to really like him, I thought you'd never believe me. '

Philippe watched the two men standing at the chalet, a

doubt still lingering in his mind. Then Christophe's words stretched across the divide.

'I borrowed your key to the map room to see if I could find any clues. But Favre was there so I couldn't even get in to look. And I know you're worried about the money you saw. You don't know how I got it but trust me, I'm not selling Swiss secrets to anyone... There's more than one way of fighting this war. And if I can profit from cheating the Nazis any way I can, then I'm in.'

Philippe swallowed. It might not be the whole truth, but at least the question was finally out in the open.

'So where did the money come from?'

Christophe was twisting his pole in the snow and didn't reply. Philippe tried one more time.

'I don't want the version of the truth you decide will stop me asking questions. I need to know what's going on. I have to be able to trust you. You're my friend.'

Christophe let out a heavy sigh and then his words came out in a rush. 'I did win some money at cards the other night. I wasn't lying to you about that. I've never told you any lies.'

'Just not the whole truth.'

'No, not the whole truth. I won a few Swiss francs but not as much as you saw. The people I play cards with in Saint-Maurice, I've got to know them quite well. They're just ordinary people working in the town, trying to get by and feed their families. A couple of them work on the railway and they discovered that the Germans have been hiding train carriages in a siding along from the station, where the main line runs into the tunnel through the cliff face above the town.'

'Why?'

'Because the carriages are full of stolen goods. My friends have managed to get past the Germans guarding the train and taken a few things back. Things we can sell...'

'So what happens when they find out items are missing?'

'They won't. My friends are very careful. They leave most

of the stuff behind. The Germans don't know anything has gone.' Christophe's irrepressible grin peeped out again.

Philippe's gaze didn't move. 'What part do you play in all this?'

'I sell some of the stuff to the soldiers in the Fort. Cigarettes and some of the fancy food. It's a ready-made market. Or I hide things for them if they can't move them on quickly. Any paintings or antiques they think are valuable I send home and get my father's old partner to sell them for me. We keep some of the money, you know my family really need it now. But I give back the rest. They have contacts in the French Resistance who are always desperate for funds.'

Christophe fell silent for a moment, then asked, 'Satisfied now?'

'I think you're mad to get involved in the whole thing. What happens if you get caught? Or the Germans find out what's happening?'

His friend grinned once more. 'We won't get caught, we're too careful.' He tossed his head. 'Anyway, life at the Fort is so boring. Pointless military exercises, walking for miles to guard bridges in the middle of the night. And I can't even talk to you because you're closeted away for hours on end. This sparks things up a bit. Particularly when it's all done under Olivier's sleepy watch. He doesn't see anything even if it's right in front of his nose. Doesn't suspect a thing.'

Philippe couldn't help smiling at Christophe's confidence, but the smile faded when they saw Favre's driver get back into his car.

'We'd better get out of here, and tell them at the Fort what's been going on under their noses. Now two of us suspect him, surely they'll have to investigate. I don't think even Favre could wriggle out of the word of two witnesses so easily.

He edged forward, ignoring Christophe's muttered warning: 'Be careful.'

But Philippe had leaned too far forward. The mound of snow on which he stood crumpled down the slope and one of his skis went with it, sliding sharply to the side. He made a wild grab for the branches in front of him to stop himself from slithering down in front of the chalet. In an instant, Christophe had seen the danger and stuck his pole on the other side of Philippe's skis, halting his slide, before hauling him back up the slope. They clung to one another for a few seconds to steady themselves before Philippe glanced down to check they hadn't been seen. He breathed a sigh of relief when he saw the car back out from behind the chalet and drive slowly down the mountain.

Suddenly a branch shuddered and broke above them with a loud crack. A thick covering of snow slid off and hit the ground with a dull thud, spraying then with frozen droplets.

'What was that?'

Before Philippe could reply, a shot rang out through the trees and this time the bullet pockmarked the snow on the slope in front of them, dark and black against the blanket of white. They instinctively ducked down.

'Move,' Philippe shouted as another shot echoed round the valley.

They scrambled further into the trees to get to an open slope, their skis floundering on the uneven snow. After an agonising few minutes in full sight of the road, they turned down into a clearing and skied away. They had to get deeper into the forest. Bending low over the rough snow, Philippe heard another shot.

'I'm hit,' Christophe cried as he twisted round and catapulted into a snow drift, his skis pointing out at sharp angles from the mound of snow. Philippe skied towards him. His friend was coughing and spitting out the powdery snow and thrashing around in panic. Philippe brushed away the snow from his face and untied his bindings to release the skis.

Christophe groaned and tried to sit up, but Philippe grasped his arm.

'Don't move... where did he get you? Just lie still until I know how badly hurt you are.'

'It's my knee.' Christophe ignored Philippe's restraining hand and pulled himself forward to brush off the snow, then let out a cry of pain when his hand touched his leg and he pulled back fingers stained with blood. He fell back into the snow, face screwed up in pain.

Philippe looked around them, scanning the area, half expecting to see someone appear out of the woods, but everything was quiet, the only sound the light breeze stirring the tall fir trees. Despite the cold, he felt clammy and his heart was thumping in his chest. They were far too exposed to the sniper and the elements up here.

He'd have to get Christophe inside as soon as he could. He winced when he looked at Christophe's leg, the blood flowing out of the ragged hole in his ski suit, staining the light material a vivid red. It might be a flesh wound or it could have hit the bone. If he could stop the bleeding, then they might manage to stagger down together.

He raked through the pockets of his ski suit and dug out his hat, folding it into a pad.

'I need your scarf.' He pulled Christophe's scarf off and tied it to his own, before leaning over his friend and tying the makeshift tourniquet above the knee. He ignored Christophe's futile attempts to push away his hands, knowing that the longer they stayed out in the open, the more danger they were in.

'Can't have you bleeding all the way down.'

Christophe smiled weakly but, by the time Philippe had finished, his face was a ghastly grey colour and beads of perspiration glistened on his brow.

Philippe took a deep breath. He wasn't at all sure he would be able to get Christophe down on his own, but he had to try.

'Come on. You need to get up.'

'Can't... Just leave me...'

'I'm not leaving you here. Come on, you should be able to stand. I'll help you.' Philippe leaned down and put Christophe's arm around his shoulder, then pulled his friend up. They stood for a moment together, Christophe's breath coming in short gasps.

'I'll take your weight. Just walk on your good leg.'

But it was no use. Christophe cried out in pain and collapsed down on to the snow again. 'Can't do it. Too painful...'

Philippe grabbed his shoulder to stop him falling back in the snow and he cried out again. This was useless. He had to go and get help and risk leaving Christophe alone in the woods. He shook his head. All his instincts told him they had to stay together.

Philippe looked up when he heard shouting coming from further down in the trees. He hesitated, not sure who was coming towards them.

The noise got louder and he strained to see who it was. Then he let his breath out in a sigh of relief,

'Philippe? Christophe?'

'We're here! Over here.' Philippe yelled at the top of his voice. Thank God it was their unit. The soldiers emerged from the trees and climbed up the slope towards them, Olivier at the front.

'Where the hell have you two been?'

'Christophe's hurt. I was just coming to find you.'

Olivier's eyes narrowed. 'What happened?'

'He's been shot.'

'Let me see him.'

Philippe moved aside as a member of his unit, a medical student before the war, knelt next to Christophe. Everyone stepped back to give him some space.

'I tried to stop the bleeding, but he couldn't walk.'

The former medical student studied Philippe's handiwork. 'Nothing more we can do up here. We need to get him down to the first aid centre to make sure the bullet isn't still in there, then assess the damage.'

'What were you two doing up there for so long? Why did somebody shoot at you?' demanded Olivier.

Some of Christophe's colour had come back.

'I'm feeling better now. Just get me off this damned slope before I freeze to death.'

Before Olivier could ask any more questions, the soldier tending Christophe nodded.

'We need to get this man to the first aid centre. His wound has to be cleaned in case it gets infected.'

'You two, carry him to the truck,' barked Olivier.

Antoine and Walter came forward to pick up Christophe and carried him between them through the trees down towards the road, where the army truck was waiting. As Philippe loaded his skis into the truck he caught a glimpse of the same black Mercedes they'd seen at the chalet, Favre's driver leaning against it and watching the scene as Christophe was laid on to a stretcher and lifted into the truck.

Philippe tried to melt into the background and avoid the driver's gaze. Bending his head, he trooped into the truck with the rest of the men, curbing the desire to look back to see whether he was still there.

The truck set off and Philippe breathed a sigh of relief, avoiding the curious stares of the other men. For once they were silent, subdued by Olivier's presence in the back of the truck. He felt icily cold and not just because of the snow trickling down inside the neck of his jacket. Christophe was lying with his eyes closed and brow creased, each jolt of the truck making him suck in his breath with pain. Philippe could hardly bear to look at his friend in so much pain. He could so easily have been killed. He prayed silently that Christophe would be fit enough to report what they'd seen to their commanding officer. They couldn't delay before they told someone. Two other soldiers had seen something that put Favre under suspicion. They would at least have to investigate, despite Favre's reputation. But what if Favre's driver had seen Philippe? The driver would have known Philippe could easily recognise him. And if he was warned quickly, Favre might have time to escape before he was captured, carrying vital information with him over to the Nazis. Their country could be attacked and it would all be Philippe's fault, because he hadn't acted quickly enough.

# FIFTEEN

## PHILIPPE

They arrived back at the Fort and Christophe was swept away
to the infirmary to see the doctor. Philippe was about to follow
the stretcher when Olivier stepped in his path.

'Where do you think you're going?'

'With Christophe, to check he's all right, because if it wasn't
for...' He bit back the admission that he was to blame for what
had happened.

Olivier shook his head. 'Not so fast. You need to see the
commanding officer first. He wants to know exactly what
happened out there and why someone would shoot at you.'

'He wants to see me now?'

'That's what I've been told.' He nodded at two soldiers
standing at the entrance to the Fort, who marched across to
them.

'Philippe Cherix?' said the taller one.

Philippe nodded.

'You need to come with me.'

They marched through the tunnels of the Fort, twisting and
turning until Philippe had no idea how deep under the mountain they had come. For all he knew, they had wound right back

to the entrance, so disorientated had he become. They passed several groups of soldiers, all looking curiously at him, making him feel like a criminal rather than an innocent witness. He remembered Christophe's story about the soldier arrested for treason protesting his innocence as he was taken away and thrust away the uncomfortable thought that he was about to end up in the same position. He shook his head to clear his brain. Why would anyone think he'd shot his own friend? He just had to tell them what he'd seen.

Finally, they reached a door that looked like all the others they had walked past, but this time the soldiers indicated a bench in the corridor. The minutes ticked by, then the hours, without anyone opening the door. Philippe began to feel hunger stabbing his stomach. He hadn't eaten anything since that morning. He wondered how Christophe was and when he would be allowed to visit him.

Philippe shuffled in his seat, uncomfortable from having to sit still for so long, glancing up every so often at the expressionless features of the two soldiers guarding him. He recognised them – had eaten with them in the dining room – but they could have been statues for all the fellow feeling they demonstrated.

The door opened and an aide slipped into the corridor, signalling to the taller soldier to approach. Philippe looked up expectantly, but the whispered conversation went on for several minutes. Finally, the soldier nodded and turned to Philippe.

'The Fort Commander can't see you now. He's been called away. He wants you to give your statement to Major Toussaint, his aide-de-camp.'

Philippe followed them into the room and looked around him. It was about the same size as the map room, but rather than the usual office furniture, cabinets and pictures, it only contained a wooden table and some chairs. A picture of Commander Guisan dominated the room and he stared at the familiar half-smile and grey moustache of the popular Vaud figure. It looked very much like an interrogation room and Philippe dropped his gaze to the man sitting behind the table, his sandy-haired head bent over the folder. After a few minutes he looked up, his expression cold and hard.

'Sit down Private Cherix. My name is Major Toussaint. I need to take a statement from you about what happened today.'

Philippe sank into a chair and swallowed a few times, his mouth suddenly dry. This was the Major he saw having lunch with Favre most days. He had seen them so many times that he almost felt he knew him, but this was the first time they'd ever spoken. Would he be making a big mistake telling this man what he'd seen? He didn't have Christophe to back him up, so why would he be believed? And would everything he said go straight back to Favre?

'What happened up there?'

His best course of action was to stick to the bare facts, so Philippe clasped his hands together and spoke clearly and calmly.

'We were skiing down with our unit just above Villars, bringing up the rear when we heard a couple of shots. We didn't see where they came from, so we tried to reach the cover of the trees, but Christophe was hit. I patched up his wound and after a few minutes, we heard our unit coming to find us. We shouted to tell them where we were and we all came back. That's all that happened really.'

The Major slowly wrote down every word Philippe said and then referred to another piece of paper in front of him.

'Your unit leader said that you took a long time to come down the mountain. That's why they came to look for you.' He looked up at Philippe. 'What were you doing up there? Why did it take you so long to ski down?'

The Major had kept him waiting until they'd taken a state- ment from Olivier. Philippe cursed his unit leader's clumsy attempts to get him into trouble. Hiding his anger, he kept his voice level.

'We didn't realise they'd gone so far ahead. It was fairly slow going down through the trees and we didn't notice the time.'

'Who shot at you?'

Philippe shrugged. 'I don't know. It could have been someone out hunting. It's the end of the season. We couldn't tell where the shots were coming from. That's why we tried to get into the trees for cover.'

'You didn't see anyone?'

'No.'

'Are you sure about that, Private?'

The Major's thin features seemed carved from stone, as he waited for Philippe to reply.

'Yes. I didn't see anyone else.'

He let his breath out slowly when the Major didn't contradict him but calmly wrote down his words.

'I understand you're one of the best marksmen in the Fort. If that's the case, I find it difficult to believe that you couldn't identify where the shots were coming from.'

He stared at Philippe, who didn't blink at the sceptical tone but kept as close to the truth as he could.

'It was all so unexpected. Everything was quiet and suddenly somebody starts shooting. We didn't know if they were shooting at us or not, so we just tried to get under cover as quickly as we could. I was looking right in front of me and didn't dare look back, so couldn't tell where the shooting was coming from. That's all I can say.'

The Major didn't reply and Philippe tried to fill the awkward silence.

'Have you spoken to Christophe yet?'

'Your friend isn't here,' came the brisk reply.

'What do you mean he isn't here? They took him to the first aid centre. He's all right, isn't he?'

The Major laid down his pen before he replied.

'Our doctors thought the bullet may have hit the bone, so he's been taken down to the hospital at Saint-Maurice for specialist care. They have proper facilities there. He may need an operation.'

Philippe stared at him, trying to take in the news. With Christophe gone, it was still only his word against Favre – one of the most respected men in the Swiss military, whose connections in the Fort reached right up to the Fort Commander himself and who was great friends with the man sitting in front of him. Was he in league with Favre too?

'You're dismissed,' said the officer coldly. He faced the soldiers accompanying Philippe. 'You can take him back to his unit.'

As they walked back through the labyrinth of cold, dank tunnels, lit only by a string of naked light bulbs, the muffled sounds of soldiers coming through the thick stone walls were the only evidence of life in the vast underground complex. Philippe no longer noticed the curious glances cast towards him but turned inwards, thinking hard about what his next steps should be. If Favre was on the run by now with all the maps, surely the whole fort would be in uproar. Maybe Favre's driver hadn't seen him? His heart sank when he thought about Christophe. If Favre wanted to make sure he was in the clear, could Christophe's life still be in danger?

Philippe felt as if he was frozen, trapped in a completely impossible situation. He would just have to wait for Christophe to return, and hope that he was safe. Then together, they would have to explain what they saw and convince the Fort Commander in person to at least investigate Favre. But for now, he needed to keep quiet and make sure Favre wasn't able to escape before they could catch him.

.  .  .

The next day, Philippe unlocked the door to the map room and saw that Favre was already working at his desk. He looked up and nodded in greeting before turning back to his desk, the silence only broken by the scratching of pens and the occasional turn of a page. *All normal so far*, thought Philippe, pulling out from the drawer the next map to be annotated. Hardly had he set the map on to the table when Favre was standing at his side and placing another sheet of paper on top of it. Philippe had never seen this map before but recognised instantly that it covered a much wider area than their usual maps, showing the most recent defences installed along the side of the valley rather than those in one small section.

He glanced up at Favre and tried to concentrate on the man's words, clamping down on the panic that was bubbling close to the surface.

'I need you to finish this map first,' said Favre smoothly. 'The Fort Commander has specifically asked for it to be ready for an important meeting this week. It is top-secret and must be completed as soon as possible.'

'Very well.' Philippe looked up at Favre but could read nothing from the other man's expression.

'I'm going down to Lavey again this evening. An unexpected trip. I would like you to stay and complete this map for me.'

'Yes, of course.'

A wave of relief flooded over him. He didn't think he could sit through another dinner trying to make small talk with the man who was betraying their country to the Nazis, whose actions could destroy everything Philippe was prepared to fight and die for. He thought of Valérie and for the first time he wondered if she had been forced to be friendly to that German to hide her involvement with the Resistance. Could he have misinterpreted what he saw that day?

'You may come with me on my usual trip next week. We'll have dinner together.'

'Thank you, that would be very good,' said Philippe with a forced smile, fervently hoping that the invitation would never become a reality and that it would all be over by then. He didn't think he could stand another week of hiding his suspicions. And the longer he stayed silent, the more secrets Favre would disclose to the enemy.

Philippe breathed a sigh of relief when he was finally alone. As soon as he had completed the map, then he'd be free to look for evidence. He wasn't the son of a policeman for nothing. It was evidence that always led straight back to the criminal.

It only took an hour to complete the last section, showing the bridges and tunnels round the mountain side towards Lac Léman, icons indicating where the charges had been laid on the side of the sweeping valley. When he'd finished, Philippe pulled out of the drawer all the other detailed maps of the area, so he could see the whole south-western flank of the Redoubt laid out before him, the strategic valley they had to protect at all costs.

He remembered Max's gloomy prediction that they wouldn't be able to hold back the Germans if they decided to invade, despite the elaborate preparations to booby trap the area. Philippe wasn't so pessimistic, but he knew they would be much weaker if the Germans discovered where they'd laid their defensive charges. Putting the maps away, he went across to Favre's desk and methodically searched through the various trays and boxes on top of it. The most interesting things he found were some bills from the Lavey hotel, covering dinners and spa treatments, including the dinner he'd attended. All it proved was that Favre was genuinely using the spa on his regular trips.

Philippe tried the drawers under Favre's table, just in case. As before, they were securely locked and the key was nowhere to be seen. This was a waste of time. Favre would never have left him alone in the map room without first making sure any evidence of his treachery was hidden away.

When Philippe let himself into the dormitory later that night he sighed with relief when he saw no sign of Olivier and sat down heavily on the thin mattress, glancing at Christophe's empty bunk.

'They said they'd taken him down the valley,' Stefano commented from across the room.

'I didn't think his wound looked that bad,' commented Antoine. He glanced at Philippe's pale face. 'I'm sure he'll be fine... He'll be back in no time.'

None of them asked who had shot at them and Philippe was grateful for their reticence. He just felt enormously tired and wanted nothing more than to let sleep take him away for a few hours.

'Someone heard one of the medics say he was taken away for his own safety.'

Philippe shifted, his sense of unease deepening. He wondered who had given the order for Christophe to be taken out of the Fort when the Fort Commander was still away.

As if he'd read his thoughts, Stefano added, 'The Fort Commander's back.'

'Are you sure?'

He nodded. 'Someone saw him drive in tonight. He was looking grim. Somebody's in for trouble.'

Philippe was about to question him further when they heard the sound of boots outside. The door was flung open. Philippe recognised the soldiers who had taken him to be questioned and behind them, Major Toussaint walked into the centre of the dormitory. They were all looking at Philippe.

'Philippe Cherix, you are arrested on suspicion of treason.'

Philippe's head jerked up. Before he could open his mouth to protest, the two soldiers had pulled him up and dragged him away from his bed into the centre of the room, their fingers digging into his arms.

'Search his belongings.'

Two other soldiers ran into the room and pulled the covering off the mattress on his bunk. They didn't go near his kit bag next to the bed but lifted the thin mattress and threw it on to the floor. It was as if they knew exactly where to look.

'What do you think you're doing?' Philippe burst out. 'What are you looking for?'

One of the soldiers stood up, holding a small square metal box in his hand. 'Found it, sir, under the bed.'

Philippe gaped at the small box, unable to believe that they had found anything or how it could have got there.

'It's a camera. We've found our traitor.'

Suddenly everything became horribly clear. That must have been what he'd seen the Germans give to Favre back at the spa. He had planted it under his mattress to incriminate him. Favre needed a scapegoat and he'd chosen Philippe.

'Wait a minute... I've never seen that before in my life. Someone put it there when I was working! Someone's trying to frame me.'

He glanced around his fellow soldiers for support, but they were all looking as stunned as he felt. Stefano even took a step away from him to put some distance between them. Olivier was standing at the doorway behind the soldiers and Philippe saw a smirk flickering at the corners of his mouth.

Philippe tried to pull his arm out of the soldier's grasp, his desperation mounting. 'You did it,' he screamed at OIivier. 'You planted the camera on me! Did Favre get you to do it? You're all in this together.'

'Take him away,' the Major ordered tonelessly.

'This is a set-up!' shouted Philippe as he was dragged from the room. 'You've got the wrong man!'

The door to the dormitory slammed behind him and the soldiers frogmarched him along the tunnels until they reached the prison in the Fort. The soldiers pushed him inside the nearest cell, slammed the door shut and turned the key in the lock. One of the soldiers hissed through the bars.

'The Fort Commander will be over to see you in the morning... then you'll get what you deserve. You'll be shot by the end of the week. Traitor.'

# SIXTEEN

## PHILIPPE

Philippe couldn't believe how quickly his life had been turned upside down. One minute he was a respected soldier and the next he was arrested like a common criminal and thrown into a cell. He looked around him at the rough stone floor and walls, the bucket in the corner and a single iron bedstead with a grubby mattress and blanket thrown on top of it. They hadn't left him any food or water and the small light left on in the corridor outside his cell was the only concession they'd made. At least he wasn't in total darkness, he thought glumly. He shivered in the damp and cold of the underground prison and sat down on the mattress, pulling the thin blanket around his shoulders.

His initial shock and anger gave way to depression and self-recrimination. Why didn't he take action more quickly and tell someone what he'd seen as soon as Christophe had been shot? But the Fort Commander hadn't been there. And he was hardly going to be able to confess everything to Favre's friend. He twisted his hands as he thought of the events over the past few hours, wishing he could get his hands around Olivier's neck. He had no doubt that his unit leader, consumed with jealousy, had played some part in the camera being planted in his belongings. But he must have been acting on Favre's orders.

Philippe swallowed a lump in his throat as he pictured the firing squad that could be waiting for him. Immediately his thoughts went to Valérie and all the plans for the future that he'd destroyed. Would she still believe he was innocent, even if he was found guilty? He wished with all his heart that he could see her again and cursed himself for that last letter he'd sent. In his dark and cold cell, he thought again about what he'd seen and whether he'd been mistaken. He'd been wrong about Christophe, so he could have been wrong about her too. Maybe they'd let him write to her again one last time and he could tell her how much he loved her.

As he attempted to slow his breathing, he tried to focus on Valérie. What would she have done, if she were in his shoes? She wouldn't have hesitated before declaring to anyone who would listen what she had seen and what she suspected. But respect for the law was so ingrained in him that he needed to be sure before he could act.

He could still hardly believe that the hard-working, patriotic professor they'd respected was prepared to betray his country. Who would the Fort Commander believe, an ordinary soldier or a revered hero?

Philippe sighed deeply and tears pricked his eyes. It would be hours before he could see the Fort Commander – hours for him to go over everything he'd got wrong. Fears for his future swirled around him and he straightened his back, determined to keep himself together.

But then he heard a key turn in the lock and Philippe looked up, expecting to see the guard. His mouth dropped in surprise when Major Toussaint came into the room accompanied by the same two soldiers who had taken him to the cell. He looked at them uneasily. This was Favre's friend. What was he going to do?

He glanced from the older man to the two soldiers who seemed tense and avoided looking at him in the eyes.

'Come with us,' said the Major.

'Where are you taking me? I need to see the Fort Commander.'

'And why is that?'

The cold eyes staring down at him chilled him more than the draughty cell.

'I need to tell him what's happening... what I saw.'

'You're accused of being a traitor. Why should he believe you?'

'Because I've been framed, none of it's true.' Philippe jumped to his feet. The two soldiers took a step forward but the Major didn't flinch.

'I need to tell him what's happening.'

'Come with me,' he replied finally, 'and do not make a sound. Do you understand, Private? If anyone hears you, you'll be right back in this cell, facing a court martial tomorrow.'

Philippe nodded, relief that he would be getting out of the dark cell mixed with fear that he was walking into a trap. He was flanked by a man on each side holding his arms in a tight grip. They were taking no chances. He looked around for the normal guards, but the corridors were empty of all life. He tried to free one of his arms, but the soldier redoubled the pressure so he had no choice but to walk between them. They filled the narrow space, obscuring the lights hanging along the wall and making the tunnel feel even smaller and darker. Philippe felt as though the walls were closing in around him. He was light-headed from lack of food, and stumbling every so often on the uneven floor; the walk along the corridors seemed to go on forever in the dimness.

Strange that they didn't meet anyone, thought Philippe. Maybe they were just going to shoot him now, quietly and without warning. He thought about his father and how ashamed he would be, the pride in his son's military service destroyed by the nasty smell of treason. And he'd never see Valérie again.

They stopped in front of another door, similar to all those they'd passed and the senior officer knocked quietly, then they went inside. Philippe was deposited on a chair in front of a large desk and was surprised and more than a little relieved to see the Fort Commander sitting across the table from him. He was a large man, encased in his uniform, and looked up from the papers in front of him, his dark, bushy eyebrows in stark contrast to the silvery-grey head of hair.

'Make sure we aren't disturbed.'

He waited until the two soldiers had left the room and the door was firmly closed behind them, before turning to Philippe.

'You know the penalty for treason?'

'Yes, sir.'

'You know how serious a situation you're in?'

'Yes, sir.'

'You've been caught with a camera that we believe has been used to capture top-secret information that has been passed to the enemy. Pictures of the maps you have been working on—'

'I know sir, but—'

'Did I ask you to speak?' the Fort Commander barked.

'No, sir.'

'You are one of the few people with access to that information.'

'Yes, sir.'

'The evidence against you is enough to get you shot.'

'Sir, I have to be able to speak!' Philippe blurted out, desperate to make the Fort Commander understand the truth. 'It's Favre who's leaking the maps. I saw him at Lavey meeting German soldiers, handing over something to them. I didn't know what it was at the time, it was dark and I couldn't see them clearly. But it must have been the camera. I suspected he was betraying us but I had no proof and I didn't think anyone would believe me.'

Philippe paused and then went on more slowly, explaining what he had pieced together during the hours he had spent locked in the cell. 'I think Favre made an extra copy of all the maps we worked on. He took some of the smaller maps out of the Fort when he went to Lavey every week. If a map was too large to take out safely, he would take photographs of it with the camera the Germans had given him.'

'Why were you shot at yesterday?'

'We saw Favre's driver at the top of the village. He gave a map to one of the Germans who had met with Favre. I slipped on the snow and they must have seen us. Then someone started shooting and Christophe got hit. You must talk to Christophe, he'll tell you what we saw.'

The Fort Commander watched him closely and said nothing to interrupt Philippe as his words tumbled out, trying to work out the sequence of events from the jumbled impressions of the previous few days.

'His driver must have recognised me and Favre realised I'd become suspicious of him. Maybe he suspected I'd seen him that night at Lavey, I don't know.'

'So you're telling me that Monsieur Favre planted the camera in your quarters?'

Philippe nodded. 'He suddenly announced he was going down to the spa tonight; he must have wanted to be out of the way when I was caught with the camera. He wanted me to finish an important map for you. Said it was top-secret.'

He leaned across the desk. 'Sir, you have to get that map to safety. It's much more important than the others, it has all our main defences marked on it. If I'm right, Favre has already made a copy of it, so he can give it to the Germans and no one will ever know. We have to get it out of there or he'll give them all the information they want.'

'And why should I believe any of this? Why should I believe that you're not just trying to shift the blame for your crimes on to an innocent man with an outstanding reputation? Perhaps you and your friend were shot at because your Nazi contacts thought they could no longer trust you? Why would Favre want to betray his country after all he has done to protect it?'

'I don't know.'

The urgency drained out of Philippe's voice and he bent his head. It was no use, he thought, they'd never believe him when there was so much evidence stacked up against him. But just as he lost all hope, Philippe thought again about Valérie. He could almost hear her voice in his head, urging him to fight for their future. He felt a new strength well up within him that made him lift his head again and look his commanding officer in the eye. They might think he was guilty but he knew he had done nothing wrong. Whatever accusations they threw at him, he was innocent and that gave him strength.

'I can prove Favre is the traitor. I know where and when he meets the Germans because I've seen them. I can help you catch him if you'll trust me.'

Philippe held his breath. He remembered the rumours about the last soldier accused of sabotage. Christophe said that he was still protesting his innocence while being dragged to the firing squad. He would have to fight hard for his future. For a chance to see Valérie again.

# SEVENTEEN

## VALÉRIE

Valérie clung to the doorframe and watched Dieter walk towards her. He must have found out she had been with Simone. Panicked, she believed she was going to be next. Executed in front of her father in their own home, the casual cruelty of war invading his carefully constructed façade of normality.

Dieter stopped a few feet away and smiled at her, his eyes gleaming with anticipation. She glanced at her father, who was also smiling, but in a fixed, tense way.

She took off her coat and draped it carefully over the back of the carved wooden chair in the hallway before going to kiss her father, linking her arm through his and looking up at Dieter.

'What happened to your arm?' Her voice was light, demonstrating just the right amount of concern as if she was inquiring about a distant but likeable acquaintance. She felt her father stiffen beside her.

He shrugged and the movement made him wince.

'A small accident. Nothing to worry about.'

Valérie smiled, masking her fierce desire for him to suffer.

Make it hurt, she felt like shouting, feel some of the pain you've made others go through. It was only her memory of Simone's brave last moments that gave her the strength to face him now and not turn and run away.

'Dieter has come over especially to see you. He has something to give you.'

She knew from her father's voice that he was pleading with her to be nice to their visitor.

The German pointed through the double doors into the dining room. He indicated that she should go in before him and she crossed the polished wooden floor, her footsteps loud in the silence. She stood at her father's workbench and looked around to see what he was making such a fuss about. Dieter flicked on the light switch and she saw a gleaming new bicycle propped against the far wall, metal glinting in the lights, out of place against the workbench and tools. It made everything else in the room look faded and old-fashioned.

'We had some new bicycles delivered to the Consulate and there was one spare. I saw you on your old one yesterday and thought you needed something better.' Dieter nodded at her father. 'We'll be increasing our German orders for watch parts, so you'll need a bike you can rely on to make your deliveries.'

Valérie couldn't suppress her first reaction, the spurt of pleasure at the sight of the new bike, all too aware of the hours she'd spent pumping up the tyres of her old bike, mending the chain and cleaning the oil stains from her clothes. She walked across and stroked the gleaming metal and leather seat. Then the fleeting pleasure gave way to anger. She could never take a gift from a Nazi, from the man who killed her friend. She kept her eyes lowered until her feelings were back under control.

'It's lovely, but it's too much. I'm afraid I can't accept it.'

'Why not?' He sounded like he'd expected the rebuff at first and the patronising tone in his voice repelled her.

'It's far too generous. And if it was intended for one of your staff, don't they need it?'

She kept smiling, but clenched her fists at her sides.

'If that's your concern, then let's say it's a loan for now. I'll let you know if we want it back.'

'Thank you. It's very kind of you.'

She almost choked on the words. How could someone commit murder one day and be kind and thoughtful the next? His actions took her breath away. At least, he didn't seem to suspect her. Not yet anyway.

Her father let his breath out in a small sigh, only audible to Valérie. His relief that she hadn't caused a scene was palpable and she looked away.

'But what's this you're saying about leaving?'

Dieter sat down again in the parlour, clearly intending to stay. Her father busied himself taking out glasses from the tall sideboard and opened a bottle of wine.

'Didn't Papa say? I'm going to stay with my aunt in Gryon. She needs help on the farm getting the cattle ready for the winter. The snow is early this year and with some of the men away, she's struggling to manage. I'm leaving tomorrow morning as soon as I can get a train.'

It was an easy excuse to make and one that would be believed. Food was scarce in Switzerland and with most of the men away from home for months at a time on military training and guarding the mountains, it was left to the women and children to grow the crops and take care of the cattle that would feed the country for as long as was needed.

Her father didn't comment on her sudden decision and just stared at her.

'I am sorry to hear that. We'll miss you, won't we Albert?' Dieter toasted her father, then put his glass down. 'Though I'm glad you'll be away from the city at a time like this. It's becoming very dangerous at night, criminals and refugees wandering the streets.'

'We heard the sirens last night,' said Valérie, sipping from her glass and watching him closely. 'I wondered what was going on.'

Her father gulped down some wine.

'We were working late,' she continued. 'Before I go away, there's such a lot to do.'

Dieter paused before answering, then seemed satisfied by Valérie's untroubled expression. 'The police caught an escaped refugee, a very dangerous woman. But they didn't catch her accomplice, I'm afraid.'

Valérie swallowed and didn't trust herself to speak.

'They're looking for her now. It won't be long before they track her down. Another Swiss citizen helping criminals to escape from the authorities and betraying her country.'

His voice lightened as he put down his glass and stood up. 'Anyway, why are we talking about such things? I hope to see you on your new bike, if not before you go to the mountains then once you come back.'

At the door, he bowed his head and shook her hand, pressing her cold fingers tightly. 'I hope you won't be gone from Geneva for too long. It will be a duller place without you.'

When he finally left, she stuck her hands into her pockets, fingers curling into small fists. She longed to punch him in his smug face but knew she had to control her temper. She didn't think he suspected she was the one helping the French Resistance nor had he asked her about Emile, though he must know he was one of her friends. She had to make sure the spark of suspicion she'd once seen in his eyes didn't reawaken.

Her father closed the parlour door and sat down on the nearest sofa, breathing heavily and wiping his forehead with a handkerchief. Valérie was aware of his eyes on her as she picked up the glasses.

'Why have you suddenly decided to go and stay with your aunt? You weren't so keen yesterday.' He hesitated and then ploughed on. 'What's happened to change your mind? Why are you going now?'

Valérie stood in the doorway and turned to look at him. She was a heartbeat away from telling him the truth about his friend Dieter, to share with him everything that had happened, from Simone's murder to her narrow escape. And most of all, to tell him about the list of names that had changed everything.

Instead, she said nothing, but took the tray through to the sink and rinsed out the fragile etched glasses that had been her mother's favourites. He followed her through to the kitchen and sat in one of the carved wooden chairs as she dried the glasses and placed them carefully on the table.

'I don't understand you anymore,' he said finally, breaking the silence. 'You lied about last night. Why did you say you were here all evening?' He swallowed before carrying on. 'Were you involved in what happened out there last night?'

The genuine worry in his voice melted her resolve and she came across to him, pulling another chair close and taking his hand. She stroked his slim fingers, capable of such delicate workmanship, but now growing lined and worn, the skin so thin it was almost translucent.

'It's best you don't know why I lied to him, Papa. But it would help me if everyone thought I was here last night.'

'Was it something to do with Emile? I thought I told you not to listen to him...'

Valérie thought about Emile in the hospital, beaten but unbowed. She hadn't trusted him enough to tell him the truth; she had lied to him because of her love for Philippe.

'I don't listen to everything he says. I only do what my conscience tells me is right...'

Her father grasped her hand. 'And what have you done?'

'It's safer if you don't know.'

He gave a small groan and muttered under his breath. 'That's just what your mother said. I can't lose you too, Valérie. I'm not strong enough.'

Valérie stared at him. 'What do you mean, Papa? Why did Maman say that?'

He paused for a second and then she saw the familiar mask coming down.

'Don't question me, Valérie. All I mean is that I couldn't bear it if anything happened to you.'

She'd always known that her father blamed himself for her mother's death. He would never talk about the night it had happened. He'd been late going to collect her; her mother had been crossing the street and was hit by a car sliding on the ice. The driver had suffered a stroke and died in hospital a few hours later. A tragic accident. Could there be more to the story than she'd been told? She stored away her questions for another time. Right now, all that mattered was rescuing Philippe.

'I'm glad you're going to your aunt's, Valérie. It will do you good and I won't have to worry about you for a while. But don't stay away too long, *ma chérie*. I need you here.'

'I know. I'll only be away for a few days, I promise.' Valérie hugged him and went up to her room to pack her small suitcase. As she filled it with clothes, she tried to push away the thought that with every step she took, she was betraying Simone and her country. While she delayed handing over the list – if she ever did hand it over – how many crucial secrets would be betrayed to the Nazis?

She abandoned her packing and sat down on the bed, picking up the framed photo of Philippe taken in front of his grandfather's house just before the war. He had his arm around her and she was laughing up at him. She remembered that day as if it had been yesterday and smiled at the memory.

She leaned across and placed the photograph carefully back on to her dressing table. She simply couldn't believe he was a traitor. But if the list ever came to light, he would be shot. Staring at his smile, she felt her resolve harden. She couldn't save Simone, but she would save the man she loved.

# EIGHTEEN

## VALÉRIE

Valérie was up early the next morning. The trains along the lakeside had been unreliable for months, their timetables thrown into disarray by last-minute troop and equipment movements. It was very unlike the punctual Switzerland she'd been brought up in. She looked for her father in his workroom. It was where he went when he was worried or upset, becoming a sanctuary in times of stress. The concentration he needed to do his work always cleared his mind of angry words and uncomfortable truths. She found him, as she had expected, head bent over his workbench, concentrating on a particularly fine watch mechanism.

'I'm off now.'

He put down his tools and hugged her fiercely. 'Send my good wishes to your aunt.'

'I will,' she responded automatically, guiltily aware that she was unlikely to go anywhere near her aunt's farm. She wasn't going to get off at their usual stop in Aigle and catch the connecting Postbus up the mountain through Villars and on to Gryon. She was going to stay on the train past the small village of Bex, where the red mountain train climbed up the hill, and on to Saint-Maurice, the station below Fort de Dailly.

'Write to me and let me know you've arrived safely.'

She nodded. She expected to be back in Geneva before any letter would arrive.

He turned to pick up some packages from the workbench. 'Could you post these for me on your way to the station? No more deliveries are due until next week.'

She frowned, knowing how long a queue there would be in the post office. But then she hid her irritation, casting her eyes down at the packages and putting them carefully into her satchel.

'It shouldn't delay you for long. You'll still be in Gryon before it gets dark.'

She didn't reply, head bent over her satchel. She just had to hope that the few hours of daylight she would have to find Philippe wouldn't be taken up waiting in line in the Geneva post office.

'And come back safe.'

Not trusting herself to speak, she gave him a fierce hug and walked quickly to the door, passing her new bicycle. She would have to decide what to do about that when she got back – whether she would use it for her deliveries and Resistance work or leave it in the workroom and face the unwelcome questions from Dieter. Earlier, she'd thought she'd never want to touch the thing, but now Valérie couldn't help the corners of her mouth lifting at the prospect of using a bike given to her by a Nazi to help Jewish refugees escape from France and contribute to the Allies winning the war. The situation had a certain irony. At least she could still find something to smile about among all the madness around her.

She paused at the door, catching sight of Agathe at the end of the street, wobbling on her stick and making slow progress across the cobbles. She was looking very old now. A sharp pang of pity made her drop the suitcase at the door and run towards the old woman to catch hold of her arm.

'Thank you, my dear.'

With a hand under her arm, Valérie walked at the slow pace towards the door.

'You shouldn't have come out so early. You know Papa said you could come in later when it's less cold outside.'

The old woman tutted her disapproval. 'How would your father manage without me?' Her sharp eyes settled on Valérie's suitcase in the doorway. She never missed much and Valérie waited for the inevitable interrogation.

'Where are you going?'

'To stay with Aunt Paulette for a few days. She wrote to Papa, asking for some help on the farm.'

'It's all a bit sudden, isn't it? I hope you haven't been arguing with your father.'

'No, we haven't argued.'

The inquisitive, dark eyes scanned her face and Valérie returned the stare unblinkingly. She was dragged back ten years to when she was getting herself out of some scrape or other and trying to convince a younger Agathe of her innocence. This time the older woman decided not to challenge her and merely patted her arm.

'Take care of yourself. I know you've done that journey many times before, but it's dangerous now wherever you go.' She nodded her head towards a group of Swiss soldiers walking along the other side of the narrow street. 'You don't know who might be sitting next to you. It never used to be like that when your mother was alive. You knew everybody in this neighbourhood, their families, friends.'

Valérie couldn't resist the opportunity. 'Agathe, when I come back, I need to talk to you about Maman.'

That assessing stare again.

'I have some questions that I can't ask Papa. You know how it upsets him to talk about her accident.'

The old woman stepped into the hall.

'Maybe I can answer your questions. You ask me again when you come back.'

And Valérie had to be content with that. Winding her scarf around her neck, she set off across the old town at a brisk pace. She had just enough time before her train departed to have a quick coffee with Geraldine and give her a letter for Marianne explaining she was going to stay with her aunt for a few days. It was the first time she'd seen Geraldine since the scene with Bernard outside the storeroom and she wondered what kind of welcome she'd get. But she was her usual chatty self, putting out the tables and chairs in front of the café, ever hopeful of attracting customers. Valérie shivered as the dark green canopy above the café door flapped in the bitter wind. She didn't think anyone would be keen to sit outside today. There was snow in the air, and they went inside into the warmth.

'Of course, I'll give your letter to Marianne. But where are you going?'

'To see Aunt Paulette for a few days. My cousin's ill and she wants some help on the farm.'

'I wish I could come with you.' Geraldine stretched out her arms. 'Up into the mountains, skiing and sledging. Stopping for hot chocolate... bliss.'

Valérie laughed and sipped her coffee. 'You're living in a dream, Geraldine. I'll be working harder up there than I do down here. And I'm unlikely to get any hot chocolate for my pains.'

Geraldine dropped her arms and shook her head at her friend. 'You have no romance in your soul. You need to dream a little. It's the only way to get through this horrible war.'

She didn't reply and glanced out of the window at the grocer's shop. There was no sign of Bernard. Geraldine followed her gaze and gave a self-conscious giggle. 'Could you believe that yesterday? I don't think I've ever heard Bernard talk like that before... so forceful and strong.'

Valérie stared at her in disbelief. Geraldine seemed to be living within the pages of a romantic novel, looking for the next hero to walk into her life, rather than facing the grim reality of wartime. It was certainly a way of avoiding reality, but no one, not even Geraldine, could completely eliminate the danger swirling around them, however much she tried to live in a fantasy world.

'Ladies, how are you today?' A handsome young Swiss soldier in uniform stood at the door and clicked his heels, bowing formally.

'I need to go, Geraldine,' hissed Valérie. 'Remember to give my note to Marianne when you see her. I don't think she's at work today so it will probably be tomorrow.'

'Yes, yes, I'll remember,' replied Geraldine distractedly, gesturing at the soldier to sit down.

Wondering how Geraldine managed to keep her admirers apart, Valérie walked back through the square and down the hill to the Rue du Rhône, waving to a few of the shopkeepers opening doors and pulling up shutters. She'd planned to walk all the way, preferring the fresh air and exercise to the packed tram carriages, but when she turned on to the wide street, she saw a tram coming towards the nearest stop so she ran the last few metres to catch it, her suitcase banging against her side. She stood wedged in next to the door, trying not to catch the eye of the well-dressed man squeezed in next to her.

A couple of stops later, she jumped off the tram at the bottom of the Rue du Mont-Blanc and stood impatiently on the pavement until a convoy of black cars made its stately way past, windows blackened to avoid the curious glances of the people watching from the pavements. She caught a glimpse of uniforms in one of the vehicles, but couldn't tell which country they represented, or whether they were the senior representatives of one of the many international organisations that had made their headquarters in the city. Everyone seemed to want a presence in Geneva these days.

'*Maman*, who's in that big car? Why do we have to wait?'

Valérie turned to see a small girl in a bright red coat jumping up and down to try to see into the darkened windows and tugging on her mother's hand.

'Stop it, Julie. Keep still.'

'Nice life for some,' an old man grumbled to his companion behind her. 'Swanning around in fancy cars and ignoring the people who live here.'

Tapping her foot impatiently, Valérie waited for the cars to pass. Finally, the road was clear and the crowd surged across.

An angry cry echoed up the Rue du Mont-Blanc. The front of the convoy had reached the edge of the lake and was turning to follow the road along the lakeside. They all looked towards the noise and saw a young man throw a heavy object into the path of one of the cars, which screeched to a halt, knocking over a group of cyclists at the side of the road. Uniformed soldiers jumped out of one of the cars and chased the protestor as the crowd around Valérie moved towards the scene, curious to see what was happening.

She heard the little girl cry out as her mother pulled her away from the road.

'Come away, it's too dangerous here.'

'But *Maman*, I want to see...'

Stifling a feeling of panic, Valérie struggled against the flow of people as she was swept down towards the lake by the crowd. She pushed her way in the opposite direction away from the loud scene unfolding behind her. The presence in Geneva of the many nationalities involved in the war provided a magnet for protestors. She couldn't afford to get caught up in any trouble now

Valérie reached the sanctuary of the imposing post office building and ran up the steps between two tall stone pillars to the nearest door. She was relieved to see that the queue inside wasn't too long, with several people abandoning their place to see what was going on outside. She fidgeted as she slowly made her way to the front of the queue, glancing at the large clock on the wall every minute or so. Finally, she was standing in front of Amélie and she handed over her packages.

'How are you today?' Amélie stared at her through her thick glasses.

'Fine, you?'

The girl shrugged and gestured towards the hall. 'It's going to be a busy day.'

She glanced at the suitcase at Valérie's feet. 'You're going away?'

'Just for a few days.' Valérie smiled to lessen the shortness of her response, but Amélie wasn't put off.

'I was sorry to hear about Emile. Marianne said he was beaten up the other night just outside here.'

Valérie wondered how much she knew, as she watched her stamp the parcels with a solid thump.

'It's not safe to be out at night these days. My father comes to meet me when I'm working late. He says it's safer.'

'I'm sure he's right.'

The girl handed Valérie her receipts.

'Well, wherever you're going, be careful. Marianne didn't say it, but I know she worries about you too, making deliveries all over the city. You mustn't go out on your own at night. It's not safe anymore. You never know who you might run into.'

'I won't. Thanks, Amélie.'

Outside the doorway at the top of the flight of steps, turning in too much of a hurry to see who was coming in, she bumped into a tall figure and stumbled until the man grasped her arm in a powerful grip and steadied her.

'Where are you going in such a hurry?'

She looked up at Henry Grant and instinctively responded to his smile.

'I'm sorry, I didn't see you.'

He glanced down at her suitcase. 'You're escaping from us?'

She stared into his face, wondering why he had used that phrase, the memories of Simone's death and her narrow escape from Dieter and his Nazi friends crowding into her mind.

Valérie flushed, remembering the list and her plan to give it to Henry, convinced he would pass it to the Allies. If only things were still so simple and she could keep her promise to Simone. But, in any case, she still didn't know anything about him. He might work in the house next to the park, but that was no reason to suppose he had any involvement in her rescue. But his next words plunged her again into speculation.

'I think it's a good idea for you to go away for a few days. Let things calm down a bit.'

As if to lend weight to his words, the sound of police sirens blared out from the edge of the lake, still chasing the protestor who had thrown the missile at the convoy.

She didn't know what to say, the lingering doubts creeping back, despite her instinctive desire to trust him.

He took her arm and led her down the steps to the side of the main door, away from the people entering and leaving the building. He spoke quietly and she had to lean towards him to catch his words, close enough to smell his aftershave. His grip on her arm tightened.

'I hear a woman was killed two nights ago and the police are hunting for her accomplice. They came to my office today asking questions, trying to find out if we had seen anything.'

Valérie swallowed a couple of times and stared into his dark eyes, trying to read the truth behind his steady gaze. 'And had you?'

He hesitated and then seemed to come to a decision, as if

weary of the fencing and the half-truths. His expression was more serious than she'd ever seen it before.

'I have many jobs in Geneva, Valérie. Only one of them is a watch dealer.'

'And the others?' she breathed.

He glanced around the busy street and back to her. 'Do you know you're being followed?'

She resisted the desire to look over her shoulder, a shiver running down her spine. 'Followed?'

'Young man, average height, blond hair, wearing a dark overcoat. He's looking at the newspapers at the kiosk on the other side of the street. Do you know him?'

She bent down to pick up her suitcase and glanced at the opposite side of the street as she stood up. She swallowed before she answered, her mouth dry. 'No, I've never seen him before.'

'I know him. He works at the German Consulate, one of the men the Germans use to do their dirty work. He looks the type, doesn't he?'

'But I'm just going to the train station, why would anyone want to...'

She stopped before she finished her sentence, unable to continue. They both knew why she was being followed.

The Englishman's deep voice calmed the thoughts buzzing inside her brain. 'You'd better not be seen talking to me for too long. Just be careful, Valérie. Don't go anywhere alone and if he follows you on to the train, try to lose him.'

She nodded.

'And when you're back in Geneva, come and see me. We need to have a proper talk.' He raised his voice. 'Give my best wishes to your father.' Then he shook her hand and turned away. Valérie watched his tall frame move among the crowds until he disappeared from view.

She resisted the urge to look in the direction of the blond man across the street, grasped her case more firmly in her hand

and strode away from the post office up the hill towards
Cornavin station. She stared doggedly in front of her, weaving
through shoppers and office workers until she reached the
station, the plain façade of the building stretching along one
side of the Place de Cornavin. She went into the station and
crossed the large rectangular concourse. Shafts of sunlight
streamed through the tall windows casting a geometric pattern
on to the dark floor. Valérie made her way through the throng of
people to buy her ticket, hoping Henry was wrong but not
daring to look behind her.

# NINETEEN

## VALÉRIE

Valérie was lucky. By the time she'd bought her ticket, there was a train due to depart for Brig which would stop at Saint-Maurice. The train was at the platform furthest from the station concourse and she forgot the man following her as she raced to catch it.

She walked past the other passengers to one of the middle compartments and found an empty seat. Clutching her suitcase on her lap, she watched the door. Her heart pounded as the seconds ticked by and she closed her eyes briefly, willing the train to leave. It remained in the station for a few more agonising minutes and she opened her eyes to watch the last few passengers run for the train.

Finally, they left the station. Valérie leaned her head back and breathed a sigh of relief. As her heart rate calmed down, she looked around at the faces in the compartment, from the businessmen discussing in low voices the terms of a major contract they hoped to win, to a young mother and her children storing their bags in the overhead luggage compartment, to a group of soldiers returning from leave. Everyone seemed relieved that their journey was underway and the carriage filled with quiet chatter, though she noticed that the group of children stayed unnaturally subdued. Rather than excitedly looking out of the window as the first glimpses of green fields appeared, their heads were bent and eyes downcast.

Valérie relaxed into her seat and stared out of the window as the outskirts of Geneva flashed by. Soon the familiar names of the Swiss Riviera towns would come into view, Lausanne, Vevey, Montreux. She had a couple of hours on the train, time to work out what she was going to do once she reached Saint-Maurice. She glanced at her watch. It was almost noon. She would only have a few hours of daylight left when she reached her destination. Maybe she should go up to Gryon, stay with her aunt overnight and try to find Philippe the next day. But there was no time to lose. In any case, she knew that her aunt would ask why she was so desperate to leave the moment she'd arrived. She'd have to find a room in Saint-Maurice for the night. Or even better, she could go and see Max and his wife at the shooting range and stay with them for the night. He was the person she knew best in the town, had known since she was a small girl. He would help her.

She frowned for a moment as she thought about Max's formidable wife, Sofia, who'd always resented his interest in his star pupils. They'd never had children and Max had welcomed Valérie and Philippe into his home as if they were his family. Sofia never seemed to like them being around, but she couldn't let that stop her. Max was the strongest link she had in the valley and he would know where to find Philippe.

She realised with a jolt that the train had stopped at Nyon, one of the smaller Swiss stations running along the north side of the lake and only twenty kilometres or so from Geneva. It wasn't a scheduled stop and she looked up to the door as two Swiss border guards came into the compartment.

'Papers, please. *Billets, s'ils vous plaît...*'

They worked their way along the carriage, checking tickets

and speaking to each of the passengers. Outside the train window, Valérie saw two police cars with more officers inside, watching the train. She glanced around the compartment at her fellow travellers, expressions of weary resignation on most of their faces.

The younger guard had reached the group of children and was examining their papers. She saw the mother hand over her identity card with a shaking hand, holding her smallest child close to her chest. He was barely more than a toddler and crying quietly in her arms.

The guard stared at the identity card and then at the group of children.

'Come with me please...'

'But Monsieur, my husband is meeting us at Lausanne. He will wonder where we are.'

He was shaking his head.

'Your papers are not in order. You must come with me.'

Everyone in the carriage watched, appalled, except for one group. The two businessmen had averted their eyes, waiting for the scene to play out, one of them checking his watch and muttering to the other about the delay to their plans.

The woman clutched the guard's sleeve.

'Please, Monsieur, have pity on us. Take me if you will, but let the children go.'

The guard seemed to hesitate, a flash of pity crossing his face. Valérie held her breath. Escapees from France could be sent back if they were found within ten kilometres of the border. Everyone knew that the Swiss authorities had clamped down on refugees entering the country since the Germans had taken over Vichy France. It was why Jean had approached Emile in the first place. The *passeurs* known to the Resistance who already operated in that section of the border area could hardly cope with the flood of refugees trying to escape.

Before he could decide what to do, the guard was joined by

two older guards, one of whom put out his hand to take the identity papers from his colleague.

'What's the problem?'

Everyone in the carriage held their breath, waiting for him to respond to the abrupt challenge. He glanced at the woman again and cleared his throat, handing the papers back to her rather than into the outstretched hand of his colleague.

'No problem, sir. Their papers are in order.'

Without looking back, he carried on through the carriage and came to Valérie. When he handed back her identity card, she looked into his eyes and saw such a bleak look of despair that she opened her mouth to speak, to say something to thank him. But he shook his head imperceptibly and she said nothing, knowing the risk he was taking to save the family.

Valérie knew that protests against the rigid policy of returning refugees across the border were growing, including among the police who were tasked with implementing the policy, and she felt a spurt of pride and gratitude that someone had made his own individual protest that day.

But behind him, the older guards hadn't moved. Suddenly they approached the woman again.

'Come with us.'

'But Monsieur, my papers are in order.'

'We need to check your papers again. We cannot delay the train any longer.'

The woman seemed to crumble before their eyes. No one in the carriage said a word as they collected their bags and the woman ushered the children out. Valérie bit her lip as she watched them pass, but she knew there was nothing she could do to save them. She couldn't risk being taken off the train, she needed to get to Philippe. As they passed Valérie, she pressed the sandwich she'd brought to eat on the train into the hands of one of the children, a young boy with round metal glasses and a winter coat that was too big for him. He smiled shyly at her before he was pulled away with the others.

Fighting back the tears and praying that the children could somehow escape, she looked into the next compartment and saw the blond man who had been following her in Geneva talking to one of the guards.

She turned back in her seat to face forward, heart thumping, knowing she would need to lose him before they got to Saint-Maurice. She watched as the border guards drove the children away. Neither the mother nor her children had uttered the slightest sound, even when they knew they would be taken by the authorities and sent back into occupied France. Valérie's resolve hardened. If they were able to be so brave, then she would be too. The train lurched forward, and she started to plan how to lose the man following her, picturing the stations along the lakeside where the train stopped to unload goods and trying to work out the best place to make her attempt.

The train was pulling out of Morges, the last stop before Lausanne, when Valérie decided to act. She knew it was risky to get off the train, but it was the only way she could lose him. Lausanne was her best chance, the busiest station on the route where the train would stop for longer than at the smaller stations. The station buildings comprised a handsome art deco main building, and low extensions stretching to either side with plenty of places to hide.

When the train arrived at the station and the passengers were preparing to disembark, she jumped out before it had completely stopped and strode into the main station building, aware of the man following her. She threaded her way through the groups of people standing in the large concourse, light streaming through the high windows, and avoided the ticket collector who was demanding to see an old lady's ticket. She went past the wood-panelled station buffet out of the main building and turned immediately to the right and back through one of the single-storey extensions.

There was a goods yard on that side, which led straight back on to the platform. She ducked behind a trolley carrying large crates and held her breath, glancing nervously at the train that stood motionless in the station. If they kept to their usual timetable, she had a few minutes before they finished loading supplies. She just had to hold her nerve and hope that the man following her had headed towards the front of the station.

The seconds ticked by and when the railway workers hoisted the last crate on to the train, she darted out of the siding and jumped on again as the doors were slammed shut, claiming a corner seat at the back of the last carriage. The train was much busier now, with passengers standing in the aisles and grumbling as more people pushed past them. She held her breath, rubbing the cold from her fingers.

The train pulled away from the station and Valérie slunk further down into her seat when she saw the man standing on the platform staring at the train as it gathered speed. Closing her eyes in relief, she didn't sit up until they were well clear of the station.

As the adrenaline slowly drained away, Valérie's mind kept coming back to the children who had been taken away, dwelling on the little boy with his sweet smile and owl-like glasses. Could they avoid being sent back to France? If not, would they be taken away on a train to the camps, never to return? Should she have done something, could she have saved them? First Simone died on her watch, and now she had let her own countrymen lead those children away. Even though they all knew what the Nazis did to children like them. She had failed them all. What made her think she could save Philippe now?

# TWENTY

## VALÉRIE

Lulled by the motion of the train, Valérie abandoned her worries for a few moments and gazed out of the window at the expanse of blue water stretching across to France. She missed the old paddle steamers which used to criss-cross Lac Léman before the war. There was nothing to disturb the glassy blue water now, except for the small border guard vessels she could see in the distance policing the French shoreline. Even that couldn't spoil the beauty and grandeur of the lake and Valérie felt that she could drink in the view forever, blotting out the dangers facing her at every turn. Already she felt closer to Philippe, surrounded by the mountain scenery they had enjoyed together. She longed to see him. Despite his cold letter, she couldn't bring herself to fully believe his feelings towards her had changed.

The train came inland from the edge of the lake and drew into Vevey station. Most of the people who'd been standing in the carriage got off the train and she looked out at the bustling scene as they streamed towards the Grande Place in the heart of the old town and the centre of the weekly market, the scene set against the hills across the lake. Women with empty baskets pulled their coats tightly around them against the cold and chatted to one another as they walked. A few tardy stall-holders pushed carts holding barrels of the local white wine, pouring out a glass for people who stopped them on the way. She even glimpsed a group of men in traditional costume carrying alphorns, excited children jumping along beside them.

She hadn't realised it was market day and smiled at the buzzing excitement. She might feel trapped within her country's borders, but she had to admire the determination of her fellow countrymen. It would take more than a world war raging around them to stop the Swiss from carrying on their centuries-old traditions. Market day was one of the most treasured. As the train pulled out of the station, the compartment filled with the smells of fresh cheese and fruit. She remembered other market days, when she and Philippe, with her cousins, had been just as excited as the children she'd seen.

All too quickly, the train swept past the steep terraces of vineyards scaling the hillside and stopped at Villeneuve, the station at the east end of the lake. This was the last stop before the line turned away from the French border and snaked along the Rhone valley towards Brig, leaving behind the elegant lake-side towns and cutting through farmland. On each side, jagged mountain peaks, white with fresh snow, soared majestically up from the valley floor.

The train pulled out of Villeneuve and gathered speed as it passed clusters of industrial buildings near the lake and then, deeper into the countryside, farm buildings dotted along the edges of the snow-covered fields, the barns where the cattle had been brought down for the winter. Despite being late in November, groups of men, mostly prisoners of war or interned refugees from Nazi-occupied France, were still working in the fields. Beyond the ten-kilometre border and no longer at risk of being sent back to France, refugees were housed in internment camps, the men split up from their wives and children and put to work to help grow food.

Here and there, she saw horses dragging carts of straw to feed the cattle, the heat coming from their bodies forming clouds in the air. The train slowed down and she could see, in the field next to the railway line, a young man encouraging his horse to keep walking against the bitter wind blowing down the valley and the snow – lifted from the hedgerows – that whipped his face.

Valérie dragged her gaze from the first stunning view of the mountains towards the dark clouds rolling down the valley towards them. The weather didn't look promising. Not only was the afternoon light dimming, the crisp sunlight giving way to cloud, but it felt much colder in the train carriage and Valérie pulled up the collar of her coat. The snow had fallen right down to the valley floor and it looked like there was more to come.

The train stopped at Aigle station, where she would usually have changed on to the local Postbus climbing up to Gryon but Valérie didn't move, clutching her suitcase on her lap. At Bex, she watched the deep red train arrive to pick up the passengers disembarking from the main line and start its steep ascent up the mountain to Villars and Gryon, quelling the pang of regret that she wasn't on a simple trip to visit her aunt and cousins. She was getting even colder, despite the number of people on the train, and realised that she was also very hungry, having given away her sandwich to the little boy. She'd have to find somewhere in Saint-Maurice to eat before turning up at Max's house unannounced.

Valérie stood up before the train pulled in to Saint-Maurice, the town at the narrowest point between the tall mountains. She looked up at the cliff faces on each side, which hid the Swiss defences, and sighed. She still had no idea how she would get herself into one of the most heavily guarded places in all of Switzerland.

She stood outside Saint-Maurice station, clutching her suitcase, and looked around her as flakes of snow began to fall from
the low cloud swirling around the mountainside. A group of
soldiers got off the train and were met by three trucks taking
them up to the Fort. She almost went across to ask if she could
hitch a lift with them, but her courage failed her when the
soldiers looked at her speculatively and she heard some
muttered comments and a bark of laughter as they clambered
into the trucks. The vehicles roared out of the town and she
stared again at the sheer cliff above Saint-Maurice, straining to
see any evidence of the Fort below the cloud line, but nothing
was visible to the naked eye, so well camouflaged were the
entrances and gun turrets she knew were lurking behind the
trees.

How she wished she were disguised as a man right now.
This wasn't Geneva, a city where you could be anonymous and
a solitary woman wouldn't attract a second glance. There, the
casual passer-by would assume she was on her way to work,
maybe in a hospital or for one of the aid organisations headquar-
tered in the city. But this was a small town where its inhabitants
took more notice of strangers. A place where you couldn't hide
so easily and a woman alone was an oddity.

She glanced at the bar across the street and saw two older
men come out and look across at her. The Café de la Gare was
one of Max's favourite haunts and they served hot food there.
She walked briskly across the broad station square, crossing the
road behind a horse-drawn cart leaving the station yard. The
snow had started to fall in earnest now and she ran the last few
steps through the tables lying forlornly outside into the café,
shutting the door quickly behind her to keep out the cold air.
She looked around to find an empty chair and felt her heart
jump when she saw Max staring up at her from one of the
corner tables.

'Valérie? What are you doing here?'

She walked across and sank on to the wooden bench, kissing his cheek and smelling the familiar tobacco he always used. The strong smell of cognac was new. She gazed at him, hardly able to believe she'd found him so quickly.

'Thank goodness you're here. I need your help...'

He looked around, glancing at the barman watching them. 'You're lucky I was in town. I was meeting someone and just stopped by for a few minutes.'

When she looked more closely, she could see some subtle differences. A bit older and greyer she had expected, but it wasn't just that. Max had always been a jovial character, full of life and energy, but he seemed diminished, quieter and more watchful, the lines on his face deeper and the bones in his cheeks more prominent.

'How's Sofia?' she asked.

'She's ill. That's why I came into town, to try to get her the medicine she needs.' His expression darkened. 'Not that I had much success. I haven't enough money or influence.'

'I'm sorry.'

He shook his head, then abruptly changed the subject. 'Are you hungry? Have you eaten?'

'Not since this morning.' She was starving, the smell of rabbit stew coming from the kitchen irresistible.

'Wait here. I'll get us something to eat.'

He waved at the barman, who came across after a few minutes holding steaming bowls of rabbit stew and hunks of fresh bread, a luxury compared to the dry potato bread she usually ate. Valérie cast off her coat and hung it to dry on the back of the chair. They ate without speaking, sharing the comfortable silence of old friends and it was only when they were drinking coffee that he spoke.

'So why are you here?'

She leaned forward and spoke in a low voice, aware of the people sitting at neighbouring tables. 'I need to get to the Fort and speak to Philippe.' Her words trailed away under his brooding gaze.

'Why have you come all this way? You could have waited until he was on leave, back in Geneva.' He hesitated, then pressed on. 'What's so urgent, all of a sudden?'

Valérie ignored the question, pushing away the unwelcome thought that Philippe wouldn't want to see her, clinging on to the hope that he regretted sending that last letter, that something was going on that would explain everything.

'There's something very important I need to show him.'

'What is it?'

She wondered how much to reveal. 'I can't tell you Max, but he's in danger and I can help him.'

Max put his cup down with a clatter. 'I'm not sure anyone can help him now,' he said finally.

'What do you mean?'

'He's been arrested for treason. I heard about it when some members of his unit were in Saint-Maurice today. They're saying that he's been leaking secrets to the Germans, giving them information about the defences along the valley.'

Valérie struggled to take in what he was saying, the beating of her heart drowning out the sounds of the café all around them. Her breathing grew constricted as she listened to his matter-of-fact comments.

'Max, you don't believe that do you?'

He shrugged. 'People do strange things in wartime. You never know what he might have decided to do.'

'No.' Valérie's voice was louder and she glanced around, aware of the curious looks from the people next to them. She lowered her voice.

'You know Philippe. He would never betray his country, would never think of doing such a thing.'

Max leaned back.

'Tell me exactly what you heard.'

'Not much more than what I've said. They found something in his kit, no idea what, but they said it proved he was a spy. He's been arrested and is being held in the prison in the Fort. There was also talk of some shooting incident when he was skiing above Villars with his unit. It could have been an accident I suppose, but people are saying a sniper could have targeted him, that maybe his German friends were trying to get rid of him before he talked.'

'Was he hurt?'

'No, but his friend was. He's in the Saint-Amé Clinic here in Saint-Maurice. They brought him down last night.'

Valérie looked around helplessly. This was worse than she could ever have imagined. She thought that finding the list of traitors with Philippe's name on it was bad enough, but she was wrong. He was already in prison, accused of a crime that could very well lead to a firing squad. She was too late, it was all too late. She ran her fingers through her hair, desperately trying to work out what she should do now.

'You'd be better just to go back home. There's nothing you can do for him here.'

Valérie stared at his lined face, looking for a chink of hope to cling on to.

'This friend who's in hospital. What's his name? Do you know him?'

'Christophe, I don't know his surname. He's just one of Philippe's friends. They would shoot at the range together.'

'I need to go and speak to him. He might know more.'

Max shook his head. She recognised his mulish expression.

'You can't. You won't get anywhere near him. He's being guarded. They probably suspect him of having something to do with it too.'

'No.' This time she banged her fist on the table, not caring about the others in the bar or what they might hear. 'I don't believe any of it, it's all lies. Someone has made it all up to hide what they're doing and I'm going to find out who it is.'

He opened his mouth to argue, but she interrupted him.

'I didn't come all this way to give up before I'd even started. If you're not going to help me, then I'll find someone who will.'

She saw a glimmer of a grin start at the corners of his mouth, the old Max still underneath. 'You don't change, do you? Always thinking you're right, despite what anyone else says. I'll take you to the hospital, but don't expect me to help you get in.' He glanced out of the window at the dark sky and the snow falling heavily over the town. 'I need to go back home to Sofia and see she's all right.'

Valérie had to be content with that. They left the bar, trudging across to Max's truck through the large snowflakes carpeting the streets of the town, muffling the noise of the few old cars still on the road and turning them from dusty black to white. Valérie climbed into the truck and slammed the door. When Max turned on the headlights the beam only shone a few feet ahead, the large flakes of snow swirling round the vehicle. He drove off slowly, tyres slipping despite the snow chains.

'You'd better find somewhere to sleep at the hospital,' he commented finally. 'No one's going up or down to the Fort in this weather.'

She didn't reply, just stared out of the windscreen at the few feet in front of them. She would see what Christophe could tell her. If he was truly Philippe's friend, he would find a way to help her.

Max dropped Valérie at the main door to the clinic in the suburbs of the town. It looked like a low, white building, but it was difficult to tell in the heavy snow where the building ended and the snow began. Before she got out of the truck, he seemed to relent a little.

'I'll come back over here tomorrow, see if you're all right. I'm sure the sisters will give you a bed for the night.'

'You don't have to worry about me, Max. I'll be fine.'

He frowned at her in the dim light coming out of the hospital windows.

'I think you're far from being fine. I don't know what mad plan you've got in that head of yours, but my advice is to forget all about it and get yourself on the train back to Geneva tomorrow morning.'

'Go home, Max. You need to look after Sofia.'

Valérie climbed out of the truck and he waited until she had gone inside the door before driving away. She stood in the deserted entrance hall, the strong smell of disinfectant making her nostrils twitch, and felt suddenly very alone.

# TWENTY-ONE

## VALÉRIE

Set up by the sisters of Saint-Maurice, the clinic served as the local hospital for the town. But when Valérie stared ahead at the dark corridors leading away from the main entrance, it looked as if the place was deserted. She wondered why Christophe had been brought here rather than to the larger hospital in Martigny, with more medical staff and better equipment, but her musings were interrupted when she heard a soft voice address her.

'Can I help you, mademoiselle?'

She turned to see a woman gliding towards her, the slim figure dressed all in white and wearing a large crucifix around her neck. She must have been in her forties and her manner was calm and assured. For an instant, Valérie considered barging past this latest obstacle and forcing her way into the hospital to search for Christophe herself, but she dismissed the idea as quickly as it had entered her head. The place couldn't be as deserted as it appeared. There must be some kind of security presence and she'd never get back in if they threw her out.

The nun smiled, looking younger than she had first thought.

'Is everything all right?'

Valérie sat down on one of the hard chairs, her suitcase at her feet, and stared up at the picture of General Guisan which dominated the reception area. She turned her gaze to look directly at the older woman.

'I'm here to see my brother Christophe, he was brought down from the Fort yesterday. I must see him. I've come all the way from Geneva.'

Although she was lying, the very real worry and strain in her voice hung between them. The nun continued to stare at her and Valérie clamped her mouth shut. The more lies she uttered, the more difficult it would be to hold that clear gaze. Valérie told herself not to be fanciful but those grey eyes seemed to stare into her very soul.

'He is here, isn't he?' she said finally, unable to bear the silence any longer. 'Please tell me.'

'It's very late. I think you would be better to come back tomorrow.'

'But Madame, I have nowhere to stay.' Valérie glanced out of the window. 'And the roads will be impassable until morning.'

'Very well. Come with me.'

Breathing a sigh of relief, Valérie followed the woman through the dim corridors, seeing more signs of activity now she was inside the clinic, passing wards with sleeping patients and medical staff quietly going about their duties. Her eyes flicked from side to side, searching down every corridor and into every open doorway until she caught a glimpse of a soldier standing next to a door at the back of the clinic building.

But they walked past the soldier and stopped at the end of one of the corridors.

'You can sleep here, mademoiselle. You may be disturbed as my nurses come and go through the night, but it is the only place I have left. I will be just outside.' The nun indicated a chair and desk opposite the door, a brass lamp shining a golden beam on to the papers piled on the desk.

'Thank you,' whispered Valérie as the door swung open to a dormitory with six beds, some of which were occupied by sleeping figures, white robes lying on the chairs next to the beds. She sat down on the bed nearest to the door and watched the woman leave, then glanced at the sleeping figures around her as the door clicked shut.

She looked down at the floor and saw puddles of water spreading under her wet boots from the melting snow. She peeled off her wet socks and rubbed the cold toes to try to get some feeling back into them, then took out a pair of dry socks from her suitcase and put them on, feeling comforted by the warmth.

The sound of soft voices filtered through the door so she swung her legs around and pulled the covers up, hiding her face and leaving a tiny space where she could watch the door. A nun came into the dormitory and went to the last empty bed, dragging her habit over her head as she walked and pulling off her shoes before dropping into bed, asleep almost before her head hit the pillow. Valérie opened her eyes and sat up, listening intently for any break in the low rhythm of breathing from the beds around her. The nun hadn't closed the door properly and through the small gap, Valérie could see no one sitting at the desk. This was her chance. She had to try to find Christophe.

Moving as quietly as she could, Valérie pulled towards her the habit and shoes nearest to her bed, hoping that they would fit. After checking that everyone was still sleeping, she stuffed her pillows under the covers so that someone glancing in the door would think she was asleep. She tiptoed to the door and clasped the handle, listening for any noise outside the room.

She let out a deep breath when she saw that the corridor was deserted and quickly closed the door behind her before walking towards the back of the clinic where she had glimpsed one of the guards. She grabbed a tray with dressings from a trolley at the side of the corridor and held it in front of her as she walked.

'Nurse, where are you going?'

She turned around to face one of the doctors, who was staring at her over his half-moon glasses. Her heart was pounding in her chest so hard that she could hardly speak.

'I was asked to fetch these dressings, Monsieur.'

His eyes narrowed. 'I don't think I've seen you before...'

'I'm new, sir. I only started today.'

He came a few steps closer and Valérie tensed herself to run. He didn't believe her, she could tell. He was going to try to stop her.

They heard a shout from the clinic entrance and then the sound of ambulance sirens. The flashing lights of an ambulance passed the windows. The doctor took one look and turned back to her. 'Don't just stand there! It's an emergency. You know the drill, get to your post. Hurry up.'

She nodded and made her escape, weaving in and out of the nuns and white-coated doctors who were running towards the entrance from all directions. She kept her head down in case she ran into the matron, then turned out of the flow of medical staff towards the rear of the building near the corridor where she had seen the guard. She peeped around the corner and saw him standing at the door, his rifle propped against the wall next to him. He stood motionless but kept glancing towards the noise coming from the entrance.

Valérie took a deep breath and strode towards him, the tray held straight in front of her.

'Excuse me. I need to see the patient.'

He picked up his rifle.

'No one is allowed in. Those are my orders.'

'Well, my orders are to change his dressings.'

The young soldier looked uncertain and glanced down the corridor.

'We have to change the dressings, or his wound will become infected. You don't want that to happen on your watch, do you?'

He lowered his rifle. 'I suppose it's all right then.'

'Thank you.'

Valérie walked into the small room and closed the door firmly behind her. She stared at the blond young man lying back on the pillows, his pale face animated by lively blue eyes turned speculatively towards her. She took a deep breath and sat on the chair next to the bed.

'Are you Christophe? Philippe's friend Christophe?'

'Who wants to know?'

'I'm Valérie, I've come from Geneva.'

She glanced at the door, expecting someone to come barging in at any moment. 'I haven't got much time. If they find me here, they'll throw me out.'

He pulled himself into a sitting position. 'Pleased to meet you. Philippe's always talking about you.'

'Is he?' She looked at him eagerly, hoping he'd say more, but his next words brought her back to reality with a jolt.

'You might be able to cheer him up. He's been like a bear with a sore head recently,' Christophe grinned. 'I wouldn't like to see his face if you're just going to make everything worse.'

'I'm not sure it could be worse. He's in terrible trouble.'

His grin faded. 'What kind of trouble?'

Valérie hesitated. Although he said he was Philippe's friend, she'd never met him before and had only heard Philippe mention him once or twice the last time he was home.

'Can I trust you?'

'It's a bit late to ask that, isn't it?' he replied impatiently, all laughter gone. 'You came to see me. And if Philippe is in trouble, I want to help. So out with it. What's happened?'

Valérie bit her lip, ashamed of her doubts. 'I'm sorry, but it's hard to know who to trust these days.'

'That's all right.' Christophe's smile was kinder now. 'Tell me what's happened. Have you tried to see Philippe? I don't expect they'd just let you walk into the Fort.'

'I haven't tried to see him yet. I was going to, but when I got to Saint-Maurice I was told he'd been arrested for treason. He's in prison, everyone in the Fort knows about it.'

'Arrested?' Christophe burst out. 'What do you mean he's been arrested?' He sat up sharply and then winced as his wound protested against the movement. 'What do they think he's done?'

'Max said they found something in his kit. They think he's been giving information about the Swiss defences to the Germans. They're saying you were shot at because the Germans thought Philippe was going to be discovered and they were trying to get rid of him.'

'I see. And what do you think?' he said slowly.

She stared into his eyes. 'I can't bear to think Philippe would ever betray his country. It can't be true... but there's something else.'

Valérie took the list out of her pocket slowly and handed it to him. It seemed impossible now that she'd be able to see Philippe, but maybe his friend could help. She had no choice.

'One of the French Resistance fighters was killed in Geneva a couple of nights ago. She asked me to hand over this list of Swiss traitors to the authorities. I couldn't do it...' She stopped when he had reached the end of the list and looked up at her, his eyes wide.

She continued, stumbling over her words. 'The Resistance told us there's more than one copy so the authorities may have seen it already. Maybe that's why he's been arrested. I had to come here to see Philippe for myself. I needed to see him, to hear him explain. I don't believe he's a traitor, he must have been set up and he needs to clear his name. But then my friend Max said he was already in prison, so I'm too late. I don't know what to do.'

Valérie glanced out of the window at the snow still falling heavily outside.

Christophe was studying the list. 'But this can't be right... some of the other names certainly aren't traitors. I know for sure that one of them died saving his unit from an avalanche when they were planting explosives. We were all told he was a hero. Are you sure this came through the Resistance? If you ask me, it's a fake.'

Valérie frowned.

'All I know is that the person carrying the information escaped from France and was being hunted by the Germans in Geneva. She died to protect that scrap of paper, to stop the Nazis getting hold of it and destroying it.'

The image of Simone's pale face before she died came back into Valérie's mind.

'It must be real. But I thought if I could see Philippe, I'd know for sure that his name was just a mistake. And I could at least give him time to prove his innocence. But now he's been arrested. I don't know what to do.'

Her voice was shaking and she clasped her hands tightly together.

They lapsed into silence and then Christophe said slowly, 'I know who is behind all this. It's Favre, the cartographer in the Fort. Philippe was helping him make maps of the explosives laid along this part of the Redoubt. I was shot when we saw his driver handing over one of the maps to someone Philippe said was a German spy. And Philippe told me he saw Favre handing something over to the Nazis too. He was trying to get evidence before going to the Fort Commander.'

'So, Philippe was framed to shift the blame from Favre?'

'I'm certain of it.'

Valérie stood up, all tiredness gone. 'We have to go and tell somebody before he's convicted. Before they carry out the sentence, before he...' She swallowed a couple of times, unable to say the words.

Christophe shook his head. 'We can't do anything tonight. It's the middle of the night and, in case you've forgotten, there's an armed guard outside my door' – he glanced across the room – 'who will be coming in here to check on me before long. They've been in every hour. We'll just have to wait until they take me back up to the Fort. Let's just hope they won't do anything until they've had a statement from me, because I was there with Philippe and can tell them what I saw.'

Valérie paced back and forth across the room.

'We can't wait. They'll think they have proof. They might just go ahead and sentence him... and then...'

Before Christophe could reply, they heard the noise of footsteps outside and they both stared transfixed at the door as the handle began to turn.

'They'll kick you out if they find you in here,' hissed Christophe.

Valérie looked frantically around but the single bed and few chairs offered no hiding place.

'There isn't anywhere to hide.'

She stood at the foot of Christophe's bed and turned towards the door, taking a deep breath to steady herself. Two soldiers marched in and stood on each side of the door, backs against the wall and hands on their weapons, staring straight ahead.

A tall officer came in next, his only reaction to Valérie's presence the barely perceptible lifting of a thin eyebrow. Although he didn't speak, he seemed to dominate the small room, the stripes on his uniform indicating his seniority. The nun who'd shown Valérie into the dormitory came in after him, carrying a battered suitcase. Valérie looked away, embarrassed by her stolen clothes. She felt the suitcase being placed next to her feet.

Then Philippe limped into the room. Valérie gasped and took an unsteady step forward. His hands were bound together in handcuffs in front of him and his uniform was torn and dirty. He stared at Valérie, his hazel eyes focused on her face.

# TWENTY-TWO

## VALÉRIE

'Philippe, you're all right.'

Valérie ran across the room with a cry and threw her arms round his neck. She kissed him, tasting her salty tears before she drew back, remembering the cold words in his last letter. Her gaze dropped and she ran her fingers over the dull metal of the handcuffs as if she could melt the metal with her touch and free him from their hold. Philippe clutched her hand in a painful grip.

'Valérie, my love. I thought I'd never see you again. I'm sorry about what I wrote. I'm sure I made a mistake. Got everything wrong. Will you forgive me?'

Joy and relief flooded through her body. 'Of course I forgive you. I've made mistakes too, thought awful things. I should never have doubted you for a minute.'

She put her hand up to his face, drinking in his expressions, revelling in the tender way he looked at her.

'Max said you'd been arrested. I didn't know what they were going to do with you...'

'Nor did I.' Voice cracking, he turned his face into her palm and gave a deep sigh.

Valérie couldn't speak. Philippe was manacled and looked tired and drawn. But she hadn't lost him. He was alive.

The senior officer cleared his throat, pulled himself up to his full height and looked down his nose at them, before turning to the soldiers, 'Go outside, shut the door behind you and keep watch on this room. I want nobody to come in or go out, do you understand?'

They saluted and turned to leave.

Valérie glanced up at Philippe and frowned as she saw his wary expression. When she heard the key turn in the lock, she twisted round to face the officer.

'Why is he still handcuffed? You've arrested the wrong man. He's innocent.'

Philippe pressed her fingers to try to stem the accusations.

'Valérie, this is Major Toussaint. He's one of the senior officers at the Fort.'

The Major stared at her and she lifted her chin to meet the unspoken challenge.

'Why do you think he is here, mademoiselle? He would still be in prison if I believed he was guilty.'

Before she could question any further, he turned to the nun.

'Sister Annunciata, could you ask someone to bring us some more chairs? We're going to be here for some time and I, for one, would prefer to sit down.'

The nun walked gracefully towards the door and paused in front of him.

'I will see to it and make sure my staff keep away from this part of the building, Monsieur.'

His stern features softened before he bent his head and kissed her hand.

'I am, once again, deeply indebted to you, Madame.'

'You know Jacques, that you only need to ask.' Valérie watched, fascinated, as his hard features broke into a private smile for the woman in front of him.

Sister Annunciata moved towards the door without looking back and the spell was broken.

An orderly came in a few moments later, carrying some chairs. He bowed as he left the room. The Major folded his long limbs into one of the chairs and gestured towards the others.

'Sit.'

Philippe sat down with a weary sigh and turned to the Major, who was watching him closely. 'Sir, we can trust Valérie. And Christophe will confirm what I saw yesterday.'

The Major cleared his throat and spoke calmly, his eyes raised towards the ceiling.

'Very well. We have suspected for many months that someone in Fort de Dailly was leaking secret information to the enemy about the south flank of our National Redoubt defences. If the Redoubt is breached by the Germans and the Alps fall to the enemy then Switzerland as we know it will be destroyed. Our whole military strategy will be in tatters.

'Although I believe Philippe is innocent, others are not convinced and he was close to facing a firing squad. Favre is a national hero and has many powerful friends. But when Philippe told the Fort Commander about his suspicions of Favre and that you both saw his driver handing over an actual map, he began to believe what I have been convinced of for several weeks now. '

He looked at Christophe, who nodded. 'Yes, I can confirm that we saw him hand over a map.'

'I remembered a previous assistant who worked with him and was found dead. Allegedly because of a fight with some locals in Saint-Maurice over a girl. But something about that never felt right to me. The man was shot, not beaten and we never found the men who did it.'

'So the guards were here to protect me?'

The Major nodded.

For once, Christophe was silenced.

Valérie squeezed Philippe's fingers tightly. It could just as easily have been him lying dead in the road.

'I didn't trust the Major when he first interviewed me,' added Philippe. 'I thought he wouldn't believe me and would go straight to Favre with my suspicions.'

'We do need more evidence to convict a man of such seniority with a great many friends in high places. I'm afraid the word of two soldiers might not be enough. But now that we know where he is passing over the information, we have to try to catch him in the act. If he thinks he's been discovered, his Nazi friends could spirit him back to Germany at any moment. We have very little time to set our trap.'

'There's more, sir,' interrupted Christophe. 'Somebody else is very keen to get rid of Philippe.' He looked at Valérie, his eyebrows raised.

Valérie hesitated. The Major believed in Philippe's innocence. If she handed over the list and he saw Philippe's name, his belief could be destroyed and she could lose Philippe, for good this time.

'No, Christophe. I don't know what you mean.' She looked at him, her eyes pleading.

Her heart was beating against her ribs and she could hardly breathe. She should have just destroyed the list when she'd found it and taken the risk that the other copy would never come to light. She was a fool to have come.

They were all staring at her and she got up unsteadily from the chair to stand with her back towards them, grasping the iron rails at the end of Christophe's bed. She heard someone stand up and then felt Philippe next to her, his hands covering hers. She looked up into his hazel eyes.

'Whatever information you have, we have to trust the Major with it. It can't be that bad.'

'I think it is.' Her voice came out as a whisper.

She saw Philippe frown, shaken by her words, but she knew

it was impossible to draw back now.

'Give him the list,' urged Christophe. 'I'm telling you, it's a fake anyway. Better get it out in the open.'

Valérie clutched Philippe's hand as if she would never let it go.

'I'm sorry, Philippe. I thought I was doing the right thing coming here, but I'm just going to make things worse.'

She stepped across the room, took out the scrap of paper from her pocket and handed it to the Major. It was as if the world stopped turning for a few seconds, all three of them holding their breath, watching him as he unfolded the paper.

The Major studied the list for a few seconds, pursed his mouth in disgust, then took out a cigarette lighter and set light to the paper, holding one corner until the small flame reached his fingers, when he dropped it on to the floor and crushed it with his boot. The burning smell filled the small room.

They all stared at him, mouths open in surprise, until Valérie broke the silence.

'Someone died to protect that piece of paper. I was almost killed. And you've just destroyed it.'

He transferred his inscrutable gaze to her stormy features. 'Did you not want it destroyed, mademoiselle? It incriminates your friend here. Do you want him to be tried for treason before we are able to catch the true culprit?'

'Of course not, but what about the others on the list? Could some of them not be traitors too?'

He sighed and looked around their tense faces.

'The Resistance were tricked, I'm afraid. It was a deadly trick, mademoiselle. We know that the Germans are circulating false information about alleged traitors through the Resistance network, their spies convincing them that the information must be protected from the enemy at all costs and taken to the authorities. The names usually include some of the best fighters in the Swiss army, men we would not want to lose.'

He indicated Philippe. 'Top-class marksmen like your friend here... or strong leaders, men whose names they want to blacken. It is a nasty way to fight a war, to spin lies to convince the other side that their strongest assets cannot be trusted and are betraying them.'

Valérie thought about Simone who had been prepared to die to protect it, her ultimate sacrifice based on a lie. If she'd known it was a fake, she would have left Geneva earlier and would still be alive. She looked at the small pile of ash smouldering on the floor. So much damage caused by one small piece of paper.

She took a deep breath. 'I was told that there was more than one copy of the list, smuggled into Switzerland by different people. What if the other one is handed over?'

'There are often several copies circulating through different Resistance Groups. We've told the police to watch out for them and hand them over immediately to the military authorities if they recover them.'

Valérie shook her head.

'My Resistance contact didn't trust the Swiss authorities. She insisted that the list be given to the Americans or the English. Would they know it was a fake? How can you be so sure they wouldn't act on it?'

He turned his impenetrable gaze on her flushed features and replied smoothly to the hot accusation. 'Sometimes people take the law into their own hands, and this is always a risk. That is what the enemy hopes for, to sow as many seeds of distrust as possible.'

She was nettled by his calmness while describing the web of lies which had caught Philippe in a trap. Her voice rose despite herself. 'But the other list is still out there and it could reach someone in the military who isn't convinced of Philippe's innocence. You said he was close to a firing squad already. We have to find it somehow.'

'Mademoiselle, the best way to prove your friend's innocence is to capture Favre before he can escape. No list will be believed if it is known that Philippe played a major role in uncovering the real traitor.'

'Valérie, it's fine,' said Philippe, coming across and taking her hand. 'The Major's right. Even if there is another copy somewhere in Switzerland, it won't do me any harm if we succeed in our plan. That will convince all the doubters that I would never betray my country.'

Valérie looked at them both and then at Christophe, who shrugged his shoulders in a gesture of acceptance.

'Life is full of risks. Your friend believed in something that proved to be false. She died because of it. This is war, the stakes are high for all of us.'

Her protests exhausted, Valérie sat down heavily on the nearest chair.

'Now,' barked the Major, 'we must focus. We haven't much time before we lose what may be our last opportunity to catch Favre before Philippe faces a hasty court martial. Favre has long-standing connections everywhere, far more than me. And many of my colleagues will never believe Philippe over Favre, not without proof. The latest map summarises in one document all the key explosive sites in this part of the Redoubt. We think it's information he will leak to the Germans when he goes on his regular trip to Lavey tomorrow evening. We must intercept the handover and arrest him in the act of betrayal. It might be our last chance.'

'So what's my role? What can I do?' said Christophe, raising himself up on his pillows and rubbing his hands.

The Major shook his head. 'You've already played your part by confirming Philippe's story.'

Christophe tried to sit up. 'Let me go. I can hide in the bushes and watch for him, just like Philippe did.'

'You're injured. You must recover. We'll have men at the

main door and in the restaurant. They can watch from there, wait for them to meet outside in the same location and trap them. It's the best we can do.'

Valérie looked at their worried faces and realised the plan would never work without someone inside the hotel who could watch Favre leaving the medical centre and signal to the others. She knew the hotel grounds well, having visited with her aunt during her childhood. The route to his meeting place was on the other side of the building from the entrance and shrouded in darkness. And if he caught a glimpse of the soldiers waiting for him, Favre could escape.

'I'll be your lookout,' she said slowly, her voice quiet. 'He's never seen me. And the Nazis would never suspect a woman. I know the Grand Hotel des Bains and I could wait in an upstairs corridor and watch for him to come. When he goes off the path into the garden, I'll signal to you that they're meeting and you can catch them together.'

'No. It's too dangerous,' said Philippe immediately.

'That would work,' said Christophe at the same time.

Valérie turned to Philippe. 'It's the only way to be sure you'll succeed. He won't see me and even if he does, he won't recognise me. I can watch him go to the rendezvous and signal to you. Please, Philippe, this could be your last chance of catching him. I have to do it.'

She turned to the Major. 'You know I'm right.'

He didn't reply but waited for Philippe to speak.

After a few moments, Philippe sighed deeply and the words seemed to be dragged out of him.

'All right. I agree it's the best plan. But we'll be right outside.'

He looked up at the Major. 'I know you want him captured alive and put on trial. But I swear, if Valérie's in danger I'll kill him.'

# TWENTY-THREE

## VALÉRIE

Valérie's bedroom was on the second floor of the Grand Hotel des Bains and was kept for the sole use of senior officers from the Fort. Or more likely for their mistresses, she thought to herself as she took in the huge bed, fine antique furniture and heavy cherry-coloured drapes. Her old, battered suitcase propped up next to the damask chaise-longue looked distinctly small and out of place.

When the Major found out that Valérie had nowhere to stay, he insisted that she go straight to the hotel. It would be better if she was there for the next day, he argued. No one would question her presence when she was a paying guest. And it was true that no one had looked at her twice when she arrived so late at night only carrying a small suitcase. All it needed was a quiet word from the Major and she had been swept up to the room on a deserted corridor by the fawning general manager.

Valérie closed the thick curtains to keep the warmth inside the room and sat in an armchair opposite the door, flicking through one of the magazines left on the low coffee table. She'd unpacked the few clothes she'd brought with her and had hung up her coat to dry. The snow had finally stopped falling and, with the usual Swiss efficiency, the hotel staff had cleared the roads around the hotel and spa for the few cars that drove slowly past. Now she was just waiting and wondering why Philippe was taking so long. They hadn't had a chance to be alone since he'd walked into Christophe's room, and she ached to feel his arms around her.

She moved to sit on the chair next to the writing bureau, unable to settle. It all seemed so unreal, being pampered in luxury until she could play her part in setting the trap for Favre. She couldn't fail to appreciate how different this was to hiding refugees in her father's dusty old storeroom and running through Geneva's cobbled streets at night, cold to her very bones, looking over her shoulder for spying eyes at every street corner.

'The manager won't talk and he keeps his staff well under control,' the Major assured her when she expressed her concern that someone would wonder what she was doing there. She was exhausted and the bed looked wonderfully inviting, but Valérie fidgeted nervously, going back across the room to look out of the window, before perching on the end of the bed. She wondered if it was always like this during wartime, a mixture of reckless bravery and nervous waiting.

She heard a quiet knock on the door and ran to open it.

'You've been ages. What took you so long?'

Philippe flicked the snow off his dark hair and threw his heavy overcoat on to a chair, before turning towards her and opening his arms wide. She ran to him and hugged him fiercely, lifting her head for his kiss.

After a long while, he pulled himself away. 'Valérie, *mon amour*, I can't stay long.'

He led her towards the chaise-longue and they sat down, Valérie keeping hold of his hands.

'Do you have to go so soon?'

'You know I do. The Major is waiting for me outside.'

'Stay a bit longer, I don't want you to go...' She pulled his head down and kissed him again, desperate to hold him there for a few more minutes and forget for a fleeting moment the risks they were planning to take. But he groaned and unclasped her hands, threading his fingers through hers and holding them tightly.

'I need to go back to the Fort. The Major is worried that Favre will suspect something if I'm not securely locked up. We don't know who he has to spy for him, but if it's one of the guards, then he might realise what's going on. We can't afford to let him slip through our fingers this time.'

She hung her head. 'I know...'

'And the Major needs to go back to make sure Christophe stays where he is and doesn't decide to help us. He's very unhappy he doesn't have a part to play, but it would ruin everything if Favre saw him. Besides the fact that he really shouldn't be walking on that leg.'

She gave a shaky laugh, remembering Christophe's crestfallen features when he realised he wouldn't be allowed to leave his hospital room.

'From what I've seen of your friend, I wouldn't be so sure he won't find a way to get over here tomorrow.'

He smiled in response, but the fleeting laughter couldn't hide his true feelings and he looked down at her, his hazel eyes dark and troubled.

'Are you sure about this, Valérie? You don't have to do it you know. We can find another way...'

She shook her head. 'I am sure. I can't lose you, Philippe. Nothing worse could happen to me than that.'

Then she asked the question that had been in her mind all evening.

'Why did you send me that awful letter?'

He frowned, sighing. 'I came back to Geneva again a few days after I saw you. I visited my grandfather and then I came to find you. You were in the café with that German, Dieter Runde.'

She stared at him before speaking. 'But why did you go without telling me you were there?'

Then she pulled away from him, wondering why he was looking so grave and hesitant.

'Because I saw you with him.' His voice hardened slightly. 'You were smiling up at him, holding his hand.'

'And you left without saying anything? Oh, Philippe.'

He leaned forward and spoke haltingly as if the words were being dragged out of him.

'You were laughing with him, it looked like you were really enjoying his company.' He shook his head. 'I was so angry.'

Valérie jumped up from the chaise-longue. How could he have thought such a thing?

'And you didn't stop to think there might have been more to it? That I have to get on with German citizens in Geneva because of my father's business and to disguise my work for the Resistance? Philippe, what you saw meant nothing. He was talking about his late wife, I was talking about my mother, about you! It was not what you thought, not at all.' Her voice wavered and she choked back a sob.

'I realised there must have been more to it when I was in prison, everything seemed very clear to me then and I just knew there would be an explanation. But Valérie, if you knew the things the Canton police suspect that man of being involved in, you wouldn't go anywhere near him...'

She couldn't speak for a moment and then the words burst out. 'I know exactly what he's capable of. I know now, Philippe, but I didn't know it then. I saw him kill a Resistance fighter. My friend. One of his men even followed me out of Geneva on my way here. I had to lose him at Lausanne. Don't you understand, Philippe? The Germans already suspect me of helping refugees escape across the border, which is exactly why I have to get on with him. Even now. But I would never have done what you thought you saw, never.'

The last words came out in a sob. Valérie angrily wiped away a tear and glared at him. 'I thought he was harmless and my father wanted me to be nice to him. Said I could help him build back his business. And I thought he was just being friendly.'

She bit her lip, angry with herself for feeling she had to explain.

'Valérie, I'm sorry.' He got to his feet in front of her and grasped her hands again, forcing her to look up at him, stopping her from pulling away. 'I was jealous and angry when I saw you. I've been an idiot. And you came all this way to warn me. Now you're putting yourself in danger to clear my name.'

His mouth twisted in a bitter smile. 'If I hadn't been too slow to act, I'd have exposed Favre myself and you wouldn't need to risk your life for me.'

Before she could say anything else, she was crushed against his tall frame, and she responded to his hungry kiss, pressing her body close to his, all their arguments forgotten. She didn't want him to stop, wanted nothing more than to lock the world out and forget about the war, the Nazis, the looming invasion. *You could die tomorrow*, said a small, insistent voice inside her head, *grab everything you can tonight in case it's ripped away forever*.

'Philippe, stay with me. I know we said we'd wait, but I don't want to.'

Her trembling fingers started to unbutton his tunic as he kissed her neck and took off her jacket, throwing it on to the floor. He stroked her breast through her thin blouse and she moaned softly.

They heard a car horn blare outside and Philippe lifted his head.

'I have to go. They're waiting for me.'

She slowly came to her senses, her heart still thumping

crazily in her chest and watched him bend down to pick up her jacket and hand it to her. The simple action steadied her and she took a deep breath.

'You're right, I know. But once we've caught Favre, I'll have to go back to Geneva. We'll be apart all over again.'

'Don't think about that. Let's get through tomorrow first.'

He picked up his coat and as she followed him to the door, he turned towards her.

'You're clear about the plan?'

'Yes. Leave my room at half past six, wait in the corridor at the side of the building for Favre to come out of the spa and walk towards the restaurant. When I see him go round the corner of the building come back to the front and signal to you that they're about to meet.'

'Three short flashes of the torch towards the road, that's the signal.'

She nodded. 'Three short flashes.'

'We'll be outside, some of us at the main door and others in the gardens outside the lounge. Once you've given the signal, go straight back to your room and wait until it's all over. Someone will come back for you and take you to the station to get the train back to Geneva.'

'Will I see you again before I go?'

'I don't know. I'm not sure who will take you to the station, but there's a train in the evening we'll try to get you on. You've got to leave immediately because you can't be linked to any of this. We don't want the Germans to find out you played any part in removing their best spy.'

She opened the door a few inches. Philippe kissed her again and then slipped out into the corridor. The door closed with a dull click and she was alone. She leaned her head against the wood, listening to the sound of his footsteps grow faint and then fade away.

# TWENTY-FOUR

## VALÉRIE

Valérie woke up the next morning, aware that she was in a strange bed, surrounded by quietness, rather than the noises of her father's workshop and the city streets. She blinked a couple of times and looked around the strange room, wondering for a few seconds where she was. As the events of the previous day came flooding back she sat up in bed, clutching her knees. She put a hand up to touch her lips and remembered with a shiver the passion that had flared up so quickly between her and Philippe.

Despite the risks she knew she still had to face, a warm glow spread through her body when she remembered Philippe's words and his touch. She had no doubt now that he still loved her and thanked God silently for giving her the chance to see him again. Even though she would be leaving Saint-Maurice that night, it was enough for now that the air was cleared between them and she could play her part to keep him safe and clear his name.

Valérie threw off the bedcovers and jumped out of bed. She was hungry and needed to go down for breakfast. 'Act like a normal guest,' the Major had said the previous evening. 'You must not draw attention to yourself, so do what everyone else does, go for breakfast, go into the hot pools, have one of the treatments. You just have to be ready at six o'clock.'

She pulled her tailored navy skirt towards her, tucked her white blouse into the waistband and pulled on her jacket, then glanced at herself in the tall mirror, smoothing down her outfit and checking her appearance with a critical eye. At least she wouldn't look too out of place.

A few minutes later, she took her first sip of excellent coffee and bite of fresh bread, lathered with butter and jam. She could get used to this – proper bread two days in a row. Glancing around the restaurant, she saw some older couples quietly having breakfast and a group of Swiss officers at a table in the corner. She looked towards the door and saw two men, wearing heavy black overcoats, come in and walk towards her table. They matched Philippe's descriptions perfectly. She put her coffee cup down, trembling in its saucer, and watched as they passed by her table. The leading man, younger than his bulkier companion, gave her a small bow as he passed, to which she responded with a tight smile.

When she finished her breakfast, the draw of the outdoors was too great and she decided to get some fresh air and walk through the grounds. The paths around the hot pools had been cleared of fresh snow and the day was clear and cold, with little wind remaining. She walked briskly along the path until she found a bench, slightly apart from the others and sat down to watch some children splashing around in the hot pools, their shrieks and squeals filling the air when too much skin was exposed to the air. Those men were still sitting in the restaurant at the table by the window, next to the doors opening out on to the pool. The scene was so peaceful that she had to pinch herself to remember what was at stake under the surface of bourgeois normality.

She gazed up at the steep mountainsides towering above her. The trees around the hotel and right up the valley sides were heavy with snow and every so often she heard the soft thud as melting snow toppled off one of the lowest branches. She glanced towards the nearest village where she knew Max's shooting range was and wondered if he had gone back to find her at the clinic.

Valérie wandered out of the entrance of the hotel and watched white-coated attendants leading an elderly man through the corridor to the medical centre. That was where Favre had his treatments. She stared at the twisting narrow road leading up the hill to the Fort and back in the other direction towards the village of Saint-Maurice. The only vehicle she could see coming along the road was a horse-drawn cart full of cattle feed, heading for the barn opposite the spa.

Philippe and the other soldiers would be waiting there, ready to intercept the German soldiers when they met with Favre.

'Mademoiselle, can I help you?'

Valérie jumped when the girl's voice interrupted her thoughts. She turned to see one of the receptionists, a kind-faced girl who was looking at her with concern.

'No, I'm fine thank you. It's the...' She fell silent when she saw a woman in a wheelchair pass the desk towards the medical centre. It was Max's wife, Sofia. Valérie recognised the thick grey hair bundled into a bun, tendrils of white escaping around her face and the unmistakeable fur coat she always wore. She looked beyond the reception desk and saw Max standing at the edge of the lounge, his back to her, shaking hands with someone just out of sight.

'Poor woman,' said the receptionist. 'She's very ill but couldn't afford the treatments here. Her husband made a scene last week, demanding that one of the doctors treat her.' They watched an attendant open the doors to the clinic and the wheelchair glide out of sight before the receptionist continued. 'He said he was going to get the money, so he must have found it.'

Valérie looked around the expensive surroundings and frowned. She remembered Max's bitter words when she'd met him in the Café de la Gare and she wondered where he could have found the money.

'Are you all right, mademoiselle?' The young receptionist was staring at her.

'Yes, I'm fine thank you.'

'Can I help you with anything?'

'No, thank you. I need to go back to my room.' She didn't want Max asking lots of questions and drawing attention to her presence when she was trying to remain as inconspicuous as possible.

Back in her room, Valérie picked up her coat to check it was dry and felt a package in her pocket. She thought she'd sent off all the packages her father had given her before leaving Geneva. She took out the small brown envelope, wrapped in paper and tape and frowned when she saw the name written on the outside in her father's neat handwriting. Henry Grant. The packaging was split, the tissue paper and contents starting to come out.

Sitting down at the bureau, she tried to fix the tape on the small package, but despite her efforts the watch parts inside spilled out on to the desk. The package was full of jewel bearings. She knew how expensive they were and quickly calculated the whole package was worth thousands of Swiss francs. What did Henry Grant want with so many of them? She remembered his words in the post office when they'd met the day before. He wasn't only a watch dealer, he'd said. It seemed quite obvious to her now that he was a spy working for the Allies.

Valérie sat down suddenly and remembered something her father had said to her years before. Jewel bearings weren't only used in watches, but could also be used in weapon sighting systems. Could he be supplying them to the Allies? The words of the watch dealer in her father's workshop came back to her. 'I can't supply the number of jewel bearings you want, Albert.'

Her mind raced, turning over what had been staring at her in the face for so many months. Her father's behaviour to Dieter, his fear of the German's mistrust, his keenness to keep him happy... She had misjudged him so badly, she thought bitterly. All the time she'd criticised him for making a friend of the German and getting his help to procure export licenses to send his watch mechanisms to his German customers, he was using it as a cover to supply weapon parts to the Allies.

'Why couldn't he tell me?' she muttered out loud. 'I could have helped him.' But she knew with a pang of remorse why her father had stayed silent. It was to protect her so that if he were found out, she wouldn't have known anything about it. She should have known he wouldn't just stand by and watch the world crumble around them.

Very carefully, Valérie wrapped up the package and put it in the bottom of her small suitcase wondering why he'd slipped it into her pocket. Perhaps he'd been trying to hide it from Dieter when he'd visited without warning.

With a stab of guilt, she recalled her father's nervousness and desire for her to be pleasant to Dieter. She'd been too busy thinking about what she was doing to fight the Nazis to realise that she might be endangering her father's own war.

She shivered as she remembered the German who had followed her from Geneva and replayed in her mind Henry Grant's warning. Maybe he hadn't been following her because of her attempts to rescue refugees and help Simone. Maybe it was nothing to do with her at all but was because of her father. But if they suspected him then he must be in terrible danger. And she'd left him alone.

Feeling sick from fear, Valérie packed her suitcase and

placed it at the side of the door, ready to leave. She had to save Philippe. But had she abandoned her father when he needed her most? Was she going to lose him, too?

# TWENTY-FIVE

## VALÉRIE

The minutes crept past, the afternoon faded into darkness and at last, it was half past six. Valérie took a deep breath and looked around the room. She glanced across at the chaise-longue, where Philippe had sat next to her, his eyes blazing with desire. She would not fail him tonight.

Valérie locked the door, her heart racing already, and she fumbled with the key, almost dropping it, before slipping it into her leather shoulder bag. She mentally rehearsed her instructions as she walked along the corridor. Wait until Favre comes out of the spa building and watch him out of the window until he disappears around the corner to meet his German contacts in the garden. She knew she had to keep out of sight at all costs because if Favre thought someone was tracking his movements, he would abandon the meeting.

She might see a sign that the Germans were waiting for him, Philippe had said. Perhaps cigarette smoke drifting across the hotel lights or a torchlight beam sweeping across the grass. The moment she saw Favre reach the corner, she had to signal to the Swiss soldiers waiting at the front, then go straight back to her room to wait to be picked up and taken to the station.

'Don't come out of your room, whatever you hear,' the Major had insisted. 'Just lock the door and wait.'

It was simple, she told herself. Nothing could go wrong if she just followed her orders. She glanced out of one of the windows towards the grounds at the back of the hotel, seeing nothing through the darkness. She thought briefly of Philippe, waiting somewhere outside until she gave the signal, then shook her head to clear her mind. It was too much of a distraction to think about him now.

She'd almost reached the corridor that stretched along the front of the building when a door opened in front of her and a young woman burst out of one of the bedrooms, almost knocking into Valérie. She wasn't looking where she was going, her head still turned towards the bedroom, and her petulant voice rang out in the corridor.

'Well, I'm going down now. I'm hungry.'

There was an indistinct grumble from inside the room before the woman slammed the door behind her. Only then did she look round and notice Valérie standing in the corridor. She looked at her curiously.

'I'm sorry, I almost knocked into you. I didn't see you out here.'

She patted her dark curls into place and smoothed the skirt of her black silk dress, clearly well aware that she presented a very pretty picture, then glanced at the closed door.

'My husband isn't ready yet.' She blushed and looked suddenly very young, the words sounding clumsy and unfamiliar. 'We're on our honeymoon. We just got married yesterday.'

Valérie forced herself to smile, though she could have screamed in frustration as the minutes were ticking past. She couldn't afford to lose any time. She was going to miss Favre and ruin everything.

'Congratulations.' She could hardly believe that normal life was still going on all around her.

'Are you going down to the dining room? We could go down together.'

Valérie put out her hand in a placatory gesture. 'You go on ahead. I think I've forgotten something. I need to go back to my room.'

'I can wait for you.' The young woman gestured airily towards the bedroom door. 'He'll be ages. He still needs to get dressed. It would be nice to have some company.'

Valérie shook her head. 'I might be a while. You'd better just go down.'

The woman's mouth pursed and she gave a toss of her head. 'Suit yourself.'

She turned and walked away, the sound of her heels clicking on the polished wooden floor.

Valérie took a deep breath, waited a few moments and then followed the girl to the front of the building, stopping at the first window as instructed and turning her back towards the stairs leading down to the hotel entrance. She watched the last few lights switched off in the spa and wondered if Sofia was still in the clinic.

Glancing at her watch, she realised it was now almost a quarter to seven and there was no sign of Favre coming out of the Spa building. Where was he? She felt a heavy weight in the pit of her stomach. Maybe he'd left already and she'd failed.

She stared out of the window, looking in all directions, then froze when she heard a man's voice coming up the stairs at the end of the corridor, the peremptory German words unmistakeable. The noise of heavy boots clattered up the steps and she looked around frantically to see where she could hide. The minutes were ticking past and she was already late. The last thing she wanted was to walk into a group of German guests when she should be signalling to Philippe. But if she left her post, she might miss Favre.

Making a split-second decision, she ran lightly back the way she'd come, trying to make as little noise as she could on the polished floor. She slipped around the corner before the men reached the top of the stairs. Heart thumping loudly, she heard their steps come closer and she groped in her bag for her key. If they came much further, she'd have to hide in her room until they passed. But to her relief, the footsteps stopped halfway along the corridor, and she heard a key turning in a lock.

Taking a deep breath, she peered around the corner. She might be able to slip past and get back to the corner window if the coast was clear. It was the two men who'd been at breakfast. They were bending over the door trying to unlock it. An older, bald man hovered behind them. She jerked her head back as he turned to look in her direction and held her breath, terrified that he'd caught sight of her. She recognised Favre from the Major's descriptions. Her mind was spinning with questions. What were they doing in an upstairs corridor rather than meeting outside? And what was she supposed to do now?

Leaning back against the wall, she heard an exclamation of triumph, the sound of a door opening and closing, then silence. She glanced around the corner again and saw that the corridor was empty. She could get past now, but everything had changed. If she made the arranged signal, the Swiss soldiers would race round to the gardens and there would be no one there.

She looked feverishly around for inspiration, for something to tell her what she should do. She could run downstairs and find someone to get a message to Philippe, but then she might lose the Germans and Favre completely. She knew that if they weren't found together with his German contacts, passing over the secret information, then the whole plan was a failure. She felt a heavy cold weight pressing down on her chest.

Philippe must know by now there was a problem. She'd have to give him some kind of signal from where she was and hope that he realised she was still in the corridor and the meeting place had changed. Taking a deep breath, she went up to one of the windows at the front looking down on to the road, fear pricking the back of her neck, knowing she would be in full view of the Germans if they came out.

She took out her torch and waved it in a sweeping motion across the window. Philippe had said three short flashes towards the road, so she made two long flashes instead, hoping that he would understand the signal. She looked over her shoulder to see if anyone was coming, but the corridor was still clear.

Then she heard the sound she'd been dreading. The door opened behind her and German voices rang through the corridor. She hid her torch in her bag and turned towards them, desperate to run but knowing she had no choice but to confront them and try to keep them there for as long as she could without raising their suspicions. She just had to hope that Philippe had seen her signal and they would catch Favre before it was too late. She couldn't bear to think about what could happen to Philippe and to their country if they failed and Favre escaped.

# TWENTY-SIX

## VALÉRIE

'Mademoiselle? What is the matter?'

Her knees buckled and Valérie clung to the windowsill. She didn't have to pretend as she passed a shaking hand over her burning brow, fingers hot and clammy. She felt sick and thought she might faint.

She felt a touch on her arm and looked up to see the younger man who had been watching her in the restaurant staring down at her in concern.

'I felt faint when I was leaving my room...'

She glanced behind her towards the window and saw both of their profiles clearly reflected in the glass. If the Swiss soldiers were outside, they would surely see them. *They will come*, she prayed silently, *they will surely come*.

Favre was standing next to the older man. He looked flushed and uncomfortable, constantly glancing up and down the corridor and rocking from one foot to the other. All three were wearing heavy overcoats but she caught a glimpse of silver insignia on the older man's jacket collar.

'We need to get out of here. Leave her alone and let's go.'

'Yes, we must leave,' said the older officer, turning towards the stairs. Valérie leaned heavily against the young soldier.

'I feel so faint... if you could just help me downstairs.'

She smiled up at him and, unable to resist, he took her arm. 'Can I not take you to your room, mademoiselle?'

She saw that Favre and the older German were already walking away, so she shook her head.

'No, please take me downstairs. I'm meeting someone there and I'm already very late.'

She took a few faltering steps away from the window and let herself be led along the corridor, trying not to let the others get too far ahead.

'How long are you staying in the hotel, mademoiselle?'

'Just until tonight, I'm having dinner and then I have to leave.'

'You have no family staying with you?'

She could tell without looking up that he was frowning. Torn between the desire for the conversation to end and the need to keep him talking for longer, Valérie shook her head.

'And who are you meeting for supper, mademoiselle? Will he be downstairs waiting for you?'

She looked into his searching blue eyes and lied smoothly. 'My uncle. My aunt has been attending the clinic and I've been visiting her. He's taking me to dinner tonight before I leave.'

They reached the top of the stairs and she walked behind Favre, the older German officer leading the way down. The man beside her tightened his grip on her arm and she had to stop herself from snatching it away. They marched down in silence and the reception area slowly came into view. It was deserted. That was unusual, she thought, a flicker of hope lightening her step and making her feel stronger. There should have been guests milling around the foyer and staff behind the desk, the noise of people in the lounge.

The older German officer paused on the stairs and put his

hand inside his coat to check his gun. He whispered to Favre, who glanced back at Valérie before snatching his arm from the German and almost tripping down the last few steps. But his escape route was blocked by someone who'd appeared at the bottom of the stairs, preventing him from going any further.

'There you are,' a familiar voice echoed around the foyer.

Valérie looked at Max smiling up at her, as if he hadn't a care in the world. She cleared her throat, but she couldn't speak.

'You are this young lady's uncle?' She felt the German's fingers relax a fraction.

Max blinked and then nodded. 'I am indeed. What's the matter?'

'She felt ill. We found her upstairs.'

Valérie kept her head down but her eyes darted around the reception area for a way out and she caught her breath as she glimpsed the outline of dark figures outside the main door. She stared at Max as he took a step forward, holding her gaze.

'My dear, you really should be careful. I've told you before. You mustn't fall on these stairs, you could hurt yourself.'

In an instant, she got the message.

Before anyone could move, Valérie gave a loud moan, snatched her arm from the unsuspecting German and slumped down the last few steps, knocking Favre to the ground with her heavy fall and landing on the polished floor in a bundle of limbs. Almost before they hit the ground with a sickening crack, she heard an explosion of noise above her head, rifle shots rico-cheting against the walls in the enclosed space, then the sound of running boots and shouts from all directions. She clasped her hands to her ears to block out the painful clamour.

Valérie felt someone take her arm to lift her up from the floor and looked into Max's tense face, dust stinging her eyes. 'It's done, Valérie. It's all over.'

She let him pull her to her feet and steady her before she looked around at the scene of destruction, walls pocked with bullet holes, the air thick with the smell of gunfire. She averted her eyes from the young German officer, his body crumpled on the staircase behind her, a pool of blood spreading out from his head, one blue eye staring out of his shattered face. The other German was lying face down on the floor in front of the reception desk, his pistol lying next to him. Swiss soldiers were swarming around both bodies, searching their pockets. She looked for Philippe but couldn't see him anywhere. She felt Max move away from her and clutched his arm.

'Where are you going?'

'I mustn't be seen here.'

She looked at him uncertainly. 'I didn't know what to think, when I saw you standing there.'

His grim features softened. 'Haven't I always looked after you? I'm not going to change now.'

'But I saw Sofia earlier at the clinic. You must have got the money from somewhere.'

He pulled her closer and lowered his voice. 'I overhear a lot of things at the shooting range and the Germans pay handsomely for it. They think I'm telling them the truth, but I don't sell out my friends, Valérie, nor my countrymen. Not even for Sofia.'

The sincerity ran through his voice and she breathed a sigh of relief. 'I'm sorry, but when I saw you, I didn't know what to think.'

He glanced around them. 'You need to get out of here before the police turn up. A military affair is one thing, but they won't like civilians being mixed up in all this. They'll want to keep their hero's fall from grace very quiet. Not good for morale.'

He turned and walked away from her. Valérie stared after him, feeling suddenly very alone. Where was Philippe? Could he have been hurt?

Then one of the soldiers raised a hand. 'I've found it. The map's here. We've got him, sir.'

Another soldier hauled Favre on to a chair and he was clutching his leg, moaning quietly.

She watched the Major take the incriminating document from the soldier's hand and turn to Favre. 'I am arresting you for treason. You will be tried by a military court and sentenced for your crime.'

She heard a step behind her and Philippe whispered in her ear.

'Valérie, we've got him. You've done it.'

She twisted round into his arms. 'Philippe, you're all right. I thought you'd never come. I tried to keep them together for as long as I could, but I didn't know whether you'd understand my signal.'

The Major came up to her and shook her hand. 'Thank you, mademoiselle. Your friend's innocence is now proved beyond doubt. You may well have saved his life today.' He patted his top pocket. 'This is enough to persuade everyone.'

He glanced around the scene. 'Now you must leave. Get back to your family.'

'Yes, thank you.' Valérie said, before turning to Philippe. 'Can you take me to the station?'

'Sir?' he addressed the Major.

The other man shook his head. 'Sorry, Private. My driver will take her. I need you here. We have to get this place cleaned up.'

'Very well.'

A soldier came down the stairs with Valérie's suitcase and stepped carefully over the pool of blood around the German officer. He handed it to Philippe and they turned towards the door. Still light-headed, she clutched on to Philippe's arm as they stepped out onto the gravelled pathway. The cold night air took her breath away and Philippe took off his coat and gave it to her.

'Take this. It'll be cold in the train.'

'I wish I didn't have to go.'

He kissed her fingers. 'I know.'

'You're sure you'll be all right now?'

He nodded. 'Favre will be tried for treason. I'll go back to my unit. And it's all thanks to you, Valérie. We'd never have proved he was guilty if you hadn't managed to stay with them. But it was bloody close. You saved me.'

Suddenly, a car hurtled along the road along the front of the hotel. It was travelling far too fast and the tyres screeched as the driver swung off the road. Headlights flooded the open space with light and then veered across the front of the building as the vehicle vaulted over the grass verge and came straight towards them. It all happened so quickly that they had no time to move, and could only stare at the missile racing towards them. Philippe pulled out his pistol and shot at the windscreen and just as Valérie was convinced they would both die there together, the car flew out of control and flipped on to its side before smashing against a tree, coming to a sudden deafening stop.

In the eerie silence, Valérie was aware of soldiers running past them.

'What happened? Are you all right?' One man grasped Philippe's arm.

'Yes, I think so.' Philippe wiped his forehead with a shaking hand. 'He was coming straight for us. I didn't think he was going to stop.'

'The driver's trapped inside...' One of the soldiers tried to get close to the car but was beaten back by the flames.

'Get back! It's going to blow up.'

The soldiers backed away and stared at the car, its front caved in and the engine crackling and steaming in the cold night air. Valérie could smell the petrol leaking on to the ground and put her hand up to her face.

Philippe came to his senses and pulled her away. 'You need to get out of here.'

'Who was in that car?' Valérie asked.

'I think it was Favre's driver. He wasn't here when we arrived but we knew he was around somewhere waiting for his boss to come out. He'll have heard the shots and knew he would be arrested when we eventually found him. I suppose he was out for revenge.'

Turning away from the steaming wreck and the slumped figure behind the smashed windscreen, they walked quickly towards the Major's car, hands tightly clasped. Her relief at Philippe's safety was bittersweet – she could hardly bear to be parted from him again. If only they could have had just one day together, just one night.

'When will I see you again?' She couldn't hold back the urgency in her voice, torn between wishing she could stay with him and going back to make sure her father was safe.

'I don't know. When I get my next leave.' His eyes darkened. 'And I promise you that we'll spend more time together than the last time. I love you, Valérie Hallez.'

'I love you too, Philippe.'

They only had a few seconds for a fierce hug before Philippe helped her into the back of the car and slammed the door shut. Everything was happening so quickly and she was going to be without him again. She leaned out of the window and clutched Philippe's hand, before the driver started up the engine and drove slowly past the crowd gathering around the wrecked car, meeting two police cars racing towards them, their sirens blaring.

They drove across the bridge over the Rhone and into Saint-Maurice. A few minutes later, the driver stopped the car outside the station as the train drew into the platform and opened the back door.

'Your train, mademoiselle.'

Valérie jumped out of the car and walked quickly towards the platform. The driver put her suitcase into the train, saluted and left.

In the background, railway workers were loading the final goods on to the train and the last few passengers climbed on board, slamming the train doors behind them.

She sat down in the window seat with a heavy sigh, feeling very alone, avoiding the curious glances of her fellow travellers. She stared out of the window at the darkness outside, trying to blot from her memory the gruesome sight of the dead German lying on the stairs, his face split in two, telling herself that he deserved it, that he'd have killed her if they'd suspected for an instant what she was doing.

The train slowed down to stop at Montreux station and she looked outside as the passengers crowded into the carriages, instinctively scanning the faces to check that no one was watching her too closely.

As they continued round the lakeside, the hollow anxiety that remained from thinking that she would be too late to save Philippe had melted away, only to be replaced by the dread that something could have happened to her father. She remembered how nervous he had seemed when Dieter was there the night before she left. She had lost her mother already. She could not bear to lose her father too.

# TWENTY-SEVEN

## VALÉRIE

All along the route, people boarded the carriage recounting stories of trains cancelled and diverted, with little information available on when they might continue their journey. When they finally arrived at Cornavin station and disembarked, a large crowd surged towards the barrier. Valérie pushed through the angry travellers and heard the arguments flare up all around her.

'They told us to come to this platform, that a train would be leaving for Brig from here.'

'No, this train is not going anywhere, monsieur.'

A woman's shrill voice echoed through the open space. 'But we have to leave Geneva tonight. My children have nowhere to sleep.'

'I can't help that, Madame. We have had to run extra trains tonight and it has disrupted our timetable.'

'This never happened before the war,' the first man complained. 'All these German trains coming through Switzerland and causing problems. Why should we suffer because of them?'

Valérie weaved her way through the crowd, emerged on to

the boulevard at the front of the station and looked towards the tram stop, hoping she wasn't too late to catch the last tram heading for the old town. It only took a glance to realise that it had long gone. She would have to walk home.

Unlike the bustling station, the streets outside were quiet. Pulling her collar up around her throat, she clasped her suitcase more tightly in her cold fingers and headed down the Rue du Mont-Blanc towards Lac Léman.

The lights were still shining in the upper floors of the post office building and she looked up, wondering if Marianne was working that evening.

Then a tall, thin figure peeled away from the side of the imposing building and came limping towards her. A low voice growled in her ear and Emile grasped her wrist in a vice-like grip, stopping her in mid-stride.

'Where have you been, stranger?'

Valérie blinked and stared up at him, the angry bruises from his beating showing clearly under the glow of the streetlight.

'Let me go. You're hurting me.'

He relaxed his grip but the frown remained. 'I asked you where you'd been. We haven't seen you for two days. What game are you playing, Valérie? Why so many secrets?'

She tried to pull her arm away but his grip was too strong. The tension of the last few days, her narrow escape and the image of the dead German officer crumpled in a pool of blood filled her mind. Emile's mistrust acted like a spark to the flame.

'You want to know where I've been? What I've been doing over the past few days? I've been saving Philippe from being tried for treason and catching a traitor, that's what I've been doing.'

Once she'd started, she couldn't stop and her voice rose as the words flowed out uncontrollably. He flinched as each one hit its mark.

'And do you know what else I found out? I found out that

Simone's list was a fake. The list was planted by the Germans in the Resistance to discredit loyal soldiers like Philippe. Simone died trying to protect something that was a lie. I'm not the traitor, Emile. I just wasn't able to save her, and I'm sorry for that.'

He dragged her to the side of the street, looking around them.

'Keep your voice down, you don't know who might be listening. What do you mean the list was a fake?'

Chest heaving, oblivious of the curious stares she was attracting from the few people walking past them, she didn't even try to lower her voice.

'You're going to have to believe me because it's the truth.'

'You told us you hadn't found Simone's list.'

'Well, I did find it. And Philippe's name was on the list. I went to Saint-Maurice to see him to find out what was going on and to give him the chance to clear his name. He could have been executed.'

'Why didn't you tell me?'

She hesitated but couldn't hold back the truth. 'I wasn't sure you'd believe Philippe was innocent. I didn't know what you'd do with the list, who you would tell.'

'But Val, he's my friend. I'd never have believed he could do that.'

'Would you really have ignored the evidence and believed the list was a fake? Truly, Emile? After everything Simone did to get it to the Allies? If you'd insisted we hand it over, Philippe could have been killed. He had already been set up as a traitor and arrested. Some of the senior officers at the Fort were so convinced Philippe was the traitor that they would have accepted it as more evidence of his guilt. Just thank God his name has been cleared now.'

Emile looked appalled, his features as white as chalk.

'Was it someone in the Resistance behind this? They gave the list to Simone.'

'They don't know for sure, but it's possible.'

Emile looked shaken, talking more to himself than to Valérie.

'I keep warning Jean, but he doesn't believe me, won't investigate anything, thinks I'm just grasping at shadows. '

He looked at her again. 'I'm not making it up. It's happened too many times now. The Nazis always seem to be one step ahead of us. And he won't do anything, says he trusts everyone in the line and that they would never betray us.'

She studied his determined face. 'Do you have any idea who it could be?'

'I might have. I'm on my way to see someone tonight who says he knows who the traitor is. Then I can go to Jean with real information.'

'Be careful.'

He frowned. 'Of course. I know what I'm doing.'

'I'm sure you do. I just... I care about you, Emile. I miss how our friendship used to be. Before all this.'

He hung his head and muttered. 'I'm sorry about what I said earlier, what I implied. I know that you would never do anything to help the Nazis. It's just that Jean saw you with—'

'With Dieter Runde, I suppose?' she said bitterly.

The mention of the German brought Valérie back to the present and she pulled her arm from his grasp. 'I must go now, I need to get back to my father.'

She turned to leave but whipped round at his next words.

'I saw him earlier this evening with Runde and a couple of other men. They didn't see me, but it looked like they were arguing. I thought they were friends.'

Valérie felt sick with fear. 'When did you see them? How long ago was this?'

'An hour or so. It was on my way here.'

'Where were they going? Do you have any idea?'

'They were heading towards your house.'

Valérie turned away from him and ran down towards the lake, leaving him staring after her, mouth open. She'd saved Philippe but she had left her father alone, with the net closing around him. She brushed away angry tears as she ran through the freezing wind, her suitcase banging against her legs, praying that she would get there in time. But if Dieter and his Nazi friends really had caught her father, what could she do?

# TWENTY-EIGHT

## VALÉRIE

Valérie had to slow down when she reached the steep cobbled lanes of the old town, the sharp pain from the stitch in her side making her gasp as she climbed the hill. She stopped at the corner of their street and sighed in relief as the hall light shone through the windows. At least he was here.

The front door was unlocked so she went inside, dropped her suitcase and coat on to the floor and walked quickly through to the parlour. The door to the workshop was closed but she could hear raised voices coming from the other side. A faint smell of smoke made her nostrils twitch and she looked around to see where it could be coming from, but the kitchen was in darkness and nothing moved in the parlour. At the workshop door, the smell of smoke was much stronger and she threw open the door, staggering back at the sight that met her shocked gaze.

Her father was tied to one of the chairs in the middle of the workshop, his face bloodied and bruised. Large candles flickered around the room casting nightmare shadows on to the wall. Dieter towered over him, a metal bar in his hand and two other men stood watching him, their backs to the door. The workshop was destroyed, tools knocked on to the ground, cabinet drawers hanging open and machinery hacked into pieces.

Valérie didn't hesitate before she flung herself at the two men and elbowed them out of the way. One of them lost his balance and he knocked over a table at the side of the room, lighted candles tumbling on to the heavy curtains. Barely aware of their frantic efforts to stamp on the smouldering fabric, she ran to her father and knelt in front of him, tugging at the ropes binding his wrists to the chair. She looked up at Dieter.

'Please, Dieter. Don't do this. Let him go.'

In the glowing light from the candles, dressed in a heavy black coat, his handsome features were twisted in rage and his eyes glittered.

'Valérie, we weren't expecting you to join us.'

Her father groaned.

Dieter grabbed her hair in a sudden movement and hauled her to her feet. She screamed in pain, tears springing to her eyes.

'Isn't that fortunate? His little girl has come home to share the punishment. Perhaps we can have some fun with you first.'

'Let me go.'

She struggled to escape from his grip, but he just laughed at her efforts.

'I've had enough of being treated like a fool by you both. I'm going to get the truth out of him and if he doesn't give me what I want then I'll destroy this place. And both of you.'

'You're wrong... It's all in your mind. We've nothing to hide, there's nothing to find here.'

'We have evidence of your father's smuggling, his cosy little relationship with the English.'

'It's all lies. Dieter, you must believe me. '

He seemed amused at her denial. It was as if he were toying with them, enjoying the power he had over them. And behind the amusement, she could see his eyes darken as he watched her, attraction lurking in their depths.

'We know that your father is supplying the Allies with weapon parts hidden in his watch deliveries. This cannot continue.'

He flicked a finger and one of his men turned towards them. Valérie gasped when she recognised him as the man who had followed her on the train.

'Packages sent to *etablisseurs* in La-Chaux-de-Fonds and Le Locle containing jewel bearings,' recited the man. 'Packages sent to an English agent in Geneva containing jewel bearings and timing mechanisms.'

'My father supplies watch movements to all these customers, that's all.'

She knew that her words were having no effect; Dieter had gone beyond listening to reason and she struggled to free herself, convinced he was going to rip out her hair from its roots.

'Enough' he barked. 'We're not here to argue with you. Get another chair!' he shouted at the second man.

'Let me go!' she screamed.

But then the curtain burst into flames and thick smoke billowed across the room.

Her father was making muffled pleas, his voice giving way to coughing as the smoke swirled across his chair. But Dieter was staring down at Valérie, ignoring the growing flames.

'Maybe a kiss before we tie you up and let you burn. I've waited long enough to have you... too long.'

He bent his head and Valérie twisted and turned to escape from his grasp but she felt his hot breath on her face and his features swam before her eyes. He crushed her lips with his and she felt him relax his grip. In a flash, she freed her hand and pulled Simone's knife out of her belt, plunging it into his leg and twisting it with all her strength. He staggered back with a roar of pain and groped for the knife.

'Don't move,' a voice cut across the room. Valérie turned to see Henry Grant pointing a pistol towards them. She looked around and saw men with guns trained on the other two Germans, their arms raised in the air, glancing nervously at the flames spreading through the old curtains.

'Get out, Englishman,' snarled Dieter, still clutching his leg. 'This is none of your business.'

'Let them go. It's over.'

A deafening explosion ripped through the room and a shower of shattered glass sprayed across the floor. Horrified, Valérie realised that the flames must have reached the cans of fuel her father kept in the cupboard beneath the window. She blinked in the stinging air blown in through the shattered glass and felt her chest constrict. She could hear her father coughing and felt the heat of the flames on her face.

'Let us go, we're all going to die,' she cried and tried desperately to pull her father's chair away from the flames.

She shuddered as another loud explosion went off in the workroom, followed by a series of smaller cracks that echoed around the space. Valérie blinked down at Dieter's body lying at her feet. She kept pulling at the chair and yelled at Henry to help her, but was stopped by a restraining arm.

'We'll get him Valérie, you need to leave now.' Henry Grant turned to one of his men. 'You, take her out. I'll get Albert.'

She could feel herself losing consciousness as she was picked up by strong arms and carried out through the house. They emerged into the street, the cold night air making her gasp after the heat of the flames. She glimpsed groups of worried neighbours silently watching the flames and heard the sound of sirens grow louder until they filled the narrow space in front of their house. Before she lost her senses, she looked round to see her father being carried outside. A few steps behind him came Henry and his men. No one else came out.

She saw Henry exchange a few words with the firefighters

and police officers who had just arrived on the scene. Valérie closed her eyes, unable to battle the waves of exhaustion any longer. The last thing she was aware of was being laid carefully on a bed in what she thought dimly must be an ambulance. She heard the doors slam shut before she lost consciousness.

# TWENTY-NINE

## VALÉRIE

Valérie heard murmuring voices and slowly blinked open her eyes. A young, bearded doctor was leaning over her, stethoscope in his ears, listening intently. After a few minutes, he glanced down at her face.

'You are awake, that is good. How are you feeling, mademoiselle?'

She tried to speak, but her throat was so dry she could only whisper.

A nurse handed her a glass of water and she sipped the cool liquid, closing her eyes as it soothed her throat. Water had never tasted so sweet. When she tried again, her voice still sounded weak. 'I'm all right, but my father. He was hurt. Is he here?' She tried to sit up, the images of the fire flooding into her mind, the horror of the scene she'd discovered still vivid and raw. She winced as she pulled herself up, her bandaged wrists and bruised upper arms refusing to hold her weight. The doctor caught her before she fell back down again and gently pulled her into a sitting position.

'Thank you,' Valérie whispered, before taking another sip.

He waited for a few moments, then continued. 'Your

father is recovering but will take a while longer.' He shook his head. 'His lungs were damaged from the smoke.' His gaze fixed on Valérie. The police said that your father had an accident, that he tripped and dropped a candle which set the workshop on fire. But the injuries to his face are not injuries from any kind of fall I've ever seen. It looks as if he was beaten.'

'Thank you, Doctor,' a familiar voice interrupted him. 'We need to speak to Mademoiselle Hallez now.'

Henry came towards her bed, followed by Nicolas Cherix. She glanced up at his concerned face, wondering how much he knew. He looked uncertain and wary.

They waited until the doctor and nurse had left and only then did Henry speak.

'How are you feeling this morning?'

She raised her bandaged wrists. 'A bit bruised, that's all.'

He pulled over a chair and sat down next to her bed, looking at her without speaking. She felt suddenly overcome, knowing that she owed this man her life. She would not be sitting recovering in bed and feeling the warmth from the ray of winter sunshine through the window if he'd arrived even a few minutes later.

'Have you seen my father? Is he all right?' She swallowed, before continuing. 'The doctor seemed concerned.'

He nodded. 'Your father will be all right. He's tougher than you think. He's more worried about you than himself, so the sooner you see him and set his mind at rest the better. It will take him some time to recover completely, but the doctors have said he'll be fine.'

She breathed a heavy sigh of relief. 'If it wasn't for you, they'd have killed us, left us to die in the fire.'

'Yes. It would have been put down as a tragic accident. A candle dropped in the workshop, setting fire to some old petrol canisters, fire taking hold and trapping you both.'

She shivered and looked from one to the other. 'Did Emile tell you we were in danger?'

Nicolas nodded. 'He came to tell me, and I alerted Henry.'

She held his gaze and tried to keep her voice level 'How could you let Germans act like this in Switzerland? Did you know what they were doing?'

'No, Valérie. We didn't know who they really were. It seems that a group of Nazi spies were placed in the Consul to spy on anyone suspected of acting against Germany. Runde's cover as the official approving export licenses allowed him to monitor Swiss businesses trading with the Allies. We don't think he was ever instructed to act on his suspicions, but just to keep a record of those who would not be faithful to the Nazi doctrine if Switzerland was taken over.' He paused. 'His attack on you and Albert last night was his own decision.'

She turned to Henry. 'No one would have known what really happened if you hadn't stopped them.'

'No one will know what did happen.' He glanced at Nicolas, who nodded slightly.

'What do you mean?'

'I'm sure that you realise how important it is that your father continues his work and I am free to continue mine,' said Henry. 'What happened last night in your house must remain a secret. You mustn't tell anyone who else was there and what their intention was.'

'But how can it be hidden? There were crowds of people when we came out, watching everything...'

'Dieter and two of his colleagues were killed in a car accident last night on the outskirts of the city. Their car burst into flames and they died before anyone could reach them.'

'But when I got back home last night...'

He finished her sentence. 'Your father fell and injured himself. When he fell, he dropped a candle and the fire spread quickly in his workshop, causing an explosion. You managed to pull him out of danger and you were both rescued by people in the street who saw the flames and came in to get you.'

'But someone must have seen you there?'

'I was outside, shocked as the other witnesses were, but no one saw me in the house. I was not inside your house last night.'

He exchanged a long look with Nicolas, who stood up, cleared his throat and seemed to consider his words for several minutes before he spoke.

'I'm sorry you had to go through such an ordeal. It should never have happened. You know I have always believed that we have to work with both sides in this war, but I was wrong not to see Dieter for what he was. Concealing how he died and why is the only way to resolve the situation without creating a diplomatic incident.'

'Which nobody wants,' Henry said firmly.

Nicolas bent down and kissed her.

'My son would never have forgiven me if I'd let anything happen to you.'

He nodded at Henry and left the room.

Valérie felt like bursting into tears. She was suddenly exhausted and closed her eyes. But she could still see the swirling flames destroying their home and feel the heat of the fire from the explosion. Her eyes flew open, and she looked at Henry.

'Did they put the fire out? I don't know what we're going to do, where we're going to live...'

'Your father's workshop is destroyed, Valérie. His equipment couldn't be saved, but the house is intact. There is some smoke damage, the broken windows, but the firemen stopped the fire from spreading. You were lucky, the thick stone of the old building withstood the flames long enough for them to put the fire out.'

He leaned forward in his chair.

'I've already spoken to some of your father's customers and

they will join me in helping him rebuild his business and open up his old workshop. He is a skilled watchmaker and we must make sure that his work continues. I am sure you realise that now.'

'Yes, I do.'

'There's something else I want to talk to you about. I've been in touch with a contact of mine in the Swiss army, Major Toussaint.'

'I know him. He's Philippe's senior officer.'

'He thought this would be of interest to you.'

Henry reached into his pocket for a folded piece of paper and handed it to her.

Valérie picked it up and slowly unfolded it. She stared down at the words, identical to those she'd found in the store-room, the duplicate of the list Simone had died to protect, Philippe's name was at the bottom of the list.

'It's the copy of that dreadful list. Where did you get it? I knew there was another copy, but I didn't know where.'

'It was found on a member of the Resistance who escaped into Switzerland across the Jura mountains. He was wounded by the Germans chasing him but managed to get to a safe house. Before he died, he made the people who took him in promise to give the list to us.'

Henry took out his cigarette lighter and flicked on the flame. Valérie put the corner of the paper into the flickering flame, then dropped it on to the ashtray on the bedside table, and watched as it burned to a cinder, Philippe's name disappearing before her eyes.

'I kept it for you. I thought you'd want proof that both copies of the list would never be found.'

'Thank you.'

Henry lit up a cigarette slowly and she watched him in silence.

'Has Emile talked much about his contacts in the Resistance?'

'No, he's very careful not to. Jean is his main contact. He's the only one I know.' She frowned. 'Emile thinks someone is betraying the Resistance, that Jean won't listen to him.'

'Has he ever said who it could be?'

'No. He believes they were betrayed one night when he was taking some Jewish refugees across the border. They were ambushed and he only managed to get a few of the children out alive.'

'There are refugees still coming through the escape routes all the time. My superiors in London think they would have been stopped if the Germans had truly infiltrated the network.'

'Is that what you think?'

He didn't answer her question but pointed at the charred remains of the list in the ashtray.

'The man who carried that list also said that there was a traitor in his Resistance cell. He didn't know who but said that someone was passing information to the Germans about Resistance members, their meeting places and their plans to sabotage German operations.'

Valérie stared at him. 'You think Emile is right?'

'I don't know, but I want you both to help me find out.'

'Help you find out? What can I do?'

His gaze didn't waver. 'Speak to Emile and find out who he knows, and who he suspects. Work for us so you can meet the people we're funding. Build up a picture of everyone in the Resistance you come across.'

Valérie felt a thrill of excitement.

'I'll need to help set up my father's new workshop first.'

'Agreed.'

'And make sure Emile's happy about it.'

'I'm sure he will be.'

She held out her hand and he grasped it.

'Then I'll do it. I'll work for you.'

That afternoon, Valérie visited her father.

She had to hide her shock at seeing his bruised face. He looked so old and tired. Neither of them spoke but she ran to the bed and held him close. It was several moments before she let him go, though she kept hold of his hands, examining them carefully.

'He didn't hurt your hands... I was worried he'd damaged them.'

'You could have been killed, *mignonne*. You should not have tried to stop him.'

She felt the tears prick her eyes. 'I could never leave you alone to face him. If I hadn't left when he did, I could have stopped him or got help somehow. I'm sorry, Papa.'

A tear dropped on to his hand and he reached up and dried her cheeks.

'Don't say that. There was nothing you or I could have said to stop him.'

Valérie pulled out the package of jewel bearings and placed it on the bedcover between them.

'When I found this, I had to come back because I realised what you were doing. All the things I said, accusing you of not caring. I'm sorry I ever doubted you.'

His fingers closed over the package. 'I hid this when Dieter turned up acting suspiciously, taking too much interest in our deliveries. But I didn't want you to know. It was safer that way.' He sighed. 'I suppose it's too late now. I've failed to protect you.'

'You couldn't have protected me. They already suspected me of working against them.'

'And they've destroyed everything. The workshop, our home, all my equipment... It's all lost.'

Valérie shook her head, hoping she could put the spark back

into his dull eyes. 'We haven't lost everything. Henry Grant said that the house wasn't destroyed, only the workshop. He'll repair the house and do up your old workshop.'

'Do up the old workshop? It's possible but we'll need new equipment. That might be difficult to source in wartime.'

'Henry didn't seem to think so.'

Her father still looked uncertain, but he squeezed her hand. 'As long as you are safe, what else matters?'

He smiled for the first time and closed his eyes. 'I'm tired now. Let me sleep.'

'I'll come back to see you tomorrow.' She kissed his forehead and left him.

When she closed his door, she saw Marianne walking along the bright corridor towards her, followed by Geraldine.

'Thank goodness, you're all right.'

Marianne enveloped Valérie in a fierce hug, strong enough to make her wince.

'Not so tight,' laughed Valérie. 'You'll hurt me.'

Marianne pulled back and studied Valérie's face. 'Are you really all right? And your father? We were so worried about you both.'

'We're fine.'

They walked arm in arm the short distance back to Valérie's room and Marianne and Geraldine helped her clamber back into bed before Geraldine held out her basket.

'I brought you some cakes. Bernard got them for me. He saw them take you out of the fire.' She shook her head and her eyes filled with tears. 'Oh Valérie, we thought you were dead.'

'What really happened?' asked Marianne. 'The police said your father fell with a candle, but there was so much damage.'

Valérie didn't hesitate.

'Papa fell and injured himself and he knocked over a candle which set light to some of the chemicals in his workshop. I tried to get him out, but the smoke was so thick... we were lucky that the police and firemen came in time.'

Geraldine was munching one of the cakes, eyes wide as she stared at Valérie, caught up in the drama. 'We were so worried,' she gasped finally, then held out the basket. 'Have a cake, they're very good.'

Marianne thumped her arm. 'Is food all you ever think about?'

'I thought she'd like one!'

Geraldine's expression was so like an outraged child that Valérie started to laugh, feeling more normal than she had for days. It seemed like she hadn't laughed in a long time and it was contagious; once she started, she couldn't stop. Marianne and Geraldine joined in and their gales of laughter filled the room. Finally, Valérie clutched her sides. 'Don't make me laugh so much. It hurts.'

Geraldine sobered up first. 'When are you getting out of here, Valérie? We need to help you get your house sorted out for your father coming home, you can't do it on your own.'

She delved into the bottom of her basket and pulled out a piece of paper. 'I've started a list of things you might need. I can give you some of my coupons. And Bernard says he can slip in a few extra things. '

As her friend went through her list, Valérie stared at her, touched by the flash of thoughtfulness. Underneath it all, she did care.

# THIRTY

## VALÉRIE

Valérie discharged herself from hospital the next morning. She pushed away her reluctance to go back home and told herself she had to get the house in some sort of order before her father could leave hospital. She wanted to whisk him out of the city and into the mountains so he could recover his strength but knew she had to make sure that their house was secure enough to come back to.

She walked out of the hospital and paused on the steps as the noise of a car horn shattered the air, making people stop and stare. Glancing across the street, she broke into a smile when she saw Geraldine wave out of the window of an ancient delivery van as it swerved across the road to screech to a halt next to her; Bernard was in the driving seat. Valérie knew that the old van hardly ever left his father's garage, the scarce supplies of petrol all claimed by the army. She pushed away the thought of what he must have sold to get some.

'We've been waiting for hours,' said Geraldine, jumping out of the van. 'You said you'd be getting out this morning, so we've been here since eight.'

Valérie clambered in between them and Geraldine slammed the door shut.

'They wanted me to stay a few more days, but I discharged myself. I need to see what the house is like and try to get it ready for my father coming home.' She glanced at Bernard who was steering the car through the streets towards the old town, oblivious of the clouds of diesel smoke pumping into the air behind them.

'Thanks for coming to get me.'

He didn't look round, but she could see him flush. 'You're welcome. My dad said I could borrow the van to pick you up. And Mum gave me some food.'

Valérie looked at the slim bag of groceries on the floor, potato bread sticking out of the top, grateful for their kindness. The food shortages in Geneva were as bad as ever, so she knew that they could ill afford what they'd given her.

'There's a cake in there from Philippe's mother,' added Geraldine. 'She came into the café to find out when you were coming home and asked me to give it to you. She was almost in tears, asking if you were all right and saying how awful it was about the fire.'

Valérie didn't reply. The van was chugging up the street towards their house and it all came flooding back, the blind panic when she'd opened the workshop door and seen Dieter standing over her father. She knew she could never forget what had happened there, but she hadn't expected to be scared to walk through her own front door. The memories of the fire, of the acrid smoky air and the towering figure of Dieter almost crushed her as the van swung around the corner of the house. She clutched on to Geraldine's arm as Bernard stopped outside the door and took a deep breath as if she was drowning.

'Are you all right?'

She looked into his worried face and tried to smile. 'I'm not sure.'

'Don't worry. I'll come inside with you.' He stretched out his hand and she grasped it as if it was a lifeline. Outside the van, Geraldine took her other arm and they walked towards the front door. Before Valérie could reach out to open it, it swung wide and a workman came out. He nodded to her as he passed.

Geraldine answered her unspoken question. 'They've been here since yesterday, boarding up the back of the house, making everything secure. Didn't you ask them to come?'

Valérie hesitated, knowing that Henry Grant wouldn't want his involvement the subject of local gossip.

'I didn't know they would be starting so soon,' she said finally. 'They didn't say.'

Flanked by her friends, Valérie went inside and looked around her. She put her hand up to her mouth as she surveyed the hall. It still smelled of acrid smoke that caught in her throat and the carpet was covered in dirty boot marks from the fire-fighters' efforts to extinguish the fire before it engulfed the whole building, furniture cast to the side so they would have a clear path through. She walked into the parlour and saw that a partition had been erected to block off the workroom, the noise of banging coming from the other side. The parlour looked the same as always, eerily frozen in time, everything in its place. She wiped a finger along the dresser and it came up black with soot.

'We've cleared up a bit in here,' said Geraldine. 'But the bedrooms upstairs all need to be cleaned. There's black soot everywhere.' She started to unpack the food from the basket, keeping her eyes on Valérie, who sank on to the sofa, looking around her as if she was in a stranger's house.

'Are you sure you're all right?'

Valérie nodded. 'I think so. I just need a minute or two.' She flinched when the makeshift door to the workroom swung back on its hinges and hit the wall with a sharp crack. As a man came out, she caught a glimpse of the destruction inside. Her eyes were drawn to the room. In the cold daylight coming through the broken windows it looked very different from the night of the fire. She took a deep breath and made herself glance at the floor where the German had fallen, expecting to see bloodstains on the wood, but there was nothing to see. Damaged by flames and water, the floorboards had all been pulled up, leaving only the bare stone. She sighed with relief when she realised that there was nothing left of her nightmare, the workroom was an empty shell and all traces of the scene she'd walked into that night were gone forever.

Valérie turned her head away from the workroom and shivered. 'It's cold in here.'

She reached towards the pile of bedspreads and blankets Geraldine must have found upstairs and picked up an old patchwork quilt she recognised from her childhood, wrapping it around her shoulders and burying her nose in the soft material, the faint scent of her mother's perfume comforting her.

'Where did you find these? I haven't seen them for years.'

'In the dresser in one of the bedrooms upstairs. The one at the end of the corridor, furthest from the fire.' Geraldine picked up an embroidered blanket and swung it around her slim shoulders. 'I thought we'd need something to keep us warm in here until we get the stove back on.'

She tutted and looked around. 'I thought you might have been able to stay here, but it's no use. It will be too cold. And everything needs to be cleaned. You'll have to come back with me to the café. We have room, so you can stay there for a few days until this place gets sorted out a bit.'

Relieved that someone else was making decisions for her, Valérie absent-mindedly reached out and dragged towards her a large box that she'd spied round the back of the sofa, half out of sight.

'You could look through that,' said Geraldine. 'It came from the workshop. The men put everything in it they thought might be worth saving. It looks like a lot of old junk to me, but you may want to keep some of it.'

'This is all they managed to save?' Valérie moved aside some bills and papers at the top of the chest and uncovered parts of her father's watchmaking tools, sets of tiny screwdrivers and other watch parts he must have been working on when he'd been interrupted. 'He'll want to keep this,' she said. 'And these are some of his favourite tools.'

'Take out what you want to keep,' said Geraldine. 'And they can get rid of the rest.'

Valérie wasn't listening to her, picking carefully through the pieces of metal and paper, placing to one side the items she thought worth keeping. She sighed as she picked up a fragment of the old vice her father used to hold his watch mechanisms in place as he worked on them, its edges melted by the fierce heat and the twisted metal shape now utterly useless. She doggedly carried on, though the pile of things she kept to one side remained pitifully small compared to the items she threw back into the wooden chest.

Her hand touched a small package wrapped in brown paper, like the one addressed to Henry Grant, and she saw through the edge of the paper a small pouch of jewel bearings. At least she'd found something of value, she thought, suppressing the sharp stab of pain that so little remained. Her hand skimmed over the bottom of the chest and caught on a torn envelope with the corners of old photographs peeping out of the brown paper. She took out the photographs and turned them over, flicking through them.

She recognised photos of her mother and father and a couple of her as a small child, laughing up at the camera. She'd seen them all before and carefully placed them one by one in the pile to keep.

Finished with the box, she looked up at Geraldine.

'Have you seen Emile today?'

Geraldine nodded. 'I forgot. He gave me a message for you. Said that the person he was going to meet the other night didn't show up and he's meeting him today instead.'

She glanced up at the clock. 'Probably about now.'

'Where did he say they were meeting?'

'The Place de Bel-Air—'

Valérie threw off the patchwork quilt and grabbed her bag from the floor.

'Where are you going?'

'To find Emile.'

'But why are you going now? Don't you want something to eat first? I'm making you a sandwich.'

Valérie hugged her friend. 'I won't be long, I promise.'

Geraldine shook her head and Bernard looked worried, but they didn't try to argue.

Once outside, Valérie dodged past the people queuing along the pavements beside the shops and walked briskly down the Rue de la Cité. In the Place de Bel-Air she looked for Emile but he was nowhere in sight. She got caught up in a crowd waiting to board an approaching tram car on the narrow sliver of pavement between the tramlines. Impatient to get past, she tried to push her way through the tight group of people but they formed a solid barrier in front of her, blocking her way and resisting her attempts to push through.

'Pardon, monsieur, I need to get past. Please let me through.'

'Wait your turn, mademoiselle,' grumbled the man in front of her, refusing to move.

It was no use. The trams were running late and everyone turned towards the approaching car, eager to be on their way. Nobody would let her through and she looked helplessly around, but more people were crowding behind her, so she was completely stuck among a mass of people.

A few feet down the platform she saw Emile, buffeted by

the jostling crowd at the front of the line and teetering on the edge of the kerb. He looked uncertain and glanced behind him. When he turned towards her, she saw an expression of naked fear on his face. He was trying to move back from the kerb. She stared at the crowd behind him, wondering what he was afraid of, but it was impossible to pick out anyone in the mass of faces.

'Emile!' She shouted his name, but he couldn't hear her. She felt a chill of fear run through her as the loud noise of the tram coming into the stop drowned out the hubbub of the waiting crowd. Something was going on in front of her. Emile was afraid of someone, but she was powerless to help or get any closer to him. She didn't know what was happening but was filled with a sick dread that he was in danger and she could do nothing to stop it.

Bernard grasped her arm and she looked up into his face. He must have followed her. He tried to pull her away, mouth moving in speech, but she couldn't make out what he was saying. She shook her head and pointed towards Emile, as the tram slid into the stop in front of her. She watched in horror as fingers splayed against Emile's dark jacket and pushed him. Emile's mouth opened in a desperate shout no one could hear before he toppled over in front of the large vehicle.

'No!' Valérie screamed. The crowd recoiled from the platform, their expressions of horror confirming the worst. Mothers dragged their children away so they wouldn't look on to the rails, an old woman fainted and was helped towards a bench nearby. Others crowded in to see what had happened, adding to the confusion.

'What's going on?' a young boy asked Valérie, but she shook her head and pushed past him, eyes scanning the thinning crowd ahead of her.

'Emile... someone pushed him...'

She saw a bearded man look over the platform on to the

rails, before running away from the crowd. In an instant, he had disappeared from the square.

Bernard's grip on her arm tightened and he pulled her to the edge of the crowd, away from the accident.

'Let me go!' She struggled to pull away from his hold, but it was impossible, and she twisted round to confront him.

'Who was that man? Did you see him?' she shouted through her tears. 'The one with the beard. He pushed Emile, he killed him.'

'Valérie, we need to leave. You can't stay here.'

Her tears blinded her and she dashed them away. 'No, I won't listen to you. Someone pushed him. We have to catch him.'

She heard the sirens of the police cars coming towards the square and tried to get away, but Bernard hugged her into his body with a strength she didn't know he possessed and almost lifted her away from the crowd. They crossed the end of the lake and collapsed on to a bench at the start of the Quai du Mont-Blanc, breathing heavily. Bernard bent his head and ran shaking fingers through his dark hair.

'I had to get you out of there. You can talk to the police when everything has calmed down a bit.'

Valérie nodded, shock numbing her ability to process what had just happened. They sat in silence until Bernard lifted his head.

'I'm sorry Valérie, I need to go. Do you want me come with you to your house?'

'No. You go. I need a bit more time.'

'Are you sure you'll be all right?'

She nodded and stood up. 'I'm going to sit over there for a while.'

She hugged Bernard and walked a little way along the Quai du Mont-Blanc, her arms wrapped in front of her, hardly aware of the tears streaming down her face.

Emile was dead. She'd never speak to him again or laugh with him, see his tall figure walk towards her with his familiar limp. She wiped her eyes and sniffed loudly, hardly able to believe what had happened. Sitting on her and Philippe's favourite bench, she gazed out at the lake glimmering in the December sun, missing Philippe desperately, aching to have his strong presence next to her.

She sat for a long time gazing at the calm water of the lake, her coat pulled around her to keep warm. After a while, the noise from the Place de Bel-Air became more subdued and her eyes emptied of tears. She felt numb, as if the whole world could explode around her and she wouldn't even flinch.

'Valérie, are you okay? I was so worried.'

Her heart turned over when she heard Philippe's voice. She wondered if she were dreaming, if she was so desperate to see him that she'd somehow conjured up his presence by sheer force of will. But he was real. She looked up to see Philippe run towards her and in an instant he was holding her tight and she was swept away, forgetting where they were, only aware of his arms around her.

It was only when a laugh from a passer-by pierced their world that they looked up to see amused glances from the people around them. They both sank down on to the bench, Valérie's head on Philippe's shoulder.

'Emile,' she whispered finally, 'Philippe, Emile...'

'I know. I met a policeman I knew at the train station. I'm so sorry, Valérie.'

They sat in silence for a while, unable to say anything further.

'How did you manage to get away again so soon?' asked Valérie finally.

'The Major gave me permission. He was told you were in hospital and what had happened, what Dieter tried to do.'

She felt him shudder. 'I could have lost you.'

She pulled his head down and kissed him. 'How did you know I'd be here?'

He tightened his arm round her shoulders. 'It's the first place I always look for you.'

'I feel closer to you here.' She looked up at him. 'I saw someone push him, Philippe. It wasn't an accident.'

'The police will find out who did it.' He smoothed down her hair. 'Don't think about it. There was nothing you could do.'

She felt tears begin to spill over again. 'I'm so glad you're with me now. I needed you so much. I can't believe he's gone, Philippe.'

They sat in silence a while longer and then Philippe spoke, sounding suddenly unsure.

'It's probably not the right time for me to say this. But maybe it is. We never know what is going to happen from one day to the next, especially with the war. I don't want to miss an opportunity I might never have again.'

Valérie looked up at him.

'What do you mean?'

He looked very serious, his eyes burning with intent, but also uncertain.

'When I was held prisoner, I thought I might never see you again. I was so sure that the Fort Commander wouldn't believe my story about Favre, that he'd decided I was the traitor. I thought I might be shot within days, and I'd never get to tell you I loved you, would never get to have the life with you that we've dreamed about.'

She nodded and watched him dig into his pocket for something.

'I went to see your father in the hospital today.'

'My father? Why did you—' She stopped short when she saw him take a small jewellery box out of his pocket.

'To ask his permission, of course.'

'Permission?' she whispered, feeling suddenly short of breath.

'To ask you to marry me.'

He opened the small box and she gazed down at the familiar diamond ring in its swirling platinum setting.

'Philippe, that's your grandmother's ring.'

He took her left hand and slid the ring on to her finger.

'It's yours now. If you want it. If you want me.'

She felt the tears run down her cheeks and flung her arms round his neck.

'Of course, I want you.'

He wiped her cheeks with his handkerchief.

'I hope that's a yes.'

She gave a watery chuckle and nodded.

'A definite yes. So long as you're sure.'

'I've never been more sure of anything in my life.'

They sat silently watching the lake. Valérie saw a golden future opening up before her, when the war would one day be over and she and Philippe could live in peace. But her happiness was tinged by the painful knowledge that Emile no longer had a future at all.

'I wish my mother were here, that she knew about us. And Emile, he would have been so happy to see us engaged.'

Philippe squeezed her closer.

'Maybe she does know. And he is happy, somewhere.'

There was another silence, neither of them wanting the moment to end. Philippe picked up her hand and moved it so the ring sparkled in the sun.

'Valérie, I'm not sure what you think, but I don't want us to get married and then spend all our time apart. I think we should wait until I can come back to Geneva. This threat of invasion won't last for ever. If the Allies win, we can get back to our normal lives.'

She grasped his hand, thinking of all the people around them and across the border who were waiting, hoping one day to be able to lead a normal life again. And about all those for whom nothing could ever be normal again. Like Marianne, who must by now have learned about her brother's death. And the little girl who had leaned against Valérie after fleeing through the streets to her father's old workshop, leaving her friends dead at the border. The boy on the train who had smiled at her before being taken away by the border guards. How could she be happy among all this pain?

'Yes, we should wait. And Phillippe, I need to tell you something. I have to take over from Emile, now he's gone.' She swallowed the lump in her throat before she could continue. 'He would have saved so many more people by helping them escape from France, but he can't do that anymore. I want to do this, for him. And for them.'

She looked up to see his expression and carried on when all she saw was love and worry.

'Emile thought there was a traitor in the Resistance. That's what got him killed, I'm sure of it. I was going to help him discover who it was. That person is endangering every person, every child escaping across the border. And they're the reason Emile is dead.' Her voice broke and she swallowed, remembering how brave Emile had been, and Simone, as they risked their lives for the Resistance. 'I'll have to find the traitor myself now.'

'It'll be dangerous, Valérie.'

'I know. But I have to do it.'

He sighed.

'I wish I could help you, stay here with you.'

'If I need you, I'll ask. I'll write to you all the time, I promise.'

She kissed him deeply.

'How long can you stay for?'

'I need to go back tomorrow. So, you're invited to dinner with my parents to celebrate. If you feel up to it.'

Valérie looked out over the water and saw a bird skimming the surface and then lifting away, up into the clear sky.

'Yes, I'll come. That's what Emile would have wanted; I know it. I'd like that very much. Philippe, your parents... are they happy about us?'

He grinned. 'My mother's delighted she's going to finally have a daughter. My father's quietly pleased. He hasn't said we're too young, but I expect he's thinking it. My grandfather just asked why it had taken so long.'

Philippe touched the ring gently. 'He wanted you to have this, said you reminded him of her.'

'I wasn't sure your father approved of me.'

'I think he worries about your safety,' said Philippe, smiling, 'but he admires your courage.'

He stood up and held out his hand.

'Enough about my family. I promised your father we'd go and see him together. Come with me?'

She clasped his hand and stood up.

'Always.'

# A LETTER FROM DIANNE

Thank you so much for reading *The Watchmaker's Daughter*. If you enjoyed it, and want to keep up to date with all my latest releases, just sign up at the following link. Your email address will never be shared and you can unsubscribe at any time.

*www.bookouture.com/dianne-haley*

Before I wrote this book, I knew that Switzerland was neutral in WW2. What I didn't know was how many Swiss citizens helped Jewish refugees escape from occupied France. Despite the opposition of the Swiss authorities and often at great risk to themselves, they helped desperate people reach safety. It's a story of courage and resilience that isn't well known.

If you enjoyed the story, it would be great if you could leave a short review. I appreciate all feedback from readers. It also helps to persuade other readers to pick up one of my books for the first time.

You can also get in touch on my Facebook page, through Twitter, Goodreads or my website.

Thanks, Dianne

dian\nehaley.com

 twitter.com/dhaley30

Printed in Great Britain
by Amazon

10222569R00162